Twiste

KIM GUINAN

Copyright © 2017 Kim Guinan

All rights reserved.

DEDICATION

For my wonderful husband, Bob, love and admiration.

Chapter One

Ruth had a notion something had woken her; an odd noise, the vague and distant memory of something important she had to remember... but couldn't? Whatever it was, lacking the energy required to fully rouse herself, she succumbed to the inevitable; closed her eyes and sank back into oblivion.

Less than an hour later, Ruth awoke with a gasp. Could feel her heart pounding as she sat bolt upright in bed.

Her eyes snapping open, she was convinced she had heard a noise. A real noise, not an imagined one.

Eerily sensing there was someone in the room with her. Someone, who was about to pounce... Ruth's breath caught. Her chest heaving with effort as she struggled to breathe, she gasped down lungfuls of chilled air. Coughed explosively.

Softly moaned.

He's here... I know it.

Feeling a sense of movement stirring the air, Ruth listened, hard. Certain there was something interrupting the silence, she thought she heard the soft sound of a whispered sigh, too close for comfort.

He's watching me.

Panicked, she whimpered.

Eyes wide open with flear, Ruth forced herself to peer deeper into the subdued light as she frenziedly scanned a sepia room. Searched into every single nook and cranny as she sought for evidence of a presence — *his presence* — saw a ghostly face manifesting out of the wall, floating toward her. Cringed in terror. Yet when she looked again, there was nothing, just patterns of light and dark.

Silence.

The air now deathly still, doubt gradually began to creep over her.

Guilt has made me paranoid, either that or the damn pills.

A sinister, formless shadow moved in the corner; *a creature coming to life?*

Ruth gripped a hold of the quilt, covered her face with it. She did not want to see. Could not bear to see.

She listened.

A minute passed, two.

Silence. There was no shuffling footsteps, and no heavy breathing.

No one, there is no one, lurking in the shadows, Ruth firmly told herself.

She dropped the quilt.

I am alone.

He is not here.

He is never here.

It is only my imagination playing tricks on me, again.

But she remained on guard, for a few more seconds.

A noise on the beside table and Ruth's head instantly spun as she scanned for the source of the sound.

It was only the digital clock flipping over; *of course.*

Ruth squinted more closely at the white face with the glow-in-the-dark numbers on the black rectangular tiles. Saw the word *Saturday* spelt out across the bottom of the clock's screen and started with surprise. Then the questions flooded in.

How long have I slept?

What the hell happened to yesterday?

Have I really lost a whole day?

What time is it?

Almost ten already, but it can't be… can it?

What is it about today and the lateness of the hour that seems suddenly, so important?

Ruth shook her head at herself. *Too many questions, not enough answers.* Told herself she had to stop fretting. Whatever she had forgotten, it would come to her.

Another noise, a clicking sound from the corner of the room, then a sudden hissing.

Again, Ruth's head swivelled.

Spooked with fear, her chest heaved, then tightened.

'Breath Ruth, just breath,' she whispered into the chilled room.

Listened again, heard a familiar gurgling.

It's just the radiator expanding, filling with hot water. There is no one here, Ruth assured herself. Reminded herself that every single morning, since the day *it* had happened, it was the same. Each day, waking with a feeling of impending doom, immediately followed by one of terror, she would soon realise, it was all because she had been dreaming of *him* again. Dreaming of a husband who had been nightmarishly absent from their marriage, long before his death.

If only we hadn't argued.

If only he…

If only I hadn't…

Enough! Ruth stopped her inner dialogue, and her heartbeat slowed.

Easing herself back onto her pillow, the sweat on her brow at last beginning to dry, Ruth's teeth began to chatter.

Withdrawal? She ruthlessly challenged herself. Angrily pushed the unpalatable thought away. Then watched with a fascination bordering on the obsessive as almost of its own volition, a trembling hand, clawed its way across the top of the quilt.

Am I really that weak, that desperate? Ruth silently chastised herself.

Grabbed for a small brown bottle sat on top of the bedside cabinet.

Yes, I'm all of those things I despise. I'm weak, desperate, and a mess.

A few weeks ago, unable to function, to think, to feel, or even to sleep, Ruth's doctor had diagnosed, *'A mini breakdown, of sorts. Understandable, bearing in mind what she had been through.'* Then prescribing a course of Valium with the usual warning of *'Do not take with alcohol,'* and *'You must come back and see me in a couple of weeks,'* within a minute of Ruth's allotted ten, Dr Grange had risen from his desk, carefully lifted her from her seat as though she were a piece of broken china, and firmly manoeuvred her out of his office. The prescription now on repeat, Ruth had made a point, of not seeing him since.

Shaking out one of the innocuous looking little pills, Ruth threw back her head and though her throat was dry, determinedly swallowed it down.

Suddenly conscious, *he* would have been wagging a knowing finger in her direction, Ruth expelled a rebellious snort into the reproving silence. Felt the almost immediate, sedative effect of the drug start to spread through her. Felt a literal pulling away as she was slowly distanced from reality.

Beginning to realise that what must have woken her for the first time that morning, had to have been the alarm going off, Ruth giggled to herself. With a mocking grin, she titteringly acknowledged the absurdity of what she had put herself through. *Torturing myself with thoughts I can no longer trust. Inventing monsters who do not exist, I have to be unhinged.*

A few minutes later, gently undulating on a sea of calm, Ruth's soothed thoughts unhurriedly began to organise themselves and she slowly began to recall what it was, she had forgotten. *Sam,* Ruth mused, absent-mindedly twiddling a limp lock of greasy hair. *Isn't today the day, I'm meant to be picking up Sam from the station?*

Glancing back toward the clock, then pendulously recalling that Sam's train was due to arrive some time after ten, it did not take too much concentration for Ruth to figure out she was going to be late, possibly very late; *Oh well.*

Feeling a dreamy sense of release and calmness wash gently over her, Ruth lazily wondered if she should call ahead and warn Sam? But she could not be less bothered. Sam would wait. Of that much, she was certain.

Without warning, Ruth's head began to throb. Knowing she had to get up but with her head now pounding, for a while, she was undecided. Momentarily closed her eyes against the thought of what lay ahead, as well as the pain now pulsating behind her temples. Then had an unexpected urge, to cry.

It's all, just too much.

Opening the beside table drawer, Ruth's fingers scrabbled around the inside of it and finding a box of almost empty paracetamols, for the headache, she popped a couple more pills. Told herself with as much confidence as she could muster, *I'll be okay. It's just one more lousy day, to get through.*

A pressing need to pee, and the decision on whether she should get up or not, was made.

Forcing a reluctant body from out of the bed, Ruth took a couple of tentative steps. Behaved as if moving to fast, too soon, might fling her over. Promptly stumbling over a wine bottle buried beneath a pile of discarded clothes, Ruth crashed heavily into the bedroom doorway frame. Swore liberally, then angrily kicked out at her would be assassin. The victim fighting back, the bottle violently spewed its blood red dregs across a cream woollen rug.

'Brilliant! Just brilliant,' Ruth yelled at the rug. *We should never have bought the damn thing, totally impractical but he had insisted and whatever he wanted, he always got.*

Spinning herself crazily around, Ruth clumsily pitched forward into the corridor. Staggered across the landing and hurled herself into the bathroom, to pee.

Desperately needing a shower but not having the luxury of time, Ruth turned to face the sink. Twisting on the hot water tap, she studiously ignored a ring of grime circumnavigating the porcelain bowl, cupped her hands under the tepid water and cursorily splashed her face. Brought the flannel up over her mouth and nose, breathed slowly through it as she tried to stop a distant panic that was once again, threatening to rise.

Hastily brushing her teeth, Ruth kept her eyes cast down and firmly averted from a mirror hanging on wall above the sink. Today, of all days, she needed no reminders of how awful she looked.

Returning to the bedroom, grabbing up a pair of black skinny jeans tossed neglectfully into the corner some days ago, Ruth heaved them on. Then dragging a crumpled and oversized black hoody of *his* out, from under the tangled mess on the floor, she hurriedly wrenched it over her still tender head. Pulled it down over a screwed up khaki T-shirt and faded underwear, she had probably worn, at least the day before.

Ruth tried to relax but still, she could feel a vague and obscure dread. Knew that like a rabid dog, an insidious foreboding percolating somewhere in the deeper recesses of her mind was merely waiting for the right opportunity to rise up and attack; to bite, and sink in its teeth.

Worrying over whether she should take another pill, then realising she had no idea how many she had taken already, Ruth shook her head at herself. Silently cursed her forgetfulness. Knowing she was going to be driving, she guessed she should err on the side of caution, but the thought of being crippled by anxiety, by fear, spurred her on. She took another Valium.

Detached herself from the lurking terror.

Feeling an immediate dreamy sense of release and calmness descend, Ruth prayed that this time, the sensation of being *out of it*, of being lodged behind her usual sheet of safety glass, would stay.

Sat on the bottom stair, Ruth laced up walking boots that were caked in dried mud. Then collecting up a coat, scarf, mis-matched gloves and a leather shoulder bag from off of the floor, she stumbled along the hallway.

Ruth's phone, unexpectedly signalled a text.

She ignored it.

Trailing dirt and dust balls in her wake, Ruth slowly made her way to the front door, but had to pause momentarily as an unexpected wave of nausea threatened to rise. She caught her breath, and swallowed it down.

Catching an unwanted glimpse of her dishevelled and pallid face, a stranger's face, in the hallway mirror, Ruth felt an overwhelming sense of loneliness and self-loathing, engulf her.

I look awful.

I'm in a bottomless pit.

I can't cope.

I hate myself.

I need a drink!

Pushing forward, reaching the end of the hallway, Ruth wrenched open the heavy front door and was met by an instant blast of ice cold air. She gasped, then recoiled.

Faced with the outside world, with the infinite terror of it and what she knew was yet to come, every inch of Ruth, wanted to turn around. Her feelings of desperation, of fear, pushing for her to sprint back to the safety of her solitary bed, to hide under its covers and retreat, she fought with herself.

Today, is not a good day.

Do I really, have to do this?

Today, is not a good day.

She is waiting.

Today, is not a good day.

If I don't show soon, she will come to the house.

Her last thought, helping her to beat back the fear, Ruth forced herself to cross the threshold.

Ruth's feet slipping and sliding down a garden path that was slick with puddles of ice, her light sensitive eyes ached from a harsh winter sunlight. Sticking a hand deep into her coat pocket, fingering through a mess of tissues and fluff, of old till receipts, Ruth grabbed for her sunglasses. Shoved them on her face.

Garden snails, driven out by their usual habitats by the freezing weather conditions, Ruth squished them underfoot. She did not notice.

Stopping mid-stride, unable to keep the bitter bile down any longer, Ruth heaved and emptied her innards into a low privet hedge that bordered the path. Then wiping her mouth with the back of her hand, beseeched the weather to do its worst. Implored it to get rid of the embarrassing mess, before anyone else could see it.

Stomach aching, her head pounding as her body shook, Ruth vowed she would not bring Sam back to the house. The state the house was in - *I am in* - Sam would only gloat.

Tears of self-pity searing her frozen cheeks, for the umpteenth time since the meeting had been planned, Ruth's thoughts turned to, *why? Why, on top of everything else, would I even think to put myself through the trauma of having to see Sam again? But that was it, wasn't it? With everything else that has happened of late, I haven't been thinking. At least not in any way, that makes any sense.*

Her phone signalling the receipt of yet another text, Ruth jumped. Felt a squeeze of anxiety.

All her senses on edge, the devil inside of Ruth was screaming at her: *Turn around! Go back! Hide!*

Yet it was too late. The repeated texts meant that Sam had arrived.

She was already here, and Ruth was expected.

And so, Ruth thought bitterly, *it begins.*

Chapter Two

In the privacy of their own home, Adam wrapped his arms around Ruth and hugged her tight. Gently, he brushed away her tears.

'It doesn't matter,' he said softly. 'I'll always love you, you know that. You'll see, we'll get past this, Ruth. I promise you, we will.'

But Ruth had seen behind the mask that was his face. She had seen how terribly close to crying he was himself. Could plainly recall, in the consultant's office earlier that morning, the startled look of confusion, of shock, quickly followed by a flash of crushed disappointment, then the pain.

Ruth had always known what was expected of her. Adam had made no secret of the fact, he wanted a child. A living, breathing facsimile of himself, he could nurture and evolve.

Now, both of them struggling to pretend that nothing between them had changed when *everything*, was different. No matter what he said to her now, Ruth could glean no comfort from the emptiness of his words. His forced concern for her welfare, his hollow embrace, all of it, left her feeling needy, horribly demanding.

Although Ruth loved Adam and had told herself she would do anything for him, even jump in front of a bullet — *or at least, she would like to think she would* — privately, she had always been ambivalent toward the idea of having children. Having lived and grown up with other people's sons and daughters, she had never developed an affinity with children. Was not at all certain how she felt about having a whole other person to be responsible for, to rear, but for Adam's sake, had convinced herself she would love the baby once it was there and be glad of it. She had even visualised herself pushing their child on a swing, the baby giggling in pleasure as its toes pointed toward the sky.

Every twenty-seven or twenty-eight days of her dependable cycle, Adam had eagerly anticipated her news. Obsessively inspected her nude form whenever she had got out the shower, the bath. During their frequent and passionate lovemaking, he had optimistically skimmed his hands back and forth over the slight swell of her breasts, her determinedly flat stomach as he looked for signs of change, for signs of a secret she had yet to divulge. When his visiting parents had hinted at how they were so looking forward to one day, becoming grandparents, he had knowingly smiled.

After almost a year of unsuccessful baby-making, Adam, who did *not* do failure, of any kind, had insisted they meet with an old colleague of his, an ex pal from university who now ran a well respected and private fertility clinic, in Harley Street. Then this morning, after a barrage of tests run over a number of weeks, and with Adam nervously optimistic, whilst she felt sick, they had gone up to London to get the results.

Now, encircling herself in Adam's arms, hot tears of self-pity crept up under Ruth's eyelids as she buried her face in his crisp, blue shirt. Tried to draw at least some comfort from the warmth of his taught chest, the musky smell of his cologne, by the sheer physical and inner strength he always exuded, no matter what. But he now pulling away from her, ever so slightly, she failed to be reassured.

Their unfortunate news doing nothing for Ruth's intense, neurotic anxiety, she chastised herself. It was as she had been told over and over again as a child; *the liars of this world, always got their comeuppance.*

Thought miserably, *I deserve to be punished.*

Chapter Three

Driving into the station approach road, it was only the top of Sam's head that Ruth first saw. A couple of middle-aged men standing a few feet to the right of her, the rest of Sam's slight form was hidden from view. But from the nudges and winks being shared between the balding, rotund males, it was obvious, Ruth's younger sister was being surreptitiously ogled.

Both just over five foot four in height and weighing in just under nine stone. Each with poker straight shoulder length chestnut hair, a golden skin tone and green almond shaped eyes set in heart-shaped faces, up until grief had imprinted itself on Ruth's face, she and Sam could almost have passed for twins. Only two years separating them, and yet in spite of their visible similarities, somehow, it had always been Sam who had courted the most attention.

Endowed with a quiet confidence, an innate sense of style and elegance, to all outward appearances, Sam was one of those fortunate people who had a polished sophistication about her that was as alluring, as it was elusive. She had that added, indefinable something, that *other* quality that Ruth had inexplicably missed out on, and had always envied.

As the car drew closer to Sam, she watched her unconsciously court the attention of those milling around her, and it was in that moment, Ruth clearly saw herself and all her shortcomings. Hated the shot of envy that coursed through her chilled veins.

In spite of Ruth's tardy arrival, as soon as Sam spotted the car, she smiled. No, she more than smiled, she joyously beamed, and in a way that immediately set Ruth's teeth on edge.

Breath! Ruth told herself as her breath caught with trepidation.

It's going to be okay. Just play nice, she silently commanded herself.

Ignoring the double-yellows, Ruth cast Sam a weak return smile as she abruptly drew the car to the curb and alongside. Then smartly tapping the automatic unlock button, felt herself instinctively tense up as she waited for Sam to climb in beside her.

Relax.

Sam bringing in a sudden rush of icy air as she slipped into the front passenger seat, Ruth shivered. *Here we go. Smile.*

Unexpectedly finding herself on the receiving end of a passing, perfunctory air kiss whilst being left enveloped in a loitering wave of her sister's musky scent, Ruth was challenged not to flinch. *Since when,* she thought, *had Sam become so tactile?*

Reared in a hard school of life, both of them had learnt to control their emotions when still infants. Their parents dying young, when Ruth was eight and Sam was six, over familiarity was awkward and not something either of them had become used to, or expressed.

'Ruth,' Sam said breathlessly. As if it were not so much two estranged sisters meeting for the first time in months, but two long lost lovers coming together. 'Hey? Are you okay? Why didn't you call me, or at least answer one of my texts? You're so late, I was really getting worried.'

Sam's face morphing into one of wreathed concern as she toned down her previously exuberant face, her excitable voice, Ruth inwardly cringed with mortification. Baulked at what she saw, was an overdone concern as well as an unspoken reproach. *How could you forget me? And why didn't you care enough to at least let me know you were going to be late?*

Unhappily realising that within less than a couple of minutes, and almost without trying, Sam had managed to seed an instant germ of guilt within her already fragile psyche, Ruth struggled to reign in her turbulent emotions. Felt suddenly nauseous again, and had to gulp down hard. The last thing she needed, was for Sam's penetrating gaze to see her discomfort, her all too obvious guilt.

Acknowledging that fundamentally, it was she who was in the wrong, but determined not to give in to an almost overwhelming urge to suck up, Ruth forced a smile in Sam's direction. Then as succinctly as possible, apologised. 'I'm sorry Sam, but I overslept.'

'Sure, no worries. It's okay. What with everything that's happened to you of late, I totally understand. I just wish you'd answered one of my texts, then I wouldn't have worried quite so much,' Sam replied easily.

Too easily, Ruth thought as she listened to Sam twist the knife in. Returned her sister's concerned smile, with a hard stare.

'Oh, I'm sorry, Ruth,' Sam said, her voice sounding full of contrition. 'I've just realised how awful that must have sounded. I hope you don't think I was criticising you? Only that wasn't my intention, really it wasn't. I was just worried about you, that's all. God, I feel terrible now.' She gave a nervous little laugh.

Finding Sam's overt graciousness particularly hard to swallow, but also feeling herself starting to wither under what appeared to be, a genuine concern for her well-being, Ruth shifted awkwardly in her seat. Mumbled out, 'It's okay, you're right, of course. I should have let you know I was running late.' *And let the grovelling commence.*

'Well, you're here now. So tell me, Ruth… how are you, really?' Sam asked, sounding uncertain.

Sam's loaded question asked so quietly and so soon, after so long, Ruth instantly bridled in defence of herself. *Was she for real?* 'I'm fine,' she lied uncomfortably, and obviously. 'You?' she demanded. Aggressively determined to change the subject.

Sam shot Ruth an old fashioned look, one that said *you don't look okay, I know you're lying, and why are you being so hostile.* 'I'm okay,' she responded dully. Fell into what Ruth took to be, a slighted silence.

From the wide-eyed disbelief on Sam's face, Ruth guessed she should perhaps, have said more? It was not as if there was not plenty more to say, but how could she possibly tell Sam what she could not yet admit, even to herself? Anyway, trading confidences required a certain level of closeness and trust, neither attributes of which, Ruth felt, could be applied to Sam.

Finding Sam's seemingly determined silence somewhat unnerving, but lacking the will to break it, Ruth just drove. Jerkily pulled the vehicle away from the kerb and began to navigate the car away from the station.

Feeling utterly drained already, a sudden and almost overwhelming thirst tried to take a hold, and the saliva in Ruth's mouth dried. *Not now!* Starting to sweat in spite of the cold, Ruth felt her face turn green as she sensed the tightly wound snake of tension lying in the pit of her stomach, begin to uncoil. She needed a drink, a really drink, but it was impossible. This was neither the time, nor the place, to collude with her inexhaustible cravings.

Get a grip, Ruth silently warned herself. Focused her attention on the road ahead.

Beads of perspiration broke out along the line of Ruth's forehead as she continued to drive. Sam still silent beside her as Ruth worked on steadying her nerves, her thirst. Joined in with the flow of the Dover traffic. Now oblivious to roads, roundabouts, traffic lights, cars, her mind distracted, Ruth thought only about how best to break the strained silence. Was not up to the intense effort of talking but knew, if only to throw Sam off the scent, she had to make at least some sort of an effort. Had to try, for both their sakes.

Composing her voice, a lopsided grin on her face, Ruth forced herself to chattily ask, 'So Sam, how was your journey down?'

'Uneventful and slow,' Sam replied dismissively as she cast Ruth a prospective look. 'Look, I'm sorry but I have to say this, in spite of everything that's happened to you, between us, I've really been looking forward to seeing you today, to spending some quality time with you. It's been far too long, already.'

Knowing she had been criticised again, albeit lightly, Ruth made a point of studying the road ahead of her. Thought of all the reasons why they had not been in touch with each other, for so long. Painful reasons for the most part. *Has there ever been happier times?* Ruth did not think so. There was so much to talk about, but it was all buried deep within a confusing and difficult past. She considered how, in reality, they had nothing in common but the past and how, for now at least, it was best to leave it well alone. Made her mind up to lie as she forced herself to lightly say, 'Yeah, me too.'

Sam watched Ruth with a critical eye, then she smiled. Silently nodded her head as if satisfied with the response she had been given.

Ruth breathed out her relief, but then in her guilt, rushed to fill the ensuing gap. 'How come you were so keen for us to go up to the cliffs? You do realise, don't you, they're going to be freezing at this time of the year?'

'Yeah, I wasn't sure, but I had guessed as much. I just thought,' Sam paused, looked a trifle uncomfortable, 'after all this time, it was best to choose a neutral ground for the two of us to meet on. And I thought, the cliffs seemed as good a place as any. I know you've always enjoyed walking on them, and so I was hoping…' she faltered, shrugged her shoulders. 'Well, you know…'

Ruth heard the common sense in what Sam had said. Realised the thought Sam must have put in to how best to spend their day together, and could not disagree with her choice. She certainly did not want to have to take Sam home with her. Nor did she want to have to spend the next three or four hours in some restaurant or café, struggling to keep a conversation flowing. So a walk along the cliffs, was probably as good a distraction as any. 'Yeah, I agree, I think it's a great idea and on that note, I was going to suggest we walk first, then stop in the National Trust café on our return.

Have a late lunch before I get you back to the station? Oh, and that reminds me, what time is your train home?'

Sam appeared to contemplate what Ruth had said, then theatrically shivering, she shoved her mittened hands in front of the car's heater. 'About four, I think, but if you don't mind, I was hoping we could go to the café first? Only, standing on that frost-bitten pavement at the station for so long, I got really cold. I also left home really early this morning and without any breakfast, so I'm now starving.'

Not wanting to be in a situation where they would *have* to make polite conversation for any length of time, at least not straight off the bat, Ruth had hoped that by walking first, it would have gone some way to easing them into each other's company. But uncomfortably realising it was possibly more of an issue for her, than it was for Sam, her conscience pricked, left her with no choice but to agree. 'Sure, no worries,' Ruth said. Vigorously nodded her head with a gay enthusiasm, she did not feel.

Sam, lapsing into a companionable silence beside her, the roads busy, Ruth slowly navigated her way through the coastal town of Dover. Once again lost in her own thoughts, she mindlessly merged the car onto a dual-carriageway known as Townwall Street. To her right, behind a number of faded Georgian buildings and a nasty brutish block of ex-local authority flats boom-built in the sixties, the wide sweeping harbour was hidden from view. Directly ahead, grandly holding court high above the historic old town, was the brooding medieval mass of Dover Castle. The once magnificent crescent of Victoria Park, sitting just below its insurmountable walls.

Sitting in heavy traffic, staring at brake lights, most of the vehicles in front, behind, and to the side of Ruth, were juggernauts. Each and every one of them converging onto Townwall Street, the main artery that fed the docks, the progress was slow. Inching forward less than a metre at a time, the road seemed distant, the car sluggish. Dead tired, her attention slowly drifting away, Ruth's head nodded toward the steering wheel.

Sleep, I need sleep.

The stream of traffic suddenly moving, massive lorries undertaking as their slipstreams violently rocked the car, the sudden blast of an air horn, and Ruth squealed in fright.

Looking wildly around, her heart cantering in her chest, Ruth's drug addled brain struggled to catch up.

Beginning to realise she must have somehow drifted across into the first lane of the dual carriageway, and directly into the path of a juggernaut coming up from behind, Ruth urgently jerked the steering wheel to the right but in her haste, forgot to depress the accelerator. Abruptly stalled the car. 'Shit!'

Sam slapping a steadying hand against the dashboard in front of her as she ricocheted against her seat belt, emitted an equally high-pitched squeak. Then ejected, 'Christ Ruth, what the hell is wrong with you? Are you trying get us both killed?'

Flustered and panicked, Ruth floundered to restart the car. Waved mortifyingly at the cursing lorry driver as she appealed for his patience. A queue of angry drivers honking their horns behind her, at last, she got the damn thing going again. Sweatily kangaroo jumped the stupid car back into the correct lane.

Acutely embarrassed by her horrifying ineptitude, Ruth resolutely avoided Sam's accusatory stare. Eyes fixed firmly on the road ahead, she muttered under her hiccuping breath, 'I'm so sorry Sam, but I didn't see it coming.'

'Really? You don't say?' Sam shot back sarcastically as she threw Ruth a filthy look. 'Do you need me to take over from you?' She demanded to know, her tone scathing as her eyes pointedly watched Ruth's hands shamefully flapping against the steering wheel.

Sam's undisguised disapproval making her feel a thousand times more anxious than she already was, Ruth wanted nothing more than to sink into the footwell of the car, to disappear.

In that moment, Ruth detested herself. Loathed what she had become. Hated that she wanted to weep, that she wanted to get out of the car, and run.

But if she were to break down now, with Sam right there, sat next to her, she would never forgive herself. So she forced herself to sit up straight. She refused to allow herself to give in to her nerves, her deep seated anxieties and though her vision was blurred, gripped tightly onto the steering wheel. Used it as a prop to still her quivering hands.

Ruth's voice taking on a strange vibrato, she assured Sam she was fine. Stated that in a couple more minutes, they would be at their destination.

Not the best of starts to their reunion, Ruth thought bitterly.

Excused herself inwardly on the grounds she had had a difficult time of late.

Chapter Four

Sunday, approaching lunchtime, and Ruth was in the garden studiously doing anything she could, to avoid being in the house.

Adam's parents had arrived early yesterday morning, and were staying for the weekend. Ruth, who had cleaned and polished for a week, was now keeping well out of the way as she focused on tending flowerbeds Adam had already cleared of weeds, only a few days ago.

Getting up this morning, Adam had insisted they could no longer avoid the inevitable. Having sat on their *news* for two months already, he felt they owed it to his parents to tell them the truth, to manage their expectations.

Not long after hearing Adam's proclamation, the first opportunity she got, Ruth had bolted for the garden.

Shivering suddenly, Ruth looked up from the rose bush she had been titivating. Swiped away a couple of self-pitying tears with the back of her hand. Though it had been sunny, the sky was starting to cloud over. The beginnings of a thick fret coming in off the sea, hanging just above the distant cliffs and on the horizon like a semi-transparent veil, Ruth suddenly became cold. Experienced a feeling of dread. Today, would be challenging.

Adam called out from the house, and Ruth reluctantly left the garden. It was obviously, *that* time.

The kitchen a hive of domestic bliss, Adam, with most probably the help of his mother, had already prepared for lunch. The oven emitting the mouthwatering odour of a roasting chicken, there were three different size saucepans bubbling and simmering on the hob. The kitchen sides already wiped down and spotless, not a single unwashed utensil had been left out or in the sink. In fact, if Ruth had not smelt and seen what was cooking, she would have had trouble believing her kitchen had ever been used. A vastly different state of affairs to when she cooked. Extravagant with equipment, and much to Adam's annoyance, Ruth would frequently employ every item of kitchen paraphernalia they owned, then leave the room in chaos. She found it impossible to both cook and clean at the same time. *Cooking up a storm,* was the usual term Adam used, when describing Ruth's approach to cuisine.

Observing the trio sat intimately around the kitchen table, a couple of Sunday newspapers scattered between them as they robustly discussed some article or other to do with politics — a subject Ruth hated and was not overly familiar with — she was suddenly reminded of the fairy tale of the three bears; papa bear, mama bear and baby bear. Felt irrationally uncomfortable as she wondered where in the story, she fitted?

Although Ruth silently told herself not to be so paranoid, not one of them lifting their head to even acknowledge her presence, she hesitated. Feeling ill at ease, and not wanting to disturb their conversation mid-flow, Ruth found herself automatically detouring toward the kitchen counter. Poured herself out a cup of tea from the still warm pot as her nonexistent courage, thinned even further.

Leaning against the kitchen counter top, but the strength in her thighs threatening to give out and overwhelmed with an urgent need to sit down, Ruth was forced to walk over and join the cosy threesome.

Almost unnoticed, Ruth pulled up one of the kitchen chairs and sat motionless. Listened to the playful bickering without contribution, as they continued to ignore her.

Smoothing her hand comfortingly over the cracked surface of the aged pine table, Ruth briefly recalled how Adam had proudly sourced the it from a local auction house. How he had brought it home as a surprise for her and even though he had known, she'd had her eye on a completely different table; a more modern glass affair that he apparently, hated.

Ruth sipped her tea. Flicked Adam an occasional anxious stare as she furtively watched his every move. His frequent smiles toward his parents temporarily disguising the careworn lines of his face, she thought how much older he had grown since their marriage. How the additional lines around his eyes suited his handsome face, made him look more distinguished. Whereas the crows feet threading out from the corners of her own eyes, made her look more haggard, ancient.

Taught as a bow, Ruth tensely waited for Adam to find an opportune moment to tactfully interrupt his parents. Continued to watch him out of the corner of her eye as she allowed her mind to momentarily drift.

With no parents of her own alive, Ruth had tried to cultivate a restrained affection between herself and her in-laws. But due to her inauspicious arrival, they had uneasily accepted her into the heart of the family. Made her reservedly welcome.

Although to all outward appearances, her in-laws seemingly sought to give her all the parental nurturing she could take, still, Ruth could not help but feel there was something about their ministrations, that was *off*. Nothing she could quite put her finger on, but their avid attention for how well she took care of Adam, for how well she kept house, felt somewhat overwhelming and at times, distinctly claustrophobic. It was as though, Ruth thought, they fully expected her to fail in her duties as a good wife.

Her own parents, orphans themselves and poorly paid, had lived in a council house. Dying intestate and with no savings, nothing of any fiscal value had been left for their young offspring to inherit. And apart from Sam, there was no other family; no grandparents, no aunts, no uncles or cousins. At least, not any that Ruth knew of.

From the age of eight, passed from one foster home to another, Ruth's childhood had been disorganised at best, horrendously chaotic at worst. Sam and she separated for the majority of their time in care, it was not until she had met Adam, that the unpredictability and the loneliness of her past had slowly begun to dissipate. *At least until…*

'The garden looks fantastic, Ruth,' said Adam's tall, patrician-looking father as he broke into her thoughts.

His diminutive mother smiling broadly, nodding her head in agreement, she bragged to Adam about Ruth's obvious gardening skills. Ruth easily accepted the credit. Yet is was Adam who had pruned the trees, sorted out the borders, planned the planting. She was proficient only in pulling up weeds and rarely, when Adam let her, operating the sit on lawnmower. But knowing the direction the conversation was about to take, and already feeling a failure, Ruth was not about to admit, to any of that.

'Mum, dad, we have something important to tell you,' said Adam, using the quiet and authoritative tone he adopted for official business.

Ruth's in-laws, snapped to attention. Seemingly warned that the *something* he had to tell them was significant and consequential, Adam's parents passed a conspiratorial glance between themselves, and their eyes began to dance.

Ruth squirmed. Dropped her own eyes as she pretended to concentrate on the drink in front of her. Braced herself for what was to come. Braced herself for failure.

'A baby?' Jenny blurted out, her eyes shining with eager anticipation as her exuberance got the better of her. 'Oh Ruth, darling, you're pregnant, you clever, clever girl.'

Please, kill me now, Ruth silently sent up a plea.

'You should be putting your feet up, not gardening,' Jenny exclaimed. Sent Adam a withering, *how could you*, look.

Visibly startled, Adam paled. Looked lost for words.

Ruth refused to look at Jenny, never mind answer her. She hid her face in her mug as she furiously sipped her tea. Swallowed miserably. A huge lump developing in her neck, she tried not to choke.

Adam cleared his own throat as he hastened to correct the misunderstanding. Caught his father's now uncertain attention.

Catching a brief view of Adam's underlying torment, the pain that was etched into his face, Ruth looked quickly away again. If she didn't, she would openly cry.

'No mum,' Adam shook his head, 'Ruth's not pregnant, but that *is* sort of what we wanted to talk to you about.'

Adam obviously working out what he wanted to say next as he searched for more explicit words but initially, could not find them, an awkward and subdued silence followed.

Diligently avoiding all three pairs of eyes; two sets enquiring and confused, one pain filled, Ruth continued to sip at her tea, too fast. Tried not to suffocate on the stifled tears, closing her throat.

Was it still too early, to have just one small drink? Ruth asked herself in desperation.

Perceptibly upset, Jenny blushed a deep shade of crimson. Embarrassed by her presumptuous outburst she began to apologise, but was stopped mid-stride. Alan reaching out, he took her hand in his and gently squeezed it. Tactfully prevented her from gabbling on. From interrupting their son in what he was so obviously struggling, to get out.

Adam took an audible deep breath, and then he told them. His voice monotone and matter-of-fact, without emotion, he carefully explained that unfortunately, there would be no grandchildren, not now and not in the future, at least, not from them. His mother's mouth dropping open in shock, his father's forming the beginnings of a question, Adam held up a protesting hand. Firmly, but gently stated, he preferred not to go any further into any of the gory details.

Ruth had to hand it to Adam, not once, had he played the blame game. At no time, had he pointed the cursed finger in her direction. Not once, had he mentioned, it was all her fault. That she was a failure and the reason, they could not have a child of their own.

A small drop of wine was an incredibly attractive concept, at the moment.

Jenny, a couple of tears squeezing silently out from each corner of her stricken eyes, lifted a hand as though to cover the treacherousness of her mouth. Whilst Alan, looking devastated, his aged hands shaking with the rigours of his suffering, was unable to prevent himself from saying at least something to mark the gravitas of the occasion. Murmuring condolences, he offered his commiserations with an air of finality and mourning. Leaned across and patted Adam's shoulder whilst treating the news his son had imparted, as a bereavement of sorts.

The elderly pair almost withering away before her very eyes it was, Ruth thought, as though they had become almost transparent. Like the skeleton bones of a couple of dead leaves being shredded by a cruel wind.

Squirming with the weight of her shame but unable to see past her own pain, Ruth refused to imagine too deeply, what her pseudo-parents were going through. She firmly told herself, *it is not the end of their world. They, at least, have another son. One who can still produce the required heir and a spare, to take forward the precious family name.*

Ruth badly wanted to find a way of having that drink, but the pull of convention, the desire to do right, was too strong. She could not pluck up the courage to get up and go grab a bottle of wine from the rack, then open it in front of everyone, not before lunch. *No one, wants to look that weak and desperate.*

Ruth watched Adam get up from the table, and go put the kettle on.

Chapter Five

Feeling Ruth's arm unexpectedly link through hers as her body pressed just as intimately into her side, Sam unwittingly flinched. She had not expected Ruth to be quite so warm or tactile toward her and consequently, had to strongly resist an automatic desire to shake her sister off.

We aren't close. We have never been close. So what is she playing at?

'Let's go,' Ruth said, digging Sam in the ribs.

Hearing the strained gaiety in Ruth's tone, Sam wondered at the amount of effort, Ruth was seemingly so keen to put in. *Is she genuinely pleased to see me, or is it all a ruse?*

'Yes, sure, you lead the way,' Sam replied somewhat uneasily. Lifted her head, then forced out an equally false smile as Ruth unceremoniously tugged her across an almost empty car park.

That's it, just keep smiling, Sam silently encouraged herself. *Don't let her get to you. Today is important.*

Entering into what would become a light and airy building, glass, wood and steel everywhere, the initial walk-in space was narrow and confined. So it was with relief, Sam was able to legitimately decouple herself from Ruth's claustrophobic embrace.

Walking single-file behind her elder sister, Sam allowed Ruth to lead her into a small shop that was run by the National Trust. A tantalising aroma of freshly filtered coffee and baking immediately assaulting her nose, making it twitch with pleasure, Sam's mouth instantly began to water. Getting up at stupid o'clock that morning, then travelling for over two hours on what had to have been, the slowest train in the world, and without any breakfast, Sam was now not merely hungry, but ravenous. Barely glancing at any of the merchandise on display in the shop, Sam hurried herself up. Hastily caught up with Ruth as they headed directly toward where all the delicious smells, were coming from.

Ruth marching them toward one of the many empty tables in the café's seating area, Sam suddenly found herself standing in front of an enormous plate of glass covering the full width of the building, and gasped with surprise.

Initially not knowing where to place her eyes because there was so much to look at, looking through the window, Sam ultimately focused on the horizon. A light haze on the ocean, twenty-one miles from where she stood, Sam could occasionally see France; one minute it was there, and then it was not.

Next perusing the dramatic seascape, and the vast number of waterborne vessels rising and falling as they bumped up and down through the wind whipped tempestuous Dover Straits, Sam could not help but marvel at the view.

Dragging back her gaze. Peering down onto the Eastern docks, watching a multitude of brightly coloured dinky toys of all shapes and sizes, slowly marshalling themselves into tidy lines, again, Sam was amazed. Each vehicle waiting for the humungous roll-on, roll-off ferries to daintily pirouette into one of the empty berths, it was an arresting sight. *How come I've never been up here before, it's wonderful?*

'Wow, this is some view,' Sam said, gesticulating for Ruth to join her at the window.

'Yes, I suppose it is,' Ruth replied dismissively.

Ruth not paying an iota of attention to what lay beyond the other side of the enormous plate of glass, Sam was at first, surprised. But then she thought, *she's obviously seen it so many times, what did I expect?*

'What can I get you?' Ruth asked.

Watching Ruth's discarded scarf slither unnoticed to the floor, Sam was unable to resist the urge to pick it up. Draping it tidily on the back of a spare chair, she just as quickly grabbed at the coat Ruth was in the process of carelessly shrugging from her shoulders. Then tidily folded it too, over the chair.

So Ruth was still just as messy. Her less than tidy habits must have driven an OCD Adam, mad, Sam mused. Though it was reassuring to note that there were some things about her sister, that had not changed.

'Sam?' Ruth prodded impatiently.

'Oh, sorry, I'll have a coffee and a fruit scone please.'

'Cream and jam?'

'Yes, please,' Sam nodded, remembering to throw Ruth a grateful smile.

'Okay, I won't be a minute,' Ruth replied.

Stripping off her own coat, Sam carefully hung it over the back of her own chair and unable to believe quite how hungry she was, discreetly passed a light hand over her non-existent, grumbling stomach. Neatly folding her gloves and scarf into her capricious shoulder bag, which she then placed onto the floor, next to her feet, she took a seat.

Observing Ruth open her bag and fish into it for something, Sam briefly wondered if she should grab her own purse and offer to pay something toward the bill? Figured, Ruth could more than afford it. Sat back more comfortably into her chair.

Although Ruth had smiled cheerily before walking toward the counter, Sam could feel her tension. She could see right through Ruth's carefully constructed and unconcerned manner, and which was undoubtedly, all an act.

Savouring a few moments to herself whilst reflecting on her sister, it was amazing, Sam thought, just how much could change over a period of a few months. Ruth's already slender frame, had become so much thinner and her chestnut hair, hanging limp and loose on her shoulders, was now dull and shapeless. But much worse than Ruth's physical appearance, was her miserable ensemble; her grey and black clothes, rumpled and stained, they had the distinctly unpleasant odour, of a wet dog.

Yet up until the previous year, Ruth had always been so stylish, and she would never have left the house without her usual mask of makeup. Depending on her mood and the amount of effort she put in, Ruth had always had the ability to be plain-looking, attractive and occasionally, even beautiful.

Right now, Ruth looking not only unkempt, but noticeably vulnerable and lost, for a couple of seconds, Sam could almost feel sorry for her.

The present Ruth, a very different version of the woman Adam had so effortlessly fallen in love with, then married. Just when, Sam mused, *had Ruth become so slovenly? Was it before Adam's untimely demise, or was it after?*

Recollecting the very last time she had seen Ruth, albeit briefly, Sam cast her mind back to Adam's funeral. Could clearly recall the frozen grimace on her sister's face, that *rabbit in the headlights* stare as she was being almost dragged across the top of the crematorium steps by Adam's father, to meet and greet the mourners. Yet even then, Sam realised, Ruth had looked a total wreck with her mussed up hair falling down out of some sort of rough chignon, her bare mouth looking white and pinched, her face with mascara runs lining cheeks that were caked in too much rouge, shiny and damp. Remembering how the tip of Ruth's bright red nose had looked raw from constantly sniffling into the wad of tissue she clutched in her trembling hand, Sam allowed herself a small smile. Ruth's reverent black clothes looking as though they had been thrown on with little to no thought, she had appeared shabby and graceless, disappointing. Those all important first impressions being crucial, at least in Sam's book, the grieving widow, she thought, had badly let herself — not to mention the deceased — down.

Pulling her thoughts back to the present, Sam revisited Ruth's late arrival that morning. Pondered on Ruth's scarily chaotic and jerky driving, her frequently vacuous stare. Disagreeably recalled, with a slight wrinkle of her pert nose, the offensive taint of breath that had been soured with the strong and unmistakable smell of alcohol. Then it dawned on Sam, that Ruth was possibly still on the drunk side of sober.

That crazy bitch could have killed us both!

Whether Ruth had been indulging copiously the night before or fortifying herself that morning, Sam could not be certain. Either way, Ruth being under the influence of alcohol this morning, would go a long way explaining why she had presented herself in such an appalling physical state. An excess of drinking would also go some way to explaining, Sam realised, what might actually have been happening, on the day of Adam's funeral; *Ruth had been pissed.*

Taking the opportunity to surreptitiously search her sister's apathetic and dazed countenance for further clues of an excess of alcohol, it didn't take Sam long to find the damning and conclusive evidence she was looking for. Ruth's eyes ringed with shadows that were black as mascara, also looked reddened and sore. Her face, hard and sharp with weight loss and the signs of fatigue, was uncharacteristically marred by pimples, spider veins and rough skin, plus there was an unusual puffiness to its contours. As for her cracked and roughened lips, Ruth was constantly licking them as though they were inordinately dry.

Yes, Sam thought, lightly nodding her head at herself. The combination of grief, combined with what had to have been a sustained alcohol abuse, had mercilessly etched themselves into Ruth's twenty-four year old face; the alcohol destroying her looks, along with her dignity. Ruth was, Sam was now certain, imbibing far more than was healthy for her.

Noisily banging down a tray laden with mouth drooling goodies onto the table, it was with an unexpected vigour that Ruth commanded, 'Well come on then Sam, I thought you were hungry, tuck in.'

'Yum,' Sam said with feeling, needing no further encouragement. 'These look delicious, Ruth.'

The bitter coffee Sam had drunk in the warmth of the station café earlier whilst waiting for Ruth to appear, now uneasily floating in an empty stomach, she had begun to feel quite queasy and could not wait to eat. Helping herself to two of the four fluffy scones flecked with juicy raisins, she loaded one of them with jam followed by a tick layer of clotted cream, then bit into her first scone with an uncomplicated greed. It had been a long time since she had allowed herself such unfettered, self-indulgence; *pure heaven.*

'Yes, he…' Ruth faltered, as her jade green eyes welled with tears. 'He used to say they were the best scones in the area.'

Sam had not missed that Ruth had avoided saying Adam's name and she wondered if it was the purely the grief that was preventing her from doing so, or, if it was some other reason; *guilt, maybe?*

As Ruth's tears began to tiresomely fall, Sam reminded herself she needed to demonstrate some understanding. That she needed to be seen, to be empathetic to Ruth's visible distress.

'Oh Ruth, you poor thing, why didn't you say?' Sam said, awkwardly reaching out to lightly pat the back of her sister's quivering hand. 'If I had known that ordering these was going to upset you,' she waved a half-eaten scone Ruth's way, 'I would never have asked you to get them for me.'

On the receiving end of a watery smile, but noticing that Ruth's eyes had turned unexpectedly dead and cold, like those of a shark, Sam quashed down a nervous shiver. *Now what have I said? It sounded all right to me.*

'Don't be silly,' Ruth said, her voice cracking, 'and anyway, my life is filled with things like these.' She gesticulated toward the scones. 'Hundreds of little memories that catch me off guard when I least expect it. So unless I'm prepared to have a lobotomy, I figure I have no choice but to get used to them.'

Ah, so nothing I said then, Sam thought with a certain amount of relief. Then acknowledging from bitter experience, what Ruth had just articulated was most definitely accurate, Sam found herself suddenly caught unawares. Struggling with a subset of her own emotions, and not wanting to be exposed but temporarily unable to talk, she hastily redirected her focus onto the task of loading up her second scone with jam and cream. Hoped that Ruth, flailing around in a pool of her own misery, was oblivious to her blip in composure.

'Sam, what happened in the car, on the drive up here, I'm really sorry,' Ruth emphasised apologetically.

The subject changed, Sam was relieved. 'Hey, it happens,' she replied with a light shrug of her shoulders. 'Don't beat yourself up over it. We survived didn't we?'

'Yeah, I suppose we did,' Ruth nodded, her cheeks pinking up with embarrassment as she shifted awkwardly in her seat.

'Oh, for heaven's sake, it's not like you meant for us to be crushed by an artic lorry, did you?' Sam asked, delivering Ruth a wicked chuckle to lighten the mood.

'No, no, of course I didn't,' Ruth confirmed, throwing over the semblance of a grateful smile.

'Okay, well subject closed, then,' Sam insisted as she wondered what to talk about next.

'You know,' Ruth continued, taking the decision away from Sam, 'when we first moved down here, we used to come up here all the time. We used to get to the cliffs, by walking across the fields at the back of the house. Then before traipsing back home again, we would share a cream tea as a treat to ourselves. Ridiculous really, as we probably consumed far more calories than we actually walked off.' Obviously on the verge of tears again, Ruth blew her nose noisily. Then cursorily brushed a hand across her damp face.

Sam's ears pricked up as she made a connection. 'Ruth, what did you mean when you said that you and Adam *used* to walk the cliffs together?'

'I'm sorry?' Ruth queried, looking oddly shaken by Sam's question.

'Well, living so close to the cliffs, I'd always assumed that you and Adam would have walked them at every opportunity? I know I would, if lived here.'

Ruth vigorously shook her head. 'Nothing, I meant nothing by it. It was just a figure of speech. Of course we walked them regularly, right up until he…'

'Right,' Sam nodded, though she was certain, she had just been lied to again.

Ruth lapsing into silence as she sniffled into a tissue, Sam started to savage her second scone with relish. Wondering as to the genuineness of sister's easy tears, the dynamic of her marriage, and knowing Ruth had always been expert at manipulating her own emotions, Sam hated to think she was being put in the position of having to collude with sister's promiscuous self-pity, her easy lies.

Minutes passed.

'Ruth, why don't you talk to me. Why don't you tell me honestly, how you're *really* doing?' Sam queried as casually as she could. She hoped it had been the right question to ask, the right button to push. Her scones finished and guessing their walk was imminent, Sam felt it was time to provoke Ruth into displaying a noticeable reaction, but she had to be careful. The last thing she needed was to push so hard, she ran the risk of Ruth walking out on her.

'I'm okay.'

Liar, Sam thought as she closed her eyes and exhaled. Swallowed down her irritation. She decided to push a little harder. 'Seriously?' Sam said, throwing Ruth a disbelieving look. 'Come on Ruth, I'm not a fool,' she continued on, deliberately sounding as unconvinced as she felt. 'I'm sorry but I warn you, I'm going to be blunt. Not to be cruel you understand, but because I think you need it. You don't look okay. In fact, you look bloody awful.'

Ruth glanced down at herself, and her face angrily clouded over. 'Really! You don't say?' she snarled loudly. Looked defiantly across the table at Sam.

The words lustily sprayed from out of Ruth's mouth with an unexpected ferocity, Sam recoiled into the safety of her seat back. *Well, that worked*. Inwardly, she smirked.

Noticing the sudden and angry exchange had also caught the attention of a couple of the National Trust staff, their heads swivelling round with interest at the disturbance, Sam continued to mentally congratulate herself; *job done*.

Wordlessly thanking Ruth for the negative memory she had unwittingly created, Sam gave the staff straining to hear, an awkward smile as she silently mouthed them an apology; *sorry, she's a little overwrought*. Obtrusively handed Ruth another paper napkin as though consoling her.

'And yes, I know I look like hell,' Ruth continued indignantly on, impatiently flapping away the serviette Sam held out to her, whilst seemingly ignorant to the interest she was generating. 'But in case it's escaped your notice, I have just buried my husband.'

Bits of scone and spittle spraying everywhere, Sam shrank even further back into seat; *disgusting*. Delivered the earwigging staff another silent apology. This was going so much better than she had expected. Though she had hoped for a display of some distress and possibly even some tears, the level of vehemence that was pouring so publicly out of Ruth was working right in her favour.

'My point exactly,' Sam reasonably pointed out. 'Look, I'm sorry if I've upset you, but it's only because I am genuinely concerned for you.'

'Really?' Ruth spat out aggressively, her tone incredulous.

'Yes, and it's not just your physical state I'm worried about. I'm also concerned for your general state of mind.'

'There's nothing wrong with me, and there's certainly nothing wrong with my state of mind,' Ruth exclaimed savagely, her voice audibly rising along with her temper. 'For God's sake Sam, I'm grieving!' she hissed out loudly. 'So exactly what *state*, do you expect me to be in?'

Having forgotten just how rudely vocal Ruth could be when provoked, in spite of herself, it was now Sam, who was a little stunned. She told herself to exhale and calm down. *Think clearly, Sam. Today is important.*

Realising, Ruth's fury was escalating to the point where it had the potential to backfire, aware the staff had heard more than enough for her needs, and not wanting to provoke Ruth into walking out on her, Sam placatingly said, 'Look Ruth, I didn't come here to argue with you. And I know I can't even begin to imagine how you must be feeling after everything you've been through, but all I've ever wanted to do, is to be able to support you. So if I've offended you in any way, I'm sorry. Truly I am. I'm just worried, and as your sister, I want to help.'

Silence.

Ruth sighed heavily, and closed her eyes. Then her mouth trembling, she calmly said, 'Yes, well, if I *am* honest, you're right. Of course you're right. These last few weeks, have been terrible and a lot tougher, than I expected.'

This time, not doubting the truth in what Ruth was saying, Sam felt a rush of relief; *disaster averted.* Deciding to hold fast to the numerous questions that were on the tip of her tongue, Sam deliberately held her own council as she sought to coax Ruth's new found candidness, through silence.

'Most days,' Ruth said, 'it's all I can do to manage the day in front of me. Every day, I struggle to get out of bed and then when I do, I can't stop crying and I'll find myself curled up in the weirdest of places; typically a corner somewhere staring off into space and with absolutely no idea, how the hell I got there.'

The words flying from out of Ruth's mouth, albeit this time in a hushed whisper, Sam felt stung by the rapidity of them. Wished she could flee, but knew she had to stay. *It's taken me weeks to get to this point.*

Following the funeral, Sam had made a point of ringing Ruth at various times throughout the day. But every time, Ruth had systematically hung up on her. Ruth not answering any of Sam's texts or emails, it had been a supremely difficult time. Frustrated, running out of patience and more concernedly, time, Sam had begun to think she would have no choice but to turn up on Ruth's doorstep, uninvited and unannounced. A worrisome thought bearing in mind she had no idea as to the extent of Ruth's local support network. And the last thing Sam wanted, was to put herself at the risk of being outright rejected in front of an audience. Both considerations of primary importance if her plans for her sister, were to be successful.

Positive she was unlikely to be given a second chance, it was with a dogged perseverance, Sam had eventually worn Ruth down. Ruth finally answering one of her calls, Sam had grabbed at the opportunity; hastily organised a date and time for a visit, then quickly switched off her mobile. Made herself uncontactable, just in case Ruth should try and cancel.

So today is important, Sam reminded herself. *I have to make it work.*

'Look Ruth, I know we've had our problems but why on earth didn't you ring and talk to me? No matter what has happened between us, I am still your sister. One phone call, and I would have come running. You really don't have to manage this awful process, all on your own,' Sam stated.

Ruth maintained a strained silence. Swallowed a couple times, then looked blankly off into the distance as though she was travelling somewhere dark, unreachable.

'Ruth, is everything okay? Did you hear what I just said?' Sam asked. *God, she could be so infuriating.*

'Why Sam? Why did this have to happen to me?' Ruth implored suddenly, her eyes desperate.

Though disorientated and somewhat confused by the unexpected rawness of Ruth's conspicuous emotions, Sam forced herself to think of an appropriate response. Then unexpectedly, found herself providing an honest answer. 'Ruth, you have to forget the *why*. There is no why. The *why*, doesn't matter, because it won't help. What happened to Adam was awful, horrendous. But what is done, is done. And it can't be undone,' she pointed out, with feeling. Refused to cry.

'I get such an awful, gut wrenching ache every time I think about him,' Ruth passionately stuttered out, her voice heavy with emotion. 'I can't begin to tell you how much I miss him and I would do *anything*, anything at all, to have him home with me again. I know it probably sounds clichéd and over-dramatic, but there was *so* much that was left unsaid between us. It all ended so badly between us,' Ruth divulged suddenly. 'We had such a terrible…' Then left the sentence hanging as she bit back any further words from escaping.

For a moment, Sam's mind raced as a flood of unsettling ideas began to reveal themselves. *What? What did Ruth just say?*

There were so many questions Sam wanted to ask Ruth. But big, fat, untidy tears sliding down the length of sister's distraught face, dripping disgustingly off the end of her wobbling chin as she became lost in a world of her own again, Sam seriously doubted she would get anywhere. She needed to give her a minute.

Squashing down a desire to shudder at the state Ruth had got herself in, it was then that Sam registered, just how tired she was. Realising she had already had more than a bellyful for one day, Sam sighed. *Ruth's nervous energy and paranoia is utterly exhausting, but if I can know, I will know.*

'Ruth, what did you mean earlier, when you said it all ended so badly between you?' Sam asked as she reached out to take Ruth's hand, squeezed it. But Ruth recoiled from her touch. She hastily snatched away her hand as though she had been burned. Sam let it go. She pretended not to notice as she reminded herself that Ruth was not a woman, who invited touches or hugs.

'Oh that,' Ruth blustered. Flicked her eyes nervously away and around the room. 'I didn't mean anything by it. We might not have been married very long, but we had a good one.'

A good marriage, really? Mocked Sam's inner voice. *So why so defensive?*

'You don't sound so sure… You do know you can tell me anything, don't you? If you *were* having problems in your marriage, I promise you, I'll just listen. I won't judge.'

There was a beat of awkward silence.

Sam grinned inwardly. *So I was right,* she thought with a disguised pleasure.

'I don't know what you mean?' Ruth shook her head. 'There's nothing to tell, and as I've already said, we had a good marriage,' she stated with a finality. Broke eye contact with Sam as once again, she looked distant, thoughtful.

Sam ignored the urge to fill the subsequent gap as she held the silence. Sat back in her chair, and patiently waited. She was guessing that given time, Ruth, in her unstable frame mind, would be unable to help herself. That eventually, she would spit out the truth.

'It's just so unfair,' Ruth stated.

Ah, here it comes, Sam thought.

'He was so young and we had our whole lives ahead of us. If only...'

Again, Ruth had infuriatingly stopped mid-sentence. Crushed with disappointment, knowing that the moment for truth had been deliberately side-stepped yet again, Sam could throttle her sister. Then noticing Ruth's hands were trembling so much, she could barely lift her mug without spilling coffee all down herself, an honest compassion took over. Shoving another serviette Ruth's way, Sam shortly said, 'Here, take this.'

'You know, I still can't believe he's dead,' Ruth stuttered out. Slopped even more drink onto her already damp lap as she ineffectively dabbed at the mess. 'Everyone I meet, keeps talking about me having to come to terms with it. But what the hell is that supposed to mean, exactly? Are they saying I should come terms with his death? Or are they saying I should come to terms with living on my own, or to not knowing what my future holds, anymore? If so, I have no idea how I am supposed to do any of that,' she angrily spat out, a wad of spittle gathering at the corners of her mouth. 'I wasn't ready.'

'We're never ready,' Sam stated impatiently, but with conviction. *I'm not sure I can cope with much more of this.*

The silence again stretching out before them, this time it felt vast and insurmountable. Watching Ruth retreat into an infinite pit of misery, Sam was beginning to think that maybe, she was finally out of her depth. But then she firmly reminded herself, she was there with a purpose. That no matter what, she had no choice but to see the day through.

Suddenly, Ruth shuffled forward on her seat, leaned in closer to Sam. Flicked her eyes furtively around the room, then her lips curling, she snarled out. 'You know, every day I find myself lurching from being so upset I can't possibly function, to being so consumed by rage, it burns inside of me like an uncontrollable wildfire. To blunt, I think I'm now at that point, where I could quite easily go out and kill someone.'

Ruth's threat spat out with such evil intent, in spite of herself, Sam shuddered. She was not a paranoid woman, and yet in this moment, knowing she could never trust her sister, she felt suddenly unnerved, and anxiously on edge.

Rubbed a comforting hand back and forth across her suddenly nauseous stomach.

Chapter Six

Adam's secretary, had called Ruth about three hours ago. Ringing, at Adam's request, Lisa had officiously told Ruth the restaurant booking for that night, had been brought forward an hour. Adam's London meeting running late, he would no longer be coming home first, to pick Ruth up. The company chauffeur now dropping him off at the restaurant, Lisa had stated, Adam would meet Ruth there.

    The only problem being, up until five minutes ago, Ruth had been crashed out on top of the bed. Sleeping through the alarm she had so carefully set for five pm, she was now running late. Already eight minutes past six, and she had yet to shower, to sort out her hair, to put on some make-up, and find something to wear.

    Even though she did not have the time, Ruth changed her clothes three times before deciding on the outfit she would wear. Finally settling on a flattering black dress that skimmed her minimal curves, she hastily applied some much needed makeup to her shadowed eyes, her perspiring face and her pale lips. Then shoved her still slightly damp hair, up into a deliberately messy bun. Liberally spraying a mist of perfume into the air, Ruth stepped into it whilst wondering, if Adam would recognise the scent as the one he had recently bought her.

    Having crashed around the bathroom and the bedroom in a futile attempt to be ready on time, both rooms now looking like a tip, Ruth was infuriated with herself. It was the third time in as many days, she had slept through the alarm.

    What the hell is happening to me, and why do I feel so tired all the time?

Today, of all days, she really needed not to be late. Adam was going to be so upset with her.

Ruth rushed into the restaurant, and glanced around the room looking for her husband. His face eerily lit up from the glow of his mobile phone, he was sat on a bar stool. As she made her way toward him, Ruth silently prayed he had not noticed just how behind schedule she was. Always reliable and a stickler for being punctual himself, Adam was never late.

'Hi,' Ruth said, as she flashed her husband her best smile. Mentally crossed her fingers, her toes, and anything else that would cross.

Adam hastily shoved the phone he had been interrogating, away. Pushed it into the inside pocket of his jacket and out of sight. Getting up from his seat, he pecked her on the side of her face. His cheek as it pressed up against hers, Ruth noticed, was smooth, cool, and smelling distinctly of his particular scent; black pepper and citrus.

'You're late,' he stated impatiently.

Adam's eyes, with their tiny wrinkles at the corners, barely acknowledged Ruth. Certainly, he did not appear to take in her appearance, or any of the effort she had made, to look nice for him. 'Yes, I know. I'm sorry,' she tried to mollify.

'Well, we've lost our table.'

Even though Adam pretended to shrug it off as if it were of no matter, Ruth could tell he was supremely irritated. Adam preferred the privacy and silence of being tucked away in a their usual booth at the back of the restaurant and because of her, it had been given away to another couple. Hence, she guessed, the heavy sigh, and the chilliness of his perfunctory kiss. Pained by the upset she had caused but knowing she had no one to blame but herself, Ruth nervously bit down on her bottom lip. Hoped her lack of punctuality, would not spoil the rest of the evening.

Following a waiter to one of the smaller tables in a row of small tables which were full of people within earshot, Ruth thanked him as he courteously pulled out a chair for her. Sat down across the table from her now flagrantly disgruntled, husband.

'So, what's the special occasion?' Ruth joked, whilst lightly acknowledging they had not been out to dinner alone, for quite some time. Giving Adam her widest smile between the bud vase of roses, and the winking candle flame, Ruth scavenged for affection. She was desperate for the evening to be relaxed, fun. It had been such a long time, since they had enjoyed any real time, together.

Adam briefly flashed his teeth, more a grimace than a smile, and did not answer her question as he absentmindedly pushed a hand through his hair. Lifting the drinks menu to peruse, he instantly hid behind it.

'Are you okay?' Ruth persisted. She wanted to understand if there was perhaps more going on, than she realised.

Adam's face appearing from around the side of his makeshift screen, he rewarded Ruth a weak grin. Tiredly said, 'Yes, I'm fine. It's just been a full on day.'

When wasn't it? Ruth thought somewhat bitterly, before brushing the thought, hastily away. In the six months since they had been told of their inability to have children. *No*, she silently corrected herself, *since they had been told of her inability to have children*, their lives had proceeded quietly. The routines had returned but with one subtle difference, instead of Adam putting in an eight hour day, he now worked a ten, sometimes even a twelve hour day. The level of his business travel also growing exponentially, it was no longer unusual for sizeable chunks of their weekends to be bitten out. The sum total beginning to leave Ruth feeling as though, from one week to the next, she barely saw him.

A waiter squeezed between their table and the next one over, asked them if they wanted a drink. Adam ordered a bottle of Chardonnay. Ruth would have preferred a Merlot, or even some celebratory champagne, but she had not been asked for an opinion.

The waiter retreating, this time Adam picked up the food menu and again, slid his face behind it. Left Ruth to listen to the soft pop of corks being pulled, the sounds of ringing crystal, the clunk of metal cutlery, the low murmur of other people's conversations.

Adam's silence getting to her, Ruth appealed, 'Adam, what's wrong? I know there's something's wrong, because you're acting all weird.'

Adam shook his head at Ruth. 'I don't know what you're talking about. There is nothing wrong with *me*,' he emphasised testily. Then returned his face to the menu.

Ruth had noted Adam's avoidance of answering directly, the vagueness of his almost accusatory reply. Left feeling flat and dull, as though she was no longer worth talking to, a non-person, someone to be tolerated rather than enjoyed, it was then it occurred to Ruth, just how lonely she was feeling. How with each uneventful day that passed and the increasing lack of company, the weeks were trudging by with a dreary slowness. How, even though she could obviously come and go at will, these past few weeks, she had begun to withdraw more and more into her own private asylum; her lovely home, slowly becoming her prison.

Lately, Ruth had even considered looking for a job. Something part-time that would perhaps go some way toward filling her day, whilst helping her to construct some sort of a social circle. But Adam, old fashioned in his views, expecting her, like his mother, to be the stay-at-home wife who took care of all his personal and private needs, she had been reluctant to discuss it with him; could not face, the inevitable argument.

Now though, the bulk of her days unstructured, Ruth found she was taking longer and longer to drag herself out of bed in the mornings. Then once up, feeling unsettled and restless, she would spend a certain amount of time traipsing along the cliffs or the fields circumnavigating the house. Returning home, only when she was so weary, she could no longer think.

Afternoons, she would crash into bed, and have a little snooze to recuperate before Adam got home from work. Yet somehow, her naps had slipped into lasting quite a bit longer, than she originally planned. Anything, she supposed, to eat up the time.

On the increasingly rare occasions when Adam did come home from work, at a decent hour, and she was not already in bed, Ruth would make every attempt to engage him in normal dialogue. She would try and chit-chat with him about how his day had gone, the weather, anything. But still, their conversations were flat, often forced, and frequently strained.

The worst thing though, was their sex life. When trying for a baby, their lovemaking had been opportunistic and frequent. Yet now, almost as though it had become a pointless exercise, the sex had become fitful and at times, for days on end, non-existent.

Is that it? Ruth challenged herself, and not for the first time. *Now I can't give him the child he craves, is he slowly pulling away from me? Is he trying to shake me off?*

Ruth convinced herself she was over-analysing, seeping into paranoia. She reminded herself that Adam loved her, that the tyranny of his job was strong and all consuming, and that she should not to take his moods so personally. He was simply worn out. She would try again, extend him an olive branch.

'Adam, I know you've had a tough day and you're really tired, but it is our wedding anniversary. So couldn't you be just a little more excited?' she protested lightly. Tried to keep the nervous break from out her voice as in spite of herself, she sought his reassurance, some attention.

Adam looked at her, hard. Lowered his voice and brusquely said, '*Excited?* What are you, a ten year old child?'

Stung by Adam's overt rudeness, the light died from Ruth's eyes. She exhaled deeply, then nervously bit down her bottom lip. *I will not cry.* She took a minute. Unsure how best to respond, Ruth avidly searched for the wine waiter; she needed the distraction, but he was nowhere in sight.

'Adam, please, we've seen so little of each other lately, and I've really been looking forward to tonight,' she pleaded, her eyes glowing wetly in the flickering candlelight.

'Really? Is that why you were so late?'   He said sarcastically.

Ruth paled. 'That's not fair!' she shot back stronger than she had intended. 'You were the one who brought the time forward, not me.'

Adam's eyebrows lowered and the eyes narrowed as he leaned in toward her. 'Ruth, your voice, please lower it and please don't make a scene.' He purposely looked around, made a point of drawing her attention to the number of people within earshot.

Why is he so angry all the time, so mean?

Ruth sat silent, motionless. Blushed fiercely from her head to her toes. She had not intended to make a scene. All she had wanted for tonight, their special night, was to celebrate. To enjoy some quality time with her increasingly distant husband.

Recalling how only this morning, she had received two perfectly formed, blood red roses. How, having assumed each flower represented a year of their marriage, she had been so touched by his thoughtfulness. The thorny duo beautifully gift wrapped and accompanied by a lovely little typewritten card telling her, he loved her, the sentiment behind them, or so she had thought until this evening, could not have been much clearer.

Now feeling confused by the mixed messages she was receiving, Ruth persuaded herself, it was all her own fault. Adam was right to be upset with her. It was their anniversary and yet it was she, who had been late. No wonder, he was so irritated with her.

The wine arrived. The waiter asked for their food order and even though she had yet to glance at the menu, Adam gave him both their choices. The waiter discreetly disappeared.

Though itching to point out she would have liked to have had the chance to peruse the menu for herself, to place her own order, Ruth did not want to spoil the evening by making matters worse. So she smiled sweetly. Said nothing.

It's not deliberate, she reassured herself. *He's just tired. He's, not thinking straight.*

The white wine so cold it frosted their glasses, Adam took a dainty sip. Ruth took a fortifying gulp.

'Go easy, Ruth,' Adam said immediately.

Shocked at the warning aggression in his tone, Ruth's cheeks flamed under the candlelight, and for a minute, she could not breath or swallow properly. She spluttered, then coughed. Tears sprang to Ruth's eyes as she had no choice but to noisily clear her throat. Heads swivelled as the people around them looked to see what the disturbance was. Hands trembling with humiliation, Ruth dabbed at her mouth with her napkin. Tried to collect herself as Adam glowered across the table, at her.

Adam taking Ruth's glass from out of her hand, putting it down on the table in front of her, she saw it was empty. She did not remember finishing her wine.

As the starter was succeeded by the main, they both picked at their food. Ruth's mind churning as she dug her fork into the dressed crab in front of her, her stomach felt knotted with anxiety.

I haven't eaten all day, so I must eat something. It will soak up some of the wine, I can't remember finishing.

Ruth chewed slowly, but each mouthful was a struggle as she forced herself to swallow. Her throat tight and dry but wary of further incurring his displeasure, she drank very little; two or three glasses, at the very most.

The tide of diners ebbed and flowed around them. Ruth smiled Adam's way a few times. She tried to engage him in discourse but seemingly restless and uninterested in what she had to say, he replied in monosyllables. He kept fidgeting and glancing at his wristwatch, as though he had somewhere else to be.

Ruth tried again. 'Thanks for organising this,' she said, between mouthfuls. Bestowed him with a warm smile. Anything to break the uncomfortable silence, to the thaw the ice running through her husband's veins.

'Don't thank me, thank Lisa,' Adam replied curtly.

Ruth stopped chewing as she wrestled with an unexplained attack of fear. *All this, because I dared to be late?*

In the end, the dinner was brief. By nine-thirty their plates had been cleared. Then without asking her if she wanted a dessert or even a coffee, Adam handed his credit card to the waiter and rudely said, 'We're in a hurry.'

A few minutes later, stood on the pavement outside of the restaurant whilst she waited for Adam to return from the cloakroom with his overnight case, Ruth glanced in the window. Watched a waiter clear their table, lower on a new white tablecloth, lay cutlery, with an organised precision. A young couple approached, took over what had been their table. The waiter sweeping in to greet them at the same time as they clasped hands across the middle of the table, each looking into the eye's of the other, it appeared, Ruth thought jealousy, they were about to have a better evening ahead of them, than she and Adam had just had.

Isolation settled in. Stood there, on her own as yet again, she waited for Adam, Ruth was suddenly a very lonely woman. Tears threatened. *I will not cry.*

Adam arrived. Told her she had had too much to drink, to be able to drive. Rudely snatched the car keys from out of her hand. Then brusquely barked at her to hurry up and get on in as he impatiently over revved the engine of her startled little car.

Such an arse, Ruth thought, with a flash of spirited anger.

Chapter Seven

Ruth figured she had roughly ten minutes tops, to get her act together before Sam returned from the toilet. Having spilt some coffee on her one and only cashmere jumper, and wanting to dab the offending liquid off before it transformed itself into a stain, Sam had gone in search of water. Ruth looked briefly down at her own damp jeans; *thank God, they were black.*

Allowing all the feelings she had bottled up for months, to explode like spoilt champagne over an unsuspecting Sam, had left Ruth feeling humiliated and vulnerable. As if that was not enough, somewhere in amongst the midst of stupidly stripping her soul bare, she had also let slip, things had not exactly been all that rosy, in the garden of her marriage. A reality she was not prepared to admit to herself, never mind to Sam, or anyone else for that matter.

Ruth's brain expanded suddenly, pressed mightily against her skull and she rubbed her aching temples. It really did hurt too much, to think. Her eyes swollen from all the crying, the skin between her nose and her upper lip stinging, she could only imagine, what a mess she looked.

What had happened to being cautious, to being wary about what I should and should not, divulge?

There was no noticeable pleasure or relief in having laid herself bare. The last time secrets had been traded between Sam and herself, the pair of them had ended up having the most almighty of all arguments. One that had culminated in months of silence. For a second or two, Ruth found herself transported back to that same row. Neither of them wanting to concede to the other, she freshly recalled the recriminations, the lies, the bitter anger. Their quarrel ending so badly, Ruth had been unable to bare the thought of having to be in Sam's company, ever again. Yet here she was; *go figure?*

Similarly, seeing Sam at *his* funeral, had come as a real shock. To Ruth's knowledge, Sam had not been invited, and she had certainly not been expected. Unable to forget how her father-in-law had dragged up the aisle of the crematorium, only to leave her standing in front of her immaculately dressed sister as though she was being presented to royalty, Ruth momentarily saw red. *How dare Sam appear at his funeral as though nothing bad between them, had ever happened.* Recalling how, her back rigid and her jaw clenched, she had fought back tears of tortuous humiliation before forcing out a salutation of sorts. How the service already over, she had fled, turned smartly on her heel and ignoring the other mourners waiting on the crematorium steps to provide their commiserations, had dived into the funeral car to hide, she relived her embarrassment all over again. Wondered briefly, what Sam remembered of that awful day. *Do I really want to know? To ask?*

Two days after the funeral, Ruth's mobile had rung. Sam's caller ID showing, she had immediately shut down her phone. Then within minutes, the house phone had rung. Answering the call, establishing it was Sam, Ruth had immediately hung up on her. But Sam, relentless in her pursuit, had persistently called Ruth's mobile and the house phone numerous times throughout the day, every day; left countless voicemails and a number of text messages. Becoming desperate, it was at the point where Ruth was seriously considering unplugging the house phone and leaving her mobile permanently switched off, that she had finally relented. Reluctant to have one or other of her in-laws, or worse, the police turning up on her doorstep concerned as to why she was not answering any of their calls, she had succumbed to the inevitable. Reluctantly answered Sam's next call and within less than five minutes, had found herself fixing a date and time, for a visit.

But why though? Why, after all these months of abstinence, would Sam be so keen to ruthlessly force her way back into Ruth's life? *Was Sam really that opportunistic, she would seek to exploit his death, to her own advantage?*

Keen to believe Sam only wanted to help, that she was merely trying to be a good sister, Ruth wavered.

But isn't there, just a little too much water under the bridge, for that?

Feeling the tears of confusion, of self-pity, falling liberally down her cheeks again, Ruth angrily swiped them away. Ignored the stares of a couple of overly interested OAPs, the National Trust staff.

Ruth began to sweat as her mouth dried. *I need a drink. A real drink.* She hastily flicked the thought away, before it could take a mean hold.

More than once, during their brief phone call, Sam had insisted she only wanted to help, to be there for her but just when, Ruth continued to obsess, had Sam ever done anything without there being an ulterior motive? She sighed, heavily. Nervously picked at a bit of loose skin down the side of her index finger.

Knowing she was no where near strong enough to deal with Sam, Ruth wished with all her heart, she had not given in to today's visit. That she had not let her loneliness drive her. But if the last few weeks had taught Ruth anything, it was that she was no good left to her own devices, not anymore. *The isolation, is killing me.*

After months of accepting his lengthening absences, their controlled fights about where he had been and who he might have been with, Ruth had long been at the point where she could no longer stand her own company. His death only serving to compound her solitude, leaving her rattling around an old house that was devoid of all life, of the family for which it had been built, she found it soul-destroying.

That, and having to suffer the torture of grief; the crying, the choking, the spluttering, spending hours rocking herself back and forth as she bordered on near hysteria.

These last few weeks, her sanity, Ruth was sure, had become questionable. All decisions, even the simple ones like whether to get out of bed, whether to eat, had become completely overwhelming, reduced her at times, to a gibbering wreck.

I'm even seeing things. I see his ghost seeping out of the floorboards, his face floating out of the walls.

Spooked by her imaginations, Ruth shivered.

Turning her thoughts back to her sister, Ruth recalled how Sam hated scenes, how she hated recriminations, fuss, and especially those played out in public; finding other people's overt emotions unattractive and darkly disturbingly. Thinking about it, Ruth was astonished by how well her unexpected outburst had been handled by Sam. The Sam of old, would have walked away, long before now. Yet today, and completely out of character, Sam had stayed. She had seen the turmoil through. *Unbelievable, so again, why? Why was Sam here, and why now?*

But before Ruth could linger on her, as yet, unanswered questions, Sam returned.

'Hi, you okay now?' Sam asked solicitously, her face full of earnest concern as she took up her seat again.

Sam's head bobbing from one side to the other as she searched her face for clues, Ruth couldn't help but observe the way her sister's chestnut hair swayed on her shoulder line; Sam's hair expertly cut, as hers was not. Immediately regretted, that she had noticed.

'Yes,' Ruth nodded, 'I think I'm fine, now.' Nervously bit down on her bottom lip as she told yet another lie. Felt another apology coming on.

'Good, I'm glad.'

'I'm sorry Sam. I can promise you, I never meant for *any* of that to happen,' Ruth emphasised with conviction, whilst trying not to squirm with embarrassment.

'It's okay. Don't fret about it. If it helps you to feel any better by getting all that stuff off your chest, then great,' Sam reassured. A warm smile settling onto her lightly, but perfectly made-up face.

Ruth felt incredibly old. Still only twenty-four herself, and only two years older than the woman sat if front of her and yet all of a sudden, she felt decrepit.

Who are you, she silently asked Sam, *and what the hell have you done with my sister?*

'Thanks, Sam. Thanks for being so understanding. That was a pretty embarrassing display, earlier.' *Am I grovelling?* 'God only knows, what the staff must think?'

'The staff?' Sam looked around. 'Why are you worried about the staff? I'm sure they're too busy to worry about us.'

'I just hope they didn't hear my little outburst.'

'I doubt it, and even if they did, it is none of their business.'

Was she for real? Ruth did hope so.

'Thanks, Sam.'

Ruth studied her coffee as she thought. Though unable to undo the past, because the future kept coming at her, she was trying to work out if now, was the right time to bring up the subject of what had happened between the two of them, all those months ago?

But Sam had already read her mind. Lightly shook her head and quietly said, 'Let's not go there now.'

Ruth hesitated, then nodded in agreement. *Sam was right, it was too soon.*

The moment passed.

A little awkwardly, Ruth asked, 'Tell me about you, Sam? Bring me up to date with all that's been happening in your life.'

'There's not that much to tell.' Sam replied with a dismissive shrug of her narrow shoulders. Gave Ruth a warm smile, to soften her evasiveness.

Hoping for more, Ruth tried again. 'Are you still living in the same house share?'

Sam giving her an odd look, Ruth squirmed inwardly as she suddenly recalled the reason for it. *Perhaps, not the right question to have asked?*

In London, to buy curtains for the new house, she had taken the opportunity to drop in on Sam before catching the train home again, to Kent. The house Sam had been sharing, a shabby and faded Edwardian villa crudely converted into four bedrooms, two bathrooms and a grubby communal living-kitchen-diner, busy with what had seemed a horde of people coming and going, and located in an aggressive neighbourhood renowned for its anti-social problems, it had not been, a particularly successful visit. Ruth uncomfortable and nervous, her surroundings bringing back difficult memories she would rather forget, she had guzzled her tea and somewhat, to her chagrin, had not been back since.

'No, I moved out quite a while ago, now.'

'Oh?'

'I'm still based in Hackney but I actually have a flat of my own, now. And you'll be pleased to know… the area I'm living in, is much nicer,' Sam chided with a smile.

Unsuccessfully trying not to blush, Ruth licked her dry lips. *Has she read my mind again? I do hope not.*

'It is great, not to have to share.'

'Yes,' Ruth nodded, even though she was surprised.

The last time they had met, which was the same day they had so furiously argued and fell-out, Sam had been worrying about the precariousness of her job. The company she had been working for, in the process of restructuring and streamlining, Sam had been certain redundancy was around the corner and finances tight, she had asked Ruth if she could borrow some money. But then they had bitterly quarrelled, and Ruth's willingness to put herself out for her sister, had instantly dissipated.

Now though, Ruth's conscience was badly pricking and it was with a certain amount of reluctance, she quietly asked the obvious next question.'And your job?'

'Work's fine, a few months back, I managed to get myself a new job.'

The smile Sam flashed Ruth, bore not even the ghost, of any animosity. *So why do I feel so guilty?*

'So were you made redundant in the end?'

'Yes, I was. And I must admit, it was a bit hairy there for while but let's just say, I got there in the end.'

Ruth experiencing surges of guilt at the thought of Sam losing her job, struggling for money, perhaps even fighting to keep even a roof over her head, she was grappling for what to say next. 'Well, if it's enabled you to move into a flat of your own, this job must be a lot better paid than the last one?'

Sam nodded her head and smiled. She did not elaborate further.

'So where are you working, now?'

'Oh, nowhere flash, just a small property development company not far from where I'm living. Being a local firm, it keeps the commute costs down, meaning I have more to spend on the rent.'

'And you enjoy it, the job?'

'As much as I would enjoy any job, but yes, I suppose it's okay,' Sam shrugged indifferently.

'On reception?'

'No, I'm a PA to one of the directors running the company,' Sam retorted, sounding a little short. The smile that did not quite reach her eyes, short-lived.

For an instant, Ruth feared she had overstepped the mark and a brief silence descended, whilst she took in what Sam had told her. *Quite a jump from being a receptionist to being a PA,* she mused, uncertain. Knowing how flighty Sam had been since leaving school, how many jobs she'd already been in and out of in her short career, and how few qualifications she had, Ruth could only assume, she had got lucky.

Ruth turned her head at a sound nearby; an elderly couple taking up residence at a table just down to the left of theirs. Her train of thought broken, she asked, 'Boyfriend?'

'Pardon?'

'Is there a man on the scene?'

'Good God no,' Sam said with feeling. Rapidly shook her head as though to emphasise the point.

But Sam looked, Ruth thought, surprisingly cagey. Almost as though she had a secret, she did not want to share. Intrigued but treading lightly on this delicate ground, Ruth gently said, 'From your response, your choice, I take it?'

'Absolutely,' Sam said with conviction, her cheeks slightly pinking up as though she had shared a confidence, even though she had not. 'I'm footloose, fancy-free, and loving every minute of it.'

Finding herself thinking how wonderful it must be, to be so independent and unshackled, to have no responsibilities to anyone other than to yourself, a violent shot of envy coursed through Ruth's veins, and took her surprise. Unexpectedly coveting Sam's freedom, it came as somewhat of a shock to discover that she too, was now just as liberated as her sister. Probably, even more so than Sam as *his* death had not only discharged her from her previous duties, but it had also left her financially secure.

Ruth went suddenly cold. *Was that it? Was that the real reason Sam was here, she was after money? Surely, she wouldn't be that calculating, would she?*

Her thoughts too appalling, too dreadful to even contemplate, Ruth imperceptibly shook her head. Shook the thoughts away as she took a strong, steadying pull on the dregs of her coffee.

'Anyway, that's more than enough about me, today was meant to be all about you,' Sam stated. 'So come on, why don't we get on with what we came here to do. Let's get out and walk those damn cliffs. Clear out our heads a little, or at least your head.'

Sam chuckling wickedly as she threw an exaggerated wink her way, for no obvious reason she could put her finger on, Ruth's stomach flipped.

Chapter Eight

The lining of Ruth's coat was cold as she pushed her arms into the sleeves. Withdrawing as deep as she could into its voluminous folds, hood up, scarf tucked protectively around the bottom half of her face and gloves firmly on, she dared to venture out.

Any sensible person on such a raw day, she whinged silently to herself, *would be sat at home now, in front of a roaring fire.*

Sam walking beside her, and equally bundled up, Ruth leant slightly forward as she pushed herself into a perishing wind that instantly sliced into any exposed extremities. The air charged with frost and bitterly cold, tinged with the slightly saline odour of the sea, she swallowed it deep into her burning lungs; relished in its frigid saltines.

'It's freezing!' Sam yelled over the gusting wind.

'Yes, I know!' Ruth yelled back as she took another determined breath. The cold wind temporarily relieving her head of its customary pain, making her body want to move even faster, she hurried her pace. Even if the fresh air was whipping her cheeks and freezing the inside of her nose, it felt good. She could breath again.

For the first time since *his* death, Ruth welcomed a flicker of excitement as she began to realise that for a very long time, something important had been missing from her life; pleasure.

Surprising herself, finding she was looking forward to doing battle with the outside elements instead of her inner demons, Ruth granted herself a small, self-satisfied smile. The perpetual tiredness that had dogged her every waking hour these last few weeks and months, slowly skulking away, for once, she began to feel the stirrings of something good. Something, akin to hope.

A lemon drop sun hanging low in a peppermint blue sky that was cloud free, Ruth was thankful to note, even if they froze to death, at least they would stay dry. *Not bad*, considering it was the end of February and that for the last few days, it had rained practically day and night.

The icy conditions combined with the high winds likely to put off the most hardy of souls, Ruth guessed the walk was likely to be as dead in the winter, as it was lively in the summer. Took a delight, in the thought of having the cliffs, all to themselves.

Keeping the sea and the sun to their right, Dover Castle and the National Trust building blurring behind them, for the next few minutes, the sisters trudged up a taxing and grassy incline. Nearing the summit and needing a minor reprieve after their initial exertions, Ruth drew Sam to a stop.

They took a minute.

Knowingly surveying the rolling terrain that lay ahead of them, casting her eyes backwards and forwards over the frozen ground, Ruth could see it was hard with ruts that were covered in frost. In the distance, ice glinting on the puddles that peppered the coastal paths, Ruth speculated on the best route to take for their circular walk.

Unable to make up her mind, Ruth briefly dropped her hood and using the tendrils of hair whipping around her head and face as an improvised weather vein, roughly evaluated the direction of the thrashing wind. Having worked out it was blasting in from north-east, her mind was made up. As soon as they were at the bottom of the Langdon Hole steps, they would fork left; take the easier farm track out, then return using the cliff path. That way, they would have the wind behind them on the more arduous and exposed part of the cliff walk.

'As it's so cold and you've got a train to catch, we'll walk only as far as the South Foreland Lighthouse!' Ruth shouted, over the top of the wind.

'What?' Sam bobbed her head in toward Ruth as she strained to hear.

'I said, we'll only go as far as the lighthouse. It's a round trip of about five miles. So we should be back in under ninety minutes. Is that OK with you?'

'Yes, but can we please get going again, before I freeze my butt off.'

Sam's indistinct voice coming from somewhere deep within the folds of her scarf, Ruth nodded her ascent. 'Okay, let's go. If this gets too much for you,' Ruth threw her hands out expansively, 'just let me know and I'll cut the walk short.'

Now standing at the top of a set of deeply descending steps, muddy puddles of frost and ice sitting atop glistening chalk, Ruth knew from bitter experience, they were about to face a potentially disastrous situation. Tugging at Sam's coat sleeve to gain her attention, she pointed to the ground and yelled, 'Sam, be careful! The steps ahead are likely to be lethal underfoot! Don't slip, or you'll break your neck!'

'Yes, all right!' Sam shouted back as she encouraged Ruth to go ahead of her.

But Ruth did not want to go first. The obvious newness of Sam's boots, worried her. Not exactly hiking boots, they looked totally impractical for what lay ahead of them. If Sam lost her footing on the slimy steps, Ruth would rather not be taken down with her. 'No, you first,' she replied, but her words whipped away by the merciless Artic wind as soon as they were out of her mouth, and guessing Sam had not heard them, she deliberately hung back. Then for good measure, waved on a reluctant looking, Sam.

Sam in front of Ruth, tackling each treacherous step with due caution, before long, both surfaced safely at the bottom. Setting down into a major depression in the cliffs known as Langdon Hole, Ruth immediately veered Sam off to the left. Guided her away from the usual paths and onto a derelict road that ran a quarter of a mile or so inland, from the actual cliff edge. From here on in, until they got to the lighthouse, Ruth knew the walk would be an easy and unremarkable one. All they had to cope with, was the slamming wind.

Falling into step together, the sisters strode out and took the same long strides. The intermittent roar of the gusting wind making it too difficult to converse, they naturally fell into silence as they trod the rough and ready, former road. Previously wide, but now reduced to a cinder footpath, it was still littered with chunks of coal and coke that crunched underfoot; visible reminders of the local coal mining industry, ruthlessly shut down in the late eighties.

The terrain in front, gently rising over a distance of approximately half a mile, passing through two kissing gates — one half way up, and the second just before the top — at the T-junction, with Sam behind her, Ruth turned right onto a small tarmac road.

The protection of the cliff undulations now dropping down to her right, and the road essentially a farm track with ploughed fields running along either side of it, Ruth knew that from here on in, they would have no choice but to push forward into the full force of the wind.

Doing battle with the obstructing wind, keeping her head low and her eyes down, Ruth put one reluctant foot in front of the other as she aimed toward St. Margaret's-At-Cliff. Becoming increasingly tired after weeks of inactivity. Her home, unable to be seen, but just three miles away at the furthest end of the field immediately to her left, suddenly, its draw was strong.

Forty-five minutes later, each step of the way mercilessly pummelled by the wind, Ruth was more than relieved to arrive at the South Foreland Lighthouse.

The decommissioned building situated in its own piece of land, Ruth briefly cast an appraising eye over its austere form. Painted a startling white, and carefully positioned on the exact spot where navigation beacons had stood for over three hundred and fifty years before, this version of the building had been built in Victorian times. Purpose built, the warning beacon had helped generations of mariners to avoid the infamous Goodwin Sands; a sandbank laying approximately three miles off the coast of Deal and that had claimed, thousands of lives.

Currently closed for the season and bare of its usual throng of visitors, the old relic appeared forlorn and abandoned. Uncomfortably reminded Ruth of herself.

Sighing, Ruth plodded wearily on as she thought how things, always lasted longer than people.

Now just past the lighthouse, leaving the farm track and turning a sharp right, Ruth approached an old warning triangle marking the entrance to an alley way. The sign faded and depicting the graphic of a peeling stick man falling dramatically off the edge of a cliff, she beckoned for Sam to get behind her.

Walking single-file down the confines of a narrow passageway that ran between a high hedge to the left, and an elevated wrought iron fence on a long block of concrete to the right, Ruth found herself temporarily sheltered from the seemingly ceaseless wind.

A temporary silence cloaking itself around Ruth, like a protective mantle, her knees unexpectedly weakened. Stumbling, fearing she was about to sink to the muddied floor and knowing that if she did, she would never get up again, Ruth forced herself to keep upright. Ruth's earlier enthusiasm for the walk, long since dissipated, she was wrestling with herself on so many levels; exhaustion, a rising panic, fear, but more than anything, she was struggling under the onslaught of an irrational thirst. Licked her dry lips as Sam prodded her in the back, to get moving again. *Impatient bitch.*

Emerging onto a grassy meadow, bereft of its usual wild flowers and insects, Ruth trudged Sam diagonally down a wide and well trodden, chalk path.

Warily approaching the ancient Saxon path that ran within just a couple of metres of the crumbling cliff edge, Ruth gulped with apprehension. She hated heights.

The very first time she and Adam had walked the cliffs together, they had seemed impressive and magical. Now though, feeling tired, depressed, craving a drink, and knowing there were no fences to protect or prevent an unsuspecting walker — *or me* — from falling to their death over the disintegrating rim, they felt inhospitable and threatening.

Her palms sweating with anxiety inside her gloves, Ruth took in a deep, steadying breath. *I will be fine. I just need to keep away from the edge.*

Stopping a little way back from the *Saxon Shore Way*, turning to face the south-west, Ruth encouraged Sam to go ahead of her, to take up the outside edge of the narrow path whilst she kept a safe distance.

The gale force wind switching from smashing them in the face, to forcefully shoving them in the back, Ruth kept the meadow to her right, Sam, the cliff margins and the sea, in that order, to her left. Then concentrating on the uneven terrain ahead of her, cautious of damaging an ankle in one of the numerous rabbit holes waiting with malicious intent, she pushed forward again.

Ruth's mouth constantly salivating, she strode out as fast she was able. *I have to have a drink. Just one, and I'll be fine again. That's all I need.*

'Ruth! How much longer? My feet are killing me!' Sam yelled, having to almost run to catch up with her.

Ruth did not stop walking. Sam would just have to keep pace. 'Blisters?' she asked, unsurprised and impatient.

'Yes,' Sam miserably affirmed. Grimly nodded her head as a pained expression settled onto her face. 'These boots are fairly new, and they're seriously chewing up my feet.'

'Yes, well, unfortunately for you, we've still got another thirty or forty minutes walk ahead of us,' Ruth replied, her sympathy as short as her temper. *That'll teach her for not wearing the right boots.*

Ruth's cravings driving her, her rhythm never slowed.

'You are kidding, right?' Sam asked breathlessly as she tried to keep up.

'No, I'm not,' Ruth shook her head dispassionately. 'We're well passed the halfway point. So there's no way of cutting the walk any shorter, not now. You should have said something, sooner.'

Sam drawing up alongside of her, Ruth knew she was being scrutinised and felt suddenly, guilty. She took a deep breath and forced her features to relax. Tried to erase all traces of her growing anger, her impatience.

'Look, if you need a short break, there's a bench on top of the next headland,' Ruth said, pointing toward where she meant. But she did not want to stop. Her excesses having ruthlessly caught up with her, she was keenly suffering. Bone-tired, nauseous and parched, she felt driven to get back to the house.

'No, it's okay,' Sam responded with a shake of her head. 'If I stop now, I'll probably never get going again.'

'Great, well let's push on then.'

Sam stretched her strides to keep pace with Ruth's and again, walking side-by-side, they fell into an uneasy silence.

The worst of the warrens now behind them, Ruth lifted her eyes and allowed her gaze to roam widely over the panoramic view. Took in a wide blue sky and miles of water glistening on and off, in the sunlight. The sea alternating between a deep navy and turquoise, crests of white topped waves wrestled and crashed over themselves in their haste to batter the cliff face, below.

Realising she was being followed, Ruth briefly locked onto the cold, dead eyes of a colony of gulls. Deathly silent, beadily watching her every move, they flew just beyond the cliff face, in parallel to her. Then starting to raucously wail and moan, they slowly sank away from view.

Though she was desperate to revel in the wildness of her surroundings, to get back the fleeting feelings of elation and excitement she had experienced at the start of the hike, it was only her thirst that was paramount in Ruth's mind. Her will for enjoying the walk long since abandoned, she was now itching, to get it over with. Could not walk fast enough.

'When was the last cliff fall?' Sam asked, breaking into Ruth's thoughts as she strode alongside.

Cliff falls? Why does she want to know about cliff falls? Can't she see I'm in a hurry to get back?

'Ruth, did you hear me?'

She would have to answer. 'I don't know. I think there was one a few months ago, but nothing since as far as I'm aware,' Ruth answered curtly. Kept on walking.

'I'd love to be around when one happens. Must be quite a sight.'

Ruth snorted unattractively. 'So long as you're not too near the edge or on one the beaches below,' she said caustically.

'I didn't realise you could get down to any of the beaches from here?'

'You can't, not from here, but you can from St Margaret's at Cliffe, or Langdon Hole.'

'Langdon Hole, isn't that the big dippy bit near the start of our walk, at the bottom of the steps?'

'Yes.'

'Seriously?' Sam queried.

Ruth thought. Gave Sam a calculated stare from behind her sunglasses. She was not in the mood for conversation, had not been for some time, but if it kept her from thinking about… 'Yes, some of the locals reckon that in the summer months, like June for example, when the tide is both out and exceptionally low, if you hug yourself tight into the foot of the cliffs and you are quick enough, you can get all the way from the beach at St Margaret's at Cliffe, right through to small beach at the bottom of Langdon Hole.'

'But how would you get back up from the beach, to Langdon Hole?'

'There are some are some steps. They're built into the cliff face, but it's not a walk to be recommended. And it's certainly not advertised.'

'Why not?'

'Why do you think?' Ruth retorted rudely.

'Because, it's dangerous?'

'Yes, obviously,' Ruth replied tersely. 'For one, the tide has to be low enough. For two, it has to be at least, a five or six mile walk from St Margaret's to Langdon Hole. For three, the tides around this stretch coastline, are unpredictable and fast. At high tide, most of the beaches running along the bottom of these cliffs are completely covered.'

'Sure, I get it,' Sam nodded conversationally.

Did she ever shut up? Ruth thought as her head thumped.

'And would I be right in thinking, this might be the next bit of cliff to potentially fall?' Sam asked, stepping off the path as she nonchalantly strolled over to investigate a huge fissure, running just to the left of them.

From Ruth's vantage point, Sam looked perilously close to the yawning edge of the crevice. Too close. Ruth's spine, tingled with fear. 'Yes, and I would strongly suggest you be careful!' she yelled over the wind.

Sam rejoining Ruth on the footpath, dipping her head in close again so she could hear, she asked, 'How about jumpers? Do you get many of those up here?'

Ruth shuddered at the thought of anyone being so desperate as to deliberately throw themselves off the cliffs. *They're so high.* '*Jumpers*, what an awful word to use.'

'Yes, sorry Ruth, I didn't mean to offend, I was just being curious?'

'I take it you really mean, suicides?'

'Yes.'

'Yes, of course we do,' Ruth nodded. 'In fact, A-Adam...' she stuttered over his name, hated saying his name, '...and I had a weird experience up here, some months back.'

'Really, do tell?' Sam demanded, somewhat ghoulishly.

I should have kept my mouth shut, Ruth thought.

'We had been walking along the cliffs one Sunday, when *he...*'

'Who?' Sam interrupted.

'When A-Adam,' Ruth stammered, 'noticed a young bloke sitting right near the edge. A screw top clasped between his knees and nothing to drink out of, he was swigging the wine straight from the neck of the bottle. And he didn't exactly look dressed for the occasion, either.'

'How do you mean?'

'He was wearing the sort of clothes you might wear to the office; smart trousers, a white shirt, ordinary shoes, no jacket, and he looked suspicious. Completely out of context with the setting, and miserable.'

'So what did you do?'

'Well, I was all ready to approach him. To ask him if he was okay but before I could, he stopped me.'

'Who stopped you?' Sam cut in again.

'A-Adam, of course,' Ruth stuttered out belligerently. Missed him in that moment. 'He said it would be too dangerous, not only for the lad himself, but also for me.'

'How do you mean?'

'Well, if he was really bent on chucking himself off the cliff and I had got in his way, he could easily have taken me with him.'

'Yes,' Sam nodded. 'So what did you do?' she asked, sounding as though she was hanging onto every word.

'We hiked it home as quick as we could, then rang the police.'

Vividly recalling the insanity of that afternoon, of the upset that had been caused between the two of them, by one unsuspecting stranger, unbidden tears sprang into Ruth's shaded eyes. A good deed done and yet he had accused her of being reckless. Of putting her life at risk and potentially his, by even *wanting* to approach the boy. Retaliating with bitterness and recriminations at the unfairness of his assertions, still, and in a way that had never made any sense to her, they had torn into each other. To this day, it was not a memory Ruth particularly liked to revisit.

Her mouth beginning to uncomfortably salivate again, *just one little drink and I will feel so much better,* Ruth squeezed her eyes tightly shut for a second. Pushed the thirst away.

'So what happened next?' Sam asked keenly.

Ruth sighed, impatiently. She had forgotten she owed Sam an ending. 'It turned out, the police had been looking for him. They had received an anxious call from a distraught girlfriend explaining she'd had a row with her boyfriend and that having dumped him, he'd threatened to take his own life by jumping off the Dover cliffs.'

'Christ.'

'Yes, the idiot boy had come all the way down from Manchester on the train, to do it.'

'And did they get to him in time?'

'Yes, we were able to give the police a good description of where he was, and they located him quickly and easily. The police also called the Coastguard and between them, they talked him down.'

'Wow, that's some story,' said Sam.

'If you say so? The whole thing turned us into nervous wrecks, at the time.'

'How do you mean?' Sam asked, her tone surprised.

'Well, we thought we were going to be in terrible trouble for wasting everyone's time, and especially when we learnt the Coastguard had scrambled their helicopter out.'

'Oh yes, I remember...' Sam stalled. Looked ahead as if she had said nothing.

What did she mean? Startled and confused by Sam's unexpected response, Ruth scanned Sam's face for clues. But her sister's eyes hidden behind her sunglasses, and her cheeks already pink from the rawness of the wind, it was difficult for Ruth to gauge if they had reddened any further.

'Sorry, did you just say you *remember*?' Ruth challenged aggressively.

'Of course I didn't, how could I?' Sam replied, her face sprouting a perplexed look.

'So you're saying, I misheard what you just said?' Ruth interrogated, her temper starting to unravel.

'Yes, of course you did. It was probably the wind, it must have distorted my words.'

There's no one here to see me do it. Right now, I could shove her off the cliff and no one, would be any the wiser.

Shocked at her murderous train of thought. Ruth shook her head at herself. What was she thinking? Hadn't there been enough death in her life, already?

'So what *did* you say?' Ruth stubbornly demanded to know.

'God knows,' Sam replied with a cherry laugh. 'I haven't got the foggiest, now.' She shrugged her shoulders. 'But I'm sure,' she turned to face Ruth, 'it couldn't have been anything important.'

Though certain she had not made a mistake… still, the doubts were creeping in. No longer convinced of what she had heard as none of it made any sense, still, Ruth couldn't quite leave it alone.

'Really?' she muttered doubtfully, and under her breath. Wanting to cast off her suspicions, but not quite able to.

Why don't I trust you?

Ten minutes later, cresting the headland that would lead them into Langdon Hole, Ruth suddenly halted, mid-stride. Sam abruptly walking to within a few measly centimetres of the crumbling cliff edge, a cold hand grabbed at the back of Ruth's neck.

Was she mad?

Watching in trepidation as Sam leant precariously forward. Hung her head right over the massive drop that was falling away from beneath her feet, Ruth trembled, with dread.

'The tides out!' Sam yelled back to her. 'I can see the beach you were talking about, and the carcass of an old shipwreck. Come on Ruth, come over here and see for yourself.'

A cold sweat breaking damply out across the top of Ruth's forehead, her face bleached to white. Her irrational phobia of heights kicking in, big-time, Ruth's spine was literally crawling with fear. Her chest constricting, her breath ragged, her head swam as she began to sway with panic.

'Come on, Ruth!' Sam called out. Turned her head back to the view, the precipice.

Rooted to the spot. Forcing herself to focus on the distant horizon, Ruth fixedly watched, until the edge of the cliff, the foaming sea and the hazy outline of the French coastline beyond, all merged to create one deceptively reassuring, level landscape.

Concentrating, the sounds of the maelstrom swirling around her, slowly dropping away, in its place, a calm descended. Experiencing an irresistible pull, mesmerised, Ruth's previously leaden feet, started to move. Inched her further and further forward as an invisible force took hold. Took her closer and closer to the crumbling rim.

Don't look down, said a soothing voice in Ruth's head. *Just keep looking straight ahead, toward the horizon. Better still, close your eyes.*

A few more steps, the whispering voice softly encouraged, *and you can step off, into a peaceful oblivion. That's right, just keep on walking and soon, it will all be over.*

One more step, and all the emptiness, all the pain of being alive, will disappear…

Then, there was the most blood-curdling scream.

Chapter Nine

Adam's job taking him away more than ever, the gardener he had employed to help him keep their third of an acre garden under control, arrived just before eight that morning. Cracking on long before Ruth had risen from her bed, a rangy man of mature years, he had been hard at it, for the rest of the morning.

Rarely, did Ruth do any gardening. She had little to no knowledge of horticulture, and did not enjoy spending hours and hours pruning and weeding, any more than she did doing the housework. In fact, the last time she had done any significant work in the garden, it had almost killed her.

Jumping on Adam's ride-on mower, pushing the lever into gear, it had started off fast and in her panic, Ruth had mistaken the throttle for the brake. The machine instantly speeding up, Ruth had struggled for control. Only just missing a cherry tree, followed by the side of the garden shed, she had wrenched the machine to the right, and had ended up ploughing her way through the orchard until an immovable apple tree, had stopped her in her tracks. Unhurt, and fortunately sustaining not even a scratch, the same could not be said for the mower. The machine damaged beyond repair, Adam had promptly banned her from going anywhere near his gardening equipment, his shed, his garage, and his tools. Admonishing her as though she were an errant child, he had insisted the outside of the house was *his* domain, whilst the inside of it, was hers; *whoopee, lucky me*. Left smarting by the extent of his anger, as well as hurt by his insensitivity toward her not insubstantial ordeal, Ruth had sulked for days. *Not that Adam had noticed, or even cared.*

Now bored, needing a distraction; *who knew there could be so many hours in a day?* More than slightly desperate for some adult company and noticing Henley stop for lunch, Ruth wandered spontaneously out into the garden. Stepping out from the cool of the kitchen, through the patio doors and into the heat of the midday sun, the foliage on the apple trees rippling and shivering in a light breeze, Ruth luxuriated in the warmth of the air as it kissed her bare arms.

The translucent yellow sun bathing her face with its temperate heat, Ruth's mood slowly began to lighten. But then she remembered, the weather would be changing soon. Summer sadly about to give way to autumn, she could almost taste it.

Her hands in the front pockets of her skinny jeans, her narrow shoulders slightly hunched in her sky blue t-shirt, Ruth casually approached Henley. Her face reddening, she tentatively asked, if she could join him for a while? He, in turn, nodded his ascent. Ran his rheumy eyes over her pinked face as she gingerly perched on the opposite end of the slightly mouldy garden bench, to him.

Sipping on a glass of red wine, Ruth watched in silence and with interest as Henley carefully unpacked the contents of a small plastic lunch box. Withdrawing each item in turn, he laid out along the length of spare bench that ran between them, a quartered sandwich neatly wrapped in sliver foil, a chunk of fruit cake, a Granny Smith apple, a single square of bitter dark chocolate, and a flask of something hot and steaming that smelt like coffee.

Ruth smiled faintly to herself. *I wonder how long it took Mrs Henley to prepare her husband's lunch, this morning?*

Slipping easily into conversation, Henley commented on how early Adam must have left for work that morning. Then he said, 'Young people these days, seem to work excessively long hours. Perhaps you could you remind me, what is it your husband does for a living?'

'Adam's a lead scientist, and he loves his job,' Ruth answered. 'It takes him all over the world, and at his level in the company, the long hours are to be expected.'

What Ruth did not say, was how hard it had become for her, his leaving the house. How the act of Adam removing himself, leaving her alone for hours on end and sometimes for days at a time, was becoming especially difficult. How watching him walk out of the door with his laptop bag in his hands or slung across his body, his roller suitcase clattering on the gravel driveway behind him, she had begun to feel he was, in some deep-routed way, slowly separating himself from her. Took a sip of wine.

Henley, looking as though he knew exactly what she had been thinking and starting to look sorry for her, Ruth decided to change the subject. She could not bare his pity. 'Tell me Henley, how's your wife doing?'

Henley frowned. He said, 'Not that well.' His eyes moistening, he looked away for a moment. 'Mrs Henley,' he went on to explain, 'is now in the latter stages of dementia and soon to go into a nursing home.' He said, 'She hardly knows me anymore,' and that she had recently had a bout of pneumonia, and that she now weighed less than seven stone. Unfortunately, there were no children and after forty-five years of marriage, he could not bring himself to imagine, what he would do without her.

It was all Ruth could do, not to openly cry.

A few hours later, when the last border had been weeded, and the lawn manicured to within an inch of its life, the air starting to turn a little cool, Ruth suggested to Henley it was time he called it a day. Having said she would see him again in a couple of weeks, Henley smiled, doffed his well worn cap at her, and said, 'It's been a pleasure.'

Ruth briefly wondered what it would have been like to have had an extended family of her own; a doting grandfather, a grandmother in her life.

Felt sorry for the child weeping inside of her as she turned to go back into the house.

Entering their bedroom, the air thick with dust motes floating in the shafts of light, Ruth undressed down to her underclothes and lay across the bed for a few minutes. Calling her husband's office, she spoke briefly to his secretary and was told he was in a meeting. Lisa promised she would ask Adam to call home, as soon as he was free. *You'd better,* Ruth thought.

Awaking well over an hour later, the evening sun starting to sink toward a blushed horizon, Ruth jumped from the bed. It was almost seven and she had yet to sort out the dinner. Stepping into baggy jeans and an even bigger, sloppy jumper, she scraped back her chestnut hair, tied it into a high ponytail and make-up free, rushed downstairs. Headed for the kitchen.

An hour or so later, a Shepherd's Pie baking in the oven, Ruth rewarded her hard won labours with a large glass of red wine, then turned on the radio.

Ruth had called Adam's office at least three or four times throughout the day and as of yet, he had not found the time to return a single one of them. She thought of ringing again, but decided it was his turn. Dinner could be turned down, and they would eat whenever he got home.

Topping up her glass, Ruth grabbed the bottle and walked through to the living room. A definite cool, almost autumn chill in the air, she decided to light the wood burner. Set about laying screwed up newspaper, kindling and logs. Listened for the phone over the hiss, pop and the crack of the dancing flames. It did not ring. She called his office again, but no one answered. *Maybe, he was on his way home.*

Went back to the kitchen and checked on the pie.

Sod him.

Opened another bottle of red.

Ruth was woken by the crunching sound of a car pulling up on the gravel driveway. The fire needing wood, slowly dying, she shivered. Blearily pushed herself up from the sofa on which she had fallen asleep. An odour of something burning, and not the wood in the fire, attacking her nostrils, Ruth quickly stood up, then faltered with light-headedness. Pressed the heel of her hand to her forehead to steady herself.

Following the smell, Ruth hastened to the kitchen. The Shepherds Pie she had slaved over earlier, dried to a crisp, it was ruined. *Damn him.*

Hearing Adam's key turn in the lock, his shoes travelling up the flagstone corridor toward her, Ruth left the burnt offerings where they were, and angrily slammed shut the oven door. In her irritation, she pushed herself backwards and forwards against the kitchen counter top a couple of times.

'Why didn't you call?' Ruth demanded to know, rounding on Adam as soon as he entered into the room.

'Sorry? I was working in the lab. What time is it?' Adam asked, not bothering to look at his wristwatch.

Ruth could not help but notice how drawn and exhausted her husband looked. How he looked like a different, much older man. His tie loosened to the middle of his chest, his normally pristine trousers, looked creased and tired. Adam rubbing his eyes as he yawned, he avoided her accusatory stare. Obviously knew better than to ask what was burning, even though the whole house was reeking. Putting his hands into the pockets of his trousers as he leaned up against the kitchen wall, Adam nonchalantly crossed his legs at the ankles whilst he obviously waited, for her answer to his question.

Ruth glanced at the kitchen clock positioned on the wall above Adam's head. 'Gone eleven… You should have called.'

'I did call. No one answered,' he replied, curtly.

'When?'

'Some time between eight, eight-thirty. Why didn't you pick up?' He criticised.

Ruth did not immediately answer. Knowing she had been fast asleep on the sofa for the majority of the evening, now suddenly, she could not stand still. Moving around the room, haphazardly wiping down the kitchen surfaces, shoving used cooking utensils into the sink, the dishwasher, Ruth swallowed guiltily. Then hastily rubbed the back of her hand across the red wine stain, ghosting her top lip. Hoped, he had not seen.

Fingers of rain tapping on the window in fits and starts, Ruth pulled down the blind against the pitch black night.

She turned to face him.

'Dinner's ruined... *again*,' she confronted. It was the second time in a week their meal had ended up destined for the bin and probably, the umpteenth time, in a month.

'Have you been drinking again?' he counter-attacked.

Ruth saw him examine her as a doctor might do. Watched him search her face for signs of illness. Her cheeks pinked with embarrassment. *How dare he?*

There was a heavy beat of silence.

Moving from her face, Adam intently scanned the kitchen looking for any incriminating evidence. Ruth followed his gaze, and baulked inwardly as his eyes alighted on an empty wine bottle lying on its side, not far from the cooker hob. He harrumphed as though vindicated. Threw her, an accusatory stare.

Anxiously scouring her tired brain for a plausible excuse, Ruth felt her face blanch. Tried not to look as ashamed as she felt. 'What?' She demanded. Feigned an innocence she did not feel.

Adam nodded his head toward the kitchen counter top. Said nothing. Let the empty bottle, do its own talking.

'Oh, that,' Ruth said uneasily. Walked across and picked the bottle up as though she had only just seen it, 'I used what little was left in this,' she shook the bottle at him, 'to flavour your ruined dinner.'

'Yeah, sure you did,' Adam nodded, his tone exasperated. His eyes cold as he snapped them toward the wine rack.

Adam gently nodding his head up and down, Ruth watched him mentally counting out the number of bottles. *Note to self, tomorrow, I must replenish the wine rack,* she thought miserably. His task finished, he stared at her for a moment and his eyes seemed to say, *You lied to me.*

For the next few seconds, the air between the warring spouses, crackled with tension.

Lifting himself off the wall, Adam pushed his hands roughly through his hair, then walked over to the kettle, checked it for water and flicked it on. He ignored Ruth as though she had left the room already. In the stretched silence the kettle boiled, and switched itself off.

Ruth deeply sighed. Adam looked haggard and troubled, as though he had the weight of the world on his shoulders. *But why?*

Not for the first time, Ruth's mind started to race. *What is he hiding from me? What has he really been up to this evening, and who has he been doing it with?*

She told herself she was over-thinking the situation, that she was being irrational. This was not the first time they had been here these last few weeks, and she did not want to fight, not again. Wearily said to his resolute back, 'I'm going to bed.'

He did not respond.

Chapter Ten

The unexpected screech of a gull snatching at Sam's attention, she spun round from looking over the edge of the cliff and was just in time to catch Ruth, a hand over her mouth, stumbling drunkenly backward.

What the…?

For a couple of seconds, Sam just stood there, listening and watching in disbelief. She knew Ruth was afraid of heights. How she had infuriatingly kept to the furthest edge of the path all the way from the lighthouse, and now she had to know… *Was it really only a gull, that had just screamed?*

Sam strode out toward her sister. 'Ruth!' She yelled over the wind. 'Are you okay? Did you just scream?'

Ruth still propelling herself backward as fast as she could, a look of abject horror on her ghost white face, Sam reached out and grabbed a hold of her sister's wrist. But her fingers unwittingly digging into the exposed flesh that lay between the cuff of Ruth's coat and her glove, she was violently shaken her off. 'Ruth! Stop! What the hell is the matter with you?'

Ruth staggered one more time, then stopped. For a second or two, as though coming out of a stupor, she looked wildly around her.

'Ruth?'

'It's okay, I can hear you. I'm fine,' Ruth said, a trembling voice wheezing its way out of her chest as she visibly struggled to speak, to catch her breath.

Adrenaline? Is she hyperventilating? 'No, you are *not* fine,' Sam insisted.

'Yes, I am.' But Ruth's voice was thin with panic, and her breathing was rasping as she wobbled from side-to-side, like a drunken tar on bad sea legs.

Liar, Sam thought. *You look traumatised.*

'But you look terrible,' Sam accused. 'What the hell happened to you?'

'For the last time,' Ruth gasped out, 'nothing, nothing happened to me.' Forcefully shook her head, but then suddenly dropped down onto the sodden grass in front of Sam. Sat with her legs splayed straight out in front of her.

'But you screamed, I heard you. Then you were stumbling backwards as though you had seen something terrible. Or…,' Sam paused, 'you got too close to the edge,' she persisted. 'And look at you now.'

'I did *not* scream,' Ruth stressed. 'You must have heard a gull.'

'No, I did not hear a gull. It was a scream, a proper scream.'

'You're mistaken.'

'Am I? If I'm mistaken, why were you stumbling backwards?'

'I just got a bit too close to edge for my own comfort, and it shook me up a bit, that's all. You know how I hate heights and yet it was you, who insisted I should look down on that bloody wreck.'

Ah, so now it's all my fault, Sam thought. *No surprises there then.*

In the face of Ruth's continued stubbornness, Sam responded in the only way possible, she shrugged her shoulders, then coolly said, 'Okay, whatever you say.' But looking down into her sister's still panic-stricken eyes, watching her shiver as though her skin was being raked, it was obvious to Sam, Ruth had lied, again.

Secrets and lies, secrets and lies, Sam thought over and over in her head, like an annoying mantra. *Is that all we share you and I,* she silently asked her shocked and deeply disturbed, sister?

'Can you help me up?' Ruth asked.

Helping Ruth get shakily to her feet, Sam watched her hastily hide her still quivering hands, deep inside the pockets of her voluminous coat.

Furious with herself, her lack of attention, Sam silently berated herself for getting caught up in the childish thrill of daring herself to look over the edge, of taunting Ruth into joining her. *I've made such a colossal mistake. Ruth was going to jump, I'm sure of it. Instead of creating the perfect moment, I missed it entirely,* she reflected angrily. *If only I'd paid attention, seen what was happening, sooner. So stupid!*

Now, Sam knew she had no choice but to find another opportunity. One, if it was to be above suspicion, that was out of sight of the Coastguard Station, or the cameras at the Dover Docks and both of which, were about to appear over the crest of the next headland.

The words, *now or never,* sprang into Sam's mind.

'Look I don't know if you noticed whilst you were having your *panic attack*, but the tide is right out. So I was thinking, we should go down to that little beach at the bottom of Langdon Hole. Spend a little time down there, while we can,' Sam threw out.

That will teach her to lie to me, Sam thought spitefully.

Ruth casting Sam a disbelieving look, forced out a false laugh. Then looked distinctly panicky, all over again.

'Seriously?' Ruth asked incredulously. 'But what about your f-feet, your b-blisters?' she stuttered out.

'Oh, they're not okay, but they'll do,' Sam replied easily. 'Come on, what are you waiting for, let's go,' she chivvied.

Sensing Ruth's hesitation, but gambling on the fact she was still too disorientated and flustered by her *non-event*, to satisfactorily object, Sam threw down the gauntlet. 'Unless of course, your recent dalliance with what did *not* happen, has left you too shaken?' *Too chicken,* she did not add.

Ruth paled again. Nervously chewed on her bottom lip. 'I keep telling you, I'm fine. I just forgot for a minute, how scared of heights, I am.'

'Okay, well let's go then.' Sam moved away from Ruth. Quickly made her way toward a faded sign and wrought iron guard rail, she had spotted earlier. The sign denoting a black staircase, Sam guessed it marked the top of the hand hewn steps, Ruth had previously mentioned.

'Sam!' Ruth yelled out from behind her. 'I really don't think we should be going down there! The steps will be too slippery, possibly even deadly in places. Plus I've no idea, when the tide is due to turn!'

Perfect, Sam thought as she faked deafness. Smiled to herself as she pretended not to hear Ruth's shouts of alarm.

Her mind made up and seizing the moment, Sam began a rapid descent. Trusted Ruth's misplaced pride, her need to pretend nothing untoward had happened, would ensure she followed.

Her nerves still shot. Feeling wrecked and not wanting to think too closely about what she had nearly done but extremely disturbed by it, Ruth was fighting to concentrate on the placement of her feet.

A fall from that height, it would have been unsurvivable.
Did I really want to die?

Zigzagging her way down an almost perpendicular staircase made of pure chalk, each step frighteningly smooth, slimy, the risers unnaturally high, Ruth repeatedly had to force herself to focus. But her head distracted, all over the place, she was losing the battle.

This is madness!

Her legs heavy as lead and still weak from her recent brush with what had happened above. Trembling with the effort of keeping herself upright, Ruth's thighs were killing her. How long had it been since her near mishap; *ten, fifteen minutes at most?* Under the current weather conditions, feeling the way she did, what she was attempting was not only dangerous, but downright insane.

Is that it? Is that what this is about? I've finally snapped? I've gone insane?

'No, I'm going to be fine,' Ruth tried to pep talk herself. 'Keep going. You can do this. You know you can.'

But then, for a dark instant, she was back in that bottomless pit. Felt deathly alone…

Suffocating with guilt, with fear, with the pain of living, she suddenly wanted to end it all again. To launch herself off the steps, and out into the abyss.

The air thinned, and Ruth found it hard to breath.

But what if I don't die? What if I just paralyse myself, become trapped and motionless in a wheelchair, dependent on others for everything? Dependent on Sam, forever?

She stopped for a moment.

Concentrated on her breathing.

Her brain whirred, tingled, fluttered crazily; *bats in the belfry?*

Feeling impotent in the face of her own fear, powerless in the face of Sam's impulsivity and her blatant defiance, it hit Ruth, she was furious. That she was livid, not only with herself, but with Sam.

How could I allow myself to be so easily manipulated?

Am I really that weak?

The irony not lost on her, Ruth mentally told herself she should have stayed up top, where it was safe.

Perhaps I should turn back now? It's not too late.

But the thought of being up there on her own after her earlier recklessness, after her thoughts of just a moment ago, was too much for Ruth to bear. Left her feeling vulnerable and terrified again.

How can I ever trust myself?

Ruth's torrid emotions needing an out, *a victim*, she became consumed by the need to scream a tirade of abuse toward her selfish and delinquent sister, to lash out at her. Could quite easily have killed Sam, on the spot. But her present situation too perilous for any melodramatic physical jerks, and Sam a good few minutes ahead and well out of earshot, common sense prevailed.

Each of Ruth's pent-up frustrations left pendulously hanging; every one of them clinging to her tenuous psyche like a cloud of bloodthirsty vampire bats, she slogged on. Ignored her screaming calf muscles as she centred herself. Using her anger to propel herself forward, Ruth took one faltering step at a time. Kept a firm hold of the metal guard rail, at all times.

In spite of the icy conditions, the glacial wind that threatened the safety of her every step, the chilling violence of her fear, Ruth was sweating inside her coat.

Her leading foot stumbling down onto a large metal platform, Ruth sighed with a short-lived relief. The platform suspended approximately fifteen foot or more above the empty beach below, Ruth knew that unfortunately, for her, another of her torments was yet to be faced. She gulped in anticipatory trepidation.

I am such a coward.

Sam waiting a couple of paces away from her, Ruth finally let loose as she vented her spleen. 'Why Sam? Why the hell didn't you listen to me? We shouldn't be here,' she spat out angrily, her breath ragged with exhaustion and fear. 'Those steps were horrendous, and you know how much I hate these bloody things!' she yelled, gesticulating wildly toward a rusting ladder hanging vertically from the middle of the steel structure. 'How could you?'

Sam, stepping back from Ruth, keeping a wary distance, she projected a picture of puzzled innocence. 'Sorry Ruth, but I couldn't hear you over the noise of the wind, and I had no idea there would a ladder down here. I naturally thought the steps would go all the way down to beach.'

'Really?' Ruth challenged.

'Yes, of course, I've never been here before, so how would I know about the ladder? Anyway, the tide's well out and we're both here now, all safe and sound,' Sam finished, somewhat haughtily.

Struck dumb with fury, Sam seemingly unable to understand the seriousness of their predicament and that it had the potential to worsen, Ruth was at a loss for words. *Was she for real?*

'Come on,' Sam encouraged, as she threw Ruth a wry — *don't be such a sissy* — smile. 'I'll go first.' Made her way to the ladder, then condescendingly said over her shoulder, 'Why don't you catch your breath and steady your nerves, and I'll see you at the bottom?'

Treated by Sam as though she were a cowardly child requiring parental reassurance, Ruth continued to inwardly seethe. *How dare she? Who does she think she is?* Watched with disbelief as her reckless sister unhesitatingly, disappeared over the side of the platform.

Ruth's need to stay exactly where she was, finely balanced with her need to show Sam just what she was made of. That she was not a namby-pamby pushover. That she was in fact, a force to be reckoned with, she firmly told herself to, *grow a pair!* Then cautiously approached her nemesis.

Breathe!

I can do this.

I will not be a coward.

Peeling off her gloves, Ruth stuffed them into the pockets of her coat. Then turning a determined back to the thrashing sea pounding some distance away on the shoreline below, she grabbed a firm hold of the freezing, almost skin blistering metal sides of the ladder. Reluctantly followed in Sam's footsteps as she began a slow and deliberate descent.

'Come on Ruth!' Sam yelled up from the beach below. 'It's really easy! Just don't look down! That's it, one step at a time! You're almost there!'

In spite of herself, grateful to feel Sam's steadying hands loosely close around her ankles, move up to the backs of her calves, then her thighs as she was guided down the last couple of rungs, Ruth was torn between a futile rage and gratitude. Had to force herself to squeeze out a, *'Thank you.'* Tried to keep the irritation and the panic from out of her voice as she dropped unharmed, to the ankle twisting pebbles below. *And, relax.*

'Sure, no worries,' Sam replied, before scooting off to Ruth's left.

Guessing Sam was smartly leaving her to her own devices for a while, Ruth veered right. She could do without Sam's company for a while.

Briefly peering up at the moss smudged, *White Cliffs of Dover*, feeling small and insignificant, an unexplained foreboding coursed icily through Ruth's chilled veins. *They look so threatening, so hostile.* Knowing there was ninety plus metres of vertical chalk laced with seams of flint, looming above her and that at this time of year, the wind, the rain, the frost and ice, all had the potential to easily prise loose some of the cliff's fragile load, Ruth imagined the worst. Shivering, she quickly moved away.

A snap of stinging salt in the air. A vicious wind whipping around her body as Ruth removed herself out from under the overhanging precipice, she slowly crunched her way along the open and isolated foreshore.

Storm clouds gathering on the horizon, the sea now a gunmetal blue, monstrous waves crashed onto the shoreline. The hissing spray hitting the rocks in star-bursts, everything around Ruth appeared grey, bare and stony. The scene chilling, and comfortless, Ruth's booted feet automatically kicking and rooting through seaweed that had been left by the previous high tideline, she sank herself into the soothing task of mindlessly looking for washed-up treasures. She did not want to think.

Ten to fifteen minutes later and with nothing of value found, the sun now coming and going behind clouds flying in from the north-east, a bitter cold started to sink deep into Ruth's marrow. Wrapping her arms around herself for warmth and comfort, it was, Ruth decided, time to leave.

Turning, walking back the way she had come, Ruth slowly approached a studious Sam.

'She looks so sad and lonely, don't you think?' Sam queried, her exhaled breath clouding around her wind chafed face.

Sam cautiously picking her way through the twisted metal ribcage of an exposed wreck, laying a few metres from the base of the cliff face, Ruth flicked her eyes over the bare and rusting bones of the *SS Falcon*. Slowly nodded her head in agreement. Quietly said, 'Yes, she does.' Felt a pang of something. Felt a pang of pain.

'I guess she's only visible at low tide?'

'Yes, she is.'

Without warning, Ruth found herself assailed by an onslaught of images. Some good, but a lot of them bad, really bad, she began to struggle, to shake. The shock of the past thumping its way into the present, like a bunched fist into the pit of her stomach, she stumbled backwards. Felt the accustomed panic begin to rise as the constant state of her low-level anxiety, was suddenly replaced with a fierce adrenaline.

Jittery, Ruth began to mumble. Envisioning *him* walking across this very same beach, calling out to her, she remembered the feel of his hands running through her tangled hair as he tipped her head up to his. Felt his warm breath whispering into her mouth just before he kissed her, deeply.

The all too familiar feelings of loss and abandonment washing up over Ruth like a tsunami, engulfed her in grief.

She dropped to her knees.

Moaning, then wailing, unable to stop herself, Ruth howled into the wind, like a demented banshee. It was as though something inside of her had exploded, like a Big Bang.

Then the sobbing started. In purgatory, the anguished, visceral tears coming not from behind her eyes, but from somewhere deep within her gut, Ruth could not stop.

Some minutes later, Ruth became aware of a tentative hand squeezing her shoulder. Looking up, she saw Sam's overly concerned face gazing down on her. She hiccuped back a sob.

'Sorry, Ruth, but we have to go. I think the tide has turned. If we don't get back up that ladder soon, I think we could be in trouble.'

Ruth wiped her eyes with the back of her frozen hand. Tried to push the searing humiliation, the shame away. She had done it again. She had cried like a baby in front of Sam. 'How long, Sam? How long have I been like this?' she asked, miserably.

'Not that long, ten minutes at most but if you take a look, you can see the sea is starting to come in.'

Her knees soaked and painfully cold, the joints almost locked, Ruth got stiffly to feet. Ruefully rubbed a damp glove across her red and white blotched face. 'Sorry Sam, all this unfettered emotion.'

Sam said nothing. Visibly had her mind on other things as she cast worried eyes toward the shoreline. Smiled a thin, tolerant smile. Then pointed to the sea.

Following Sam's finger, her gaze. Checking the wildness of an encroaching sea that was cold and indifferent. That was unerringly beginning to thrash its way in toward them, Ruth saw Sam was right. The tide was definitely on the turn. In a short amount of time, the beach would disappear and they would be swimming for their lives. *Here, we could die, and nobody would know.*

Sam ahead of Ruth, already at the foot of the ladder and ready to climb, she turned and called out, 'Come on Ruth, we need to go! I'll go up first, then I can help you when you get nearer to the top!'

Wearily fighting back her forebodings, her undesired dread for a second time, Ruth took a minute as she encouraged herself to get a grip. Her fear manifesting into sweat prickling out along her hairline, she pulled down her hood, exposed her head and face to the elements. *Breath!*

'Okay,' Ruth just about managed to eject.

Watching Sam easily climb up the ladder then vanish, it took all Ruth's self-control not to betray the horror and trepidation she felt. Palms damp with fear, she reminded herself that sometimes, courage was simply a matter of putting one foot in front of the other. Hesitantly began, her own ascent.

Don't look down! Don't look down!

A few rungs from the top, Sam's head suddenly popped over the edge of the platform as she shoved an ungloved hand down toward Ruth. Shouted out, 'Ruth, grab my hand and I'll help you up!'

Reaching up to grasp a hold of Sam's outstretched hand, suddenly, Ruth was overbalanced.

Startlingly found herself waving at the air.

Her leading foot sliding off its damp metal rung, for a few short seconds, she was suspended in mid-air.

Then, she was flying backwards.

It was with a whoosh of icy air that Ruth's body, her head, agonisingly smacked into the ground.

A searing heat erupting inside Ruth's skull, before she could scream, her head exploded in pain.

Then everything, snapped into black.

Chapter Eleven

Adam's belated birthday, and they were spending it with his parents. Having left early that morning, an accident on the M2 followed by roadworks on the M25 just before the Dartford Tunnel, what should have been a two hour journey, had taken almost three. Adam's temper frayed well beyond his ability to talk, Ruth had spent most of the horrendous journey, with her head sightlessly buried in a book.

Now pulling up into the driveway in front of in-law's house, Ruth bit down on her lower lip with nervousness; the huge, detached, immaculate Edwardian villa, innocently rubbing her nose in her own disadvantaged beginnings. Gazing down at her hands, noticing they were clasped so tightly her knuckles had turned a translucent white, Ruth silently commanded herself to *relax*.

No matter how early or late they arrived, with the front door flung open in welcome, Jenny was always there, waiting. When they first got married, Ruth had teased Adam about it. She had pointed out his mother must spend her life, looking out of the windows or hiding behind the front door, waiting for unsuspecting callers. Not amused, Adam had looked offended.

September, technically autumn, small chinks of blue sky amid the darkening grey, and the air outside of the car cool and damp, Ruth's tiny mother-in-law was sensibly dressed for the unpredictability of the season. Sporting a brown tweed skirt, a powder blue twinset and pearls, tan court shoes with brown woollen tights, her cap of silver hair perfectly coiffured and her face lightly made up, as always, Jenny looked the epitome of understated elegance.

Checking out her own tan leather moccasins, worn and scuffed at the toes, her light blue skinny jeans, fashionably ripped at the knees, and the cotton navy jumper she was wearing over a pale blue t-shirt, Ruth was suddenly very much aware, of just how casual she looked. Adam in a hurry to leave that morning, she was not wearing make-up either, and had left her hair to fashionably — or so she told herself — air dry.

I have not made a faux pas of etiquette. I am adequately dressed, she tried to convince herself.

'Darling!' Jenny called out.

Discerning Jenny's wave was directed purely toward her son, Ruth stiffened in her seat. Looked straight ahead as she slapped on a smile.

'Welcome home. Come on in. Come on in. What an awful journey you've had.'

Adam kissed his mother on the cheek. Jenny then turned and kissed Ruth's left cheek. Not once, did she let go of Adam's arm as salutations were traded. Practically dragged him into the house as though it had been months, rather than a couple of weeks since she had last seen, her darling little boy.

A few minutes later, a mug of tea pressed into each of their hands and a plate of home-made chocolate chip cookies doing the rounds, Ruth anxiously watched Adam out of the corner of her eye. Hoped his black mood would lift and lighten now he was back in the bosom of his childhood home.

'Are you all right?' Jenny asked Adam. She had obviously noticed his strained and sulky look.

'Yes, thanks. We're much better now,' he replied for the both of them. Forgot himself for a moment as he flashed his mother a charming, toothy grin.

'Good,' Jenny smiled warmly back at him. 'Ruth, you look a little peaky, can I get you anything else?'

'No, no, I'm fine,' Ruth replied, immediately feeling at a disadvantage.

'Are you sure, dear?'

'Yes,' Ruth nodded. 'What with the accident, the roadworks and all the detours, it was just a long journey,' she explained, tricked into defensiveness.

'Well, if you're sure.'

Ruth gritted her teeth. Tried not to mind that Adam's mother treated her as though she did not know her own mind. Deliberately settled back into the sofa and for her mother-in-law's benefit, visibly relaxed.

The elderly tag team full of news about some relative or other who had recently died, Adam was quickly monopolised into conversation. The subject matter painfully reminding Ruth of how her own parents had been cremated, without her being present, she tried not to care. It wasn't like she really remembered them, all that well.

Ruth sipped her tea. Hands lightly trembling for some reason, she ended up slopping some into her saucer and spattered her jumper; *good job it's a dark colour.* Feeling blurred around the edges, like a wet watercolour painting, Ruth tried not to think to much. Nibbled her cookie. Attempted to chew. Her throat dry, she thought she might choke and had to force herself, to swallow.

Flicking her attention to Adam, watching him surreptitiously play the dutiful and interested son, Ruth marvelled at the ease of his duplicity. A favourite child of applauding parents, Ruth knew that in their eyes, their precious son could do no wrong. *If only they knew,* she thought, but was not about to complain as for now, Adam was distracted, occupied and out of her hair.

'I think we'd better go,' Alan said suddenly as he checked the time on the solid gold wristwatch; a family heirloom, earmarked for the firstborn grandson. Straightening his tie, patting down the pockets of his olive coloured trousers, his brown tweed jacket looking for, Ruth presumed, his car keys, he briskly stated to no one in particular, 'I rang the pub and delayed the booking when Ruth rang to say you were going to be late. But if we don't leave soon, they'll let our table go.'

God forbid.

Twenty minutes of country roads later and after a number of back-doubles Ruth would never be able to remember, Alan parked the car. Entering an upmarket restaurant in the centre of town, with crystal chandeliers, tables laid with heavy white linen and set with silver cutlery and matching china, Ruth now knew, she was most definitely underdressed. She wished Adam had been more forthcoming when she had asked him about the day's arrangements, and what he thought she should wear. His mother would have discussed the occasion with him, Ruth was sure of it. *He must have known.*

Seated at their reserved table, their three course meal pre-ordered, Alan said to Adam, 'Now son, this is on us.'

'Dad, really, you don't have to,' Adam replied, feigning objection though loving, Ruth knew, every minute of being spoilt by his parents.

'Don't be silly, son. It's our treat, for your birthday.'

Her in-laws smiling indulgently, firstly at Adam and then at each other, Ruth felt absurdly excluded, and out of place.

Inwardly cringing at the size of the main meal brought out to her, she had only wanted a small portion, Ruth already knew she would partake without enjoyment. These days, bored with eating alone more often than not, she typically fuelled up only because her body needed it. Sometimes, she had gone days without proper food.

Adam's father poured out the red wine and Ruth drank a couple of glasses in quick succession, but she struggled to make herself eat. Adam ate a hearty meal and drank little. Rubbed his belly and said he was looking forward to dessert.

'You'll put on weight,' his father warned him, good-naturedly. 'Look at me,' Alan said, patting his ample stomach. 'Though I blame your mother's cooking.'

Adam chuckled, leant across the table and stabbed one of Ruth's roast potatoes, as his answer.

'Champagne, Ruth?' Alan asked.

'Silly question,' Adam answered for her, stone-faced.

Adam's tone both pugnacious and sarcastic, Ruth determinedly stretched her mouth into a wide smile. Tried not to care that like a bossy little bully boy, he had just humiliated her in front of his parents. And not, for the first time.

Alan and Jenny briefly toasted their son a *Happy Birthday*. Then almost at the last minute, remembered to chink their glasses with Ruth's.

'So, where have you been this week?' Alan asked Adam.

Like he doesn't know already, Ruth thought with scorn. Adam rang his parents at least once a week, most weeks. They knew everything. *Well, at least everything he wants them to know,* she mentally corrected herself.

'New York, I had to go out there to deliver a symposium.'

'And when did you get back?'

'Yesterday morning, so you'll have to excuse me if I drop my head into my pudding, as I'm still a bit jet lagged.'

'You know, it still amazes me to think, my little boy is a hotshot scientist,' Alan remarked, smiling proudly. 'Why don't you tell your mother and I about the symposium? We may not understand the finer details, but I'm sure we can handle a summary.'

Ruth nervously sipped her celebratory champagne. Rotating the glass, she caught the condensation with her finger. Tried to appear as the normal loving wife who had missed her husband and was now immensely enjoying his recollection of the conference, whilst in reality, she felt a panicky, low-level anxiety, as though she had strayed too close to the edge. Her body tense with the strain of pretence, and close to saying something she knew she would probably regret, Ruth allowed the conversation to fade out. Reflected instead, on Adam's last phone call home.

Ringing from his hotel room, over three thousand miles away in New York, the line had been crystal clear. Yet Adam, had been distant and vague, sounded as though he was concentrating on something — *or someone* — else. He had called at a quarter to one in the afternoon UK time, which would have been a quarter to eight in the morning, US time. She, surfacing from a midday nap, had rubbed her eyes and groggily asked him how he was, how the symposium was going. Even though Ruth understood nothing of his work, she had tried to ask him intelligent questions but unlike the old days, where he would have laughed and teased her, their polite *chat* had been brief, distinctly uninformative and punctuated with awkward silences. In the end, unable to help herself, she had asked, '*Adam, do you still love me?*' For a moment, Adam had remained silent. Then he had said, '*Why do you ask?*' Disappointed, she had answered honestly. *'I don't know, perhaps because I haven't heard you say it in a while.'* He had said, *'Of course I love you.'* Then he had cleared his throat, left her with a heightened sense of vulnerability, of being left alone for too many days. It was only once the call had ended, she realised that not once, had he asked her about her week or how she was doing. Ruth wondered idly, what Adam would have done, had she simply hung up on him?

'Ruth dear, did you hear what I just said?' Jenny asked, lightly butting up against Ruth's arm, with her own.

With huge effort, Ruth forced herself to pay attention. All she wanted, was to lie down somewhere. To fade out.

Jenny's unexpected nudge having caused Ruth to spill some of her red wine onto the blindingly white tablecloth, somehow, she managed to rally herself. Hastily grabbed at her napkin, to blot the crimson mess. Pretending not to notice the purse of Jenny's coral pink lips - *It was your fault, not mine, you stupid bloody woman* — Ruth muttered a weak, 'Sorry.'

'I said, I can't believe you've been married for two whole years, already. My, how time flies. And what a lot of changes you've both had to deal with, newly wed and then within a matter of weeks, moving from London to Kent with Adam's super-duper new job. Buying and renovating such a lovely old house. You being able to give up work, and at such a tender age, you're so lucky.'

Ruth felt her mouth go dry. Took a fortifying slug of wine. She had no idea, what she should say. The fact that Jenny had so obviously omitted to add, *not given me a grandchild, will never give me a grandchild,* to her inexhaustible list, made her want to slither away in shame.

A waitress suddenly swooping down on them, gathering up three empty plates and one barely touched as she asked if they wanted to see the dessert menu, Ruth was neatly prevented from having to find a suitable response for her mother-in-law. From pointing out to a smug Jenny that in those same two years, work had become everything to Adam, and that she barely saw him anymore. That with no explanation, he no longer took her to any of his work dinners, or on any of his business trips. That since finding out they could never conceive a child of their own, rather than talking with her about their options, he seemed to be emotionally detaching himself from their marriage. That this *lucky woman* was bored witless, and slowly going crazy.

Suddenly maudlin, feeling tears of self-pity stabbing at the corner of her eyes, Ruth hastily blinked them away.

I will not cry, not now. I will not give her the satisfaction.

'You know, I still find it hard to believe how terribly naughty the pair of you were,' Jenny said teasingly, her words directed to Adam. 'I know you've always been protective of your privacy Adam, but to disappear off and get married the way you did. And after barely three months together, well...' Jenny gently shook her head at her son. 'I still can't quite believe, the *first* time we met Ruth, it was day *after* you'd married her.'

And your point is? Ruth silently challenged her mother-in-law.

'And Ruth, being *so* young,' Jenny emphasised with a forgiving smile, though her eyes, when she flashed them Ruth's way, were cold and steely.

To make me feel even more awful than I already do, for steeling your precious son in such an underhand way, and for cheating you out of his wedding, Ruth answered her own question.

Unsurprisingly, Adam did not answer his mother. He never went in for pointless explanations.

Maintaining her own silence, Ruth tried not to be hurt, but could not stop herself from tensely focusing on the hidden subtext in what Jenny had been saying... *It's all your fault. If it wasn't for you enticing him into marriage, Adam would have found someone more suitable. A woman more matched to his needs, his growing status in life. A woman who would given him the child — and me the grandchild — he craves, and deserves.*

'And the way you did it, darling. Married with none of your family or friends there to support you.'

Still, Adam maintained his silence. Though he did send his mother, a mildly withering look.

On a roll, Jenny would not leave it alone. 'I know, aside from her sister, Ruth doesn't have any relatives of her own to call on but you Adam, you have lots of family and friends who would have loved to have been there to support you, to share in your happy day. You young things,' Jenny tinkled out in her superior manner, 'anyone would think you were ashamed of us.'

'I know, mum,' Adam said, simply. Wisely neither agreeing, nor disagreeing with his mother, albeit at Ruth's expense.

No surprises as to where Adam got his stubbornness from, Ruth thought.

Feeling buffeted and winded as though someone had knocked into her, by Jenny's covert criticism, by Adam's indifference, again, Ruth tried not to be hurt. *What did it matter? Adam loved her. He had told her so, in his call from New York.*

Picking up her glass, Ruth took another, stabilising sip of wine. Two weeks into their marriage, Adam had warned Ruth that his mother was smarting, that she was feeling keenly insulted at having been exiled from attending the wedding, of her youngest son. Then a few weeks later, Adam had also disclosed, his mother resented not being able to readily boast about such a *significant* event, with her family and friends. That she felt acutely embarrassed by what she had taken to be, a complete lack of consideration for his parents feelings, on the matter. Mortified by her new mother-in-law's take on their hasty marriage, Ruth had immediately offered to talk to Jenny. She had suggested to Adam, she could try and smooth things over with Jenny. Perhaps even propose, they have a church blessing to appease her, but Adam had point blank refused. He had said it wasn't necessary, and that his mother would just have to come to terms with what they had done. That basically, it was his life and his mother, would just have to get over herself.

Now observing mother and son share a swift and intimate glance, Ruth was instantly envious. Turning her head away, unable to watch the codependent pair any longer, the composure Ruth had so carefully been practising, dissolved. She coughed and wretched. Could not stop.

Heads nearest to them, sharply turned; other diners glancing over at her with expressions of faint alarm as she struggled for breath.

Adam throwing her a penetrating stare, got up and whacked her on the back, hard. Quietly hissed in her ear, 'You might like to take some water with your wine.'

Jenny, looking aghast at the commotion caused, hastily shoved her napkin Ruth's way. Gesticulated for Ruth to cover her spluttering mouth.

Alan, his navy blue eyes dancing with intensity, had not missed Adam's irritation and looking particularly concerned, he swiftly signalled for the waitress to bring him their bill.

'I'm so sorry,' Ruth said as she smiled bleakly at her in-laws. 'I think my drink must have gone down the wrong way.'

'Here, have another drink,' Adam said nastily as he made a grab for the water jug, banged it down next to her plate. Returned to his seat.

Both of Adam's parents, sat stock still and silent, it was only out of the corner of Ruth's eye, she caught the slight lift of Jenny's immaculately painted mouth.

Chapter Twelve

Strange, antiseptic smells. A brightly lit warehouse of a room, with white walls and polystyrene ceiling tiles.

Stiff white sheets, she was in a bed.

Phones ringing, the distant ping of an elevator, the swooshing of automatic doors opening and closing, disembodied voices talking and laughing. Whispering and moaning, the far-off yell of a man in pain.

Assorted tubes and wires emerging from her body, lights were piercing her eyes and suddenly, she was scared.

Where was she? But Ruth knew the answer even as she asked the question. She was in hospital.

But why? What has happened to me, and how did I get here?

So confused. So frightened.

Wanting to run, to swing her feet off the bed and onto the floor, Ruth wanted to rip the line piercing her arm, and sprint for freedom. She wanted to get well away from whatever, or whomever, had put her in here. Yet every part of her body was aching, screaming; muscles, joints, even the blood pumping through her brain. It was impossible for her to move.

'Hello, can you hear me?' demanded a booming, cheery female. The disembodied voice coming from somewhere behind her head, it took Ruth a second to realise, the woman was speaking to her.

Ruth tried to respond, but her head was pounding, and her voice was gone.

Swivelling her eyes, pain piercing her brain, Ruth saw a young nurse to the right-hand side of the bed she was in. The nurse fiddling with a large beeping machine, with an array of digital displays the colour of rubies and emeralds, it surprised Ruth to see, the woman was exceptionally pretty. With long blonde hair caught up into a perfect bun, a cupid's bow mouth that was painted a deep red, eyes lined and winged with black kohl, as a nurse, she could not have looked more incongruous with her surroundings.

Ruth swallowed, clawed at the bed sheet, struggled to find her voice.

Not waiting for Ruth to answer, the nurse moved away from the bed and disappeared. She returned a couple of minutes later, with a clean cut, boyish looking doctor in a white coat and stethoscope around his neck.

Ruth felt herself shivering, could not prevent her teeth from chattering.

'Hi, welcome back,' the man said calmly. 'I'm Ben. I'm one of the A&E consultants.' He reached for her shaking hand, gave it a brief, steadying squeeze. 'You're in shock. The trembling will pass,' he said encouragingly.

Unable to answer, Ruth delivered Ben a grateful smile.

'Can you tell me your name?'

Speaking required effort and movement, neither of which, Ruth was sure she had. 'Ruth, my name is Ruth,' she hoarsely whispered. Her throat raw, Ruth's voice was weak and barely audible.

A bright light being suddenly shone into each of her eyes in turn, Ruth squinted as her vision was temporarily blurred. Tried to turn her head away, then moaned at the agony the action caused her.

'And do you know what day it is?'

Strands of thoughts floating away from her like the sticky skeins of a spider's web drifting on the wind, it was with relief, Ruth finally managed to catch onto one of them. 'Saturday,' she ejected. Felt absurdly pleased with herself as though she had won something special.

'Good, and the date?'

Ruth thought, hard. Nervously bit down on her bottom lip. Shook her head and instantly grimaced, with the pain it brought. 'No…'

'It's all right,' Ben smiled at her, 'neither do I. So don't worry about it. And your sister, can you remember what her name is?'

'Sam, it's Sam.'

Ben smiled slightly as Ruth made eye contact, silently acknowledged she had given him the correct answer. Then paternally patted her hand. 'You know, you're one very lucky young lady.'

Ruth did not feel lucky. A meat cleaver buried in her skull, aching from head to foot, she felt like she was the victim of an attempted murder. Winced at the upset that particular thought caused. Felt the tears slip out from between her eyelids, and trickle down her face.

'Can you tell me what happened to you?' Ben asked.

Two piercingly blue eyes drilling into her own, Ruth had the strange feeling he was expecting her to lie to him and wondered why, he would think that way?

Fragmented memories tugging at the corners of Ruth's confused mind, she silently repeated the consultant's question to herself. Did it over and over again as she fought to get at the truth. Slowly recalled walking with Sam. Then sharply focused on being up on the cliffs when suddenly, an icicle pierced her heart. *Ben was right to be suspicious of me.* She prepared herself, to lie.

'Ruth,' Ben tried again, 'can you tell me what happened to you, yet?'

'No,' Ruth said. Firmly shook her head and winced at the horrendous pain it caused. *I have to stop doing that.*

Ben shot Ruth a speculative, questioning look.

'No,' she repeated. Kept her head deadly still.

'Okay, humour me. Have, another little think.'

Knowing he was watching her every facial twitch, Ruth fast forwarded herself from being up on the cliffs, to being down on the beach. Realised that although she could recall walking on the beach, even studying the old wreck with Sam, beyond that, there was nothing.

'I can't remember.'

'Ah,' Ben said, pursed his lips. 'So you have no memory of walking along the cliffs?'

'No.'

'What about the beach?'

'No.'

'Your fall, or your rescue?'

What fall? What rescue? Ruth strained to absorb what Ben was saying. She fought to clear the fog from her brain but still, she could not see what had happened to her.

'Ruth?'

'No, I'm sorry. I think I have a vague memory of walking with my sister along the cliffs, and an even vaguer one of being down on the beach… But that's it. What fall?'

Did I really try to kill myself?

'Okay, so you don't remember climbing a ladder?'

Ruth thought, and thought again. Lightly pressed her hands to her temples, as she tried to think through the ache. She had to concentrate as for some reason, it felt important. 'I think I can remember walking toward a ladder, the one that hangs from that platform on Langdon Beach, but I'm not sure.'

'You're not sure?'

'No, I've been down to that beach quite a few times, and I'm worried I might be confusing my memories.'

'So you don't remember climbing the ladder, today?'

'No.'

'Or falling off of it?'

'No.'

Ruth willed for Ben to get on with it as for some reason that was beyond her grasp, she now desperately needed to know.

'Okay. Well, you were down on Langdon Beach, with Sam. And you did climb the ladder, but somehow, you fell before you reached the top. Fortunately for you, you landed on top of a bed of seaweed and it cushioned your fall.'

'Seaweed?'

'Yes, according to the rescue services, you were surrounded by the stuff. They reckon it must have been at least a foot deep. Thank goodness for the recent storms, eh? The extraordinary high tides we've been having lately, must have washed it all up.'

'Oh.'

'Hmm,' he nodded, 'I think we could have been looking at a very different set of injuries and outcome, if you had fallen onto the pebbles, or God forbid, one of the boulders that litter that beach.'

Why did I fall off the ladder? Did I deliberately let go?

Ruth unsuccessfully tried to take an inventory of her wounds, and in the end, she had to ask. 'But nothing's broken?'

'No, there's nothing broken, but you did bump you head and it seems, for a while, you lost consciousness. We've done a CT scan and there are no obvious problems. But you do have a concussion and a mild head trauma that explains your amnesia.'

'Amnesia?'

'Yes,' Ben nodded sagely.

'Will it come back? My memory?' Ruth asked. Felt the fear beginning to rise. Perhaps, it was better to forget?

'Hard to say at this stage but in a situation such as yours, the amnesia can be temporary and sometimes, permanent.'

'What?'

'You have to understand, memory is a complicated thing. Sometimes a sound, a smell, and poof, you're transported back to a moment in time. Hopefully, with time, something will trigger you into remembering what happened. Or it might even be that you wake one morning, and your memory of the event, will suddenly be there again.'

'So, it should come back?'

Why can't I let it go?

'As I've already said, I can't be certain as it may never come back. In the meantime, you're going to experience some intense headaches. Ones that are going to be with you for at least the next few days. Oh, and you can expect some nausea and dizziness. You're also going to be incredibly stiff and sore, and for quite some time as you have extensive bruising to your limbs, and torso. Okay?'

'Okay,' Ruth said slowly, though she did not feel okay. The nausea, the dizziness, both pretty natural states of being for her, of late, did not phase her. But her anxiety levels were through the roof. That, plus the horrendous pain in her head as the cleaver sank even deeper, twisted and turned, she could quite easily have curled up and died.

'As I said earlier,' Ben continued, 'you are one, very lucky young woman. Right, I'll go and get your formidable sister. She's been pacing up and down the corridor these last couple of hours. Even though I've told her you'll be fine, she's desperate to see you, for herself.'

'When can I go home?' Ruth managed to force out through her parched lips.

'Nurse, please get Ruth some water,' Ben commanded.

He has noticed my discomfort, my thirst. So perceptive, but is he too perceptive?

'Well, you're medicated up to the eyeballs at the moment, so I'm arranging for you to be kept in overnight. Bed and breakfast only, I'm afraid,' he said, chuckling infectiously at his own joke. 'Then provided you are stable through the night and tomorrow morning, I'll see to it you're discharged, soon after lunch. But I warn you, for a week at least, you're going to need painkillers and support, at home. It's going to be a tricky few days for you, and you will *need* someone to watch over you,' he emphasised. 'The nurse will give you more details on what you can and can't do, when to go to your GP versus coming back to A&E; the *red flags* you should look out for, etcetera, etcetera. Just be aware that with the concussion and the memory loss, you might not be able to trust your own thoughts for a while.'

Nothing new there then, Ruth thought, with a certain amount of irony, and trepidation.

Then, with a flurry of white coat and with the nurse right behind, Ben was gone.

Suddenly deliciously warm, almost comfortable if she was careful not to move, Ruth gave in to a comforting darkness.

Later, shaking off the cobwebs of her medically induced sleep, Ruth awoke to find Sam sat on a chair next to her bed. Sam alternately frowning and grimacing as she drank out of a brown plastic cup, Ruth almost had to smile.

Hungry, and thirsty, Ruth could not remember her last meal. *My last drink.*

'Hi,' Sam whispered. 'How are you feeling?'

Ruth checked in with herself as she scanned her body head to toe. Re-established that practically every part of her ached, or was in pain. Felt as thought she were supremely hung over. 'Awful,' she replied honestly.

Grimaced as the sound of her own voice mercilessly reverberated around her head. 'You?' she croaked out.

'Oh, I'm okay, It's you I'm worried about.' Sam pressed a plastic beaker with a straw in it, into Ruth's hands. 'Drink. I'll get you some sandwiches, once we've talked.'

Ruth sipped, passed the beaker back. 'What time is it?' she asked, trying to clip her words and not sound like a drunk.

Sam glanced down at her wristwatch. 'It's a little after seven.'

'Seven at night?' Ruth queried listlessly. The ward she was in, artificially lit and lined with beds that were full with other patients, the window curtains closed, she had no way of knowing, whether it was morning or night.

'Yes.'

'But it is still Saturday, isn't it?'

'Yes,' Sam replied, with a reassuring smile. 'The staff transferred you up here, to the ward, a short while ago. But you were fast asleep at the time.'

Disorientated by the day's events. Revisiting what had happened to her, Ruth cast an anxious look around the room. Without understanding why, she shrank back against the bed as if she was expecting someone to jump out her, like some sort of freakish jack-in-the-box. *My nerves are shredded.*

Sam picking up on her distress, said, 'It's okay, Ruth. If you're looking for the police, they've gone, and they won't be coming back.'

Thinking hard, vaguely recollecting the persistent presence of a young policeman sent to interview her about the accident, the feelings of awkwardness and guilt, every time she found herself having to repeat, '*I can't remember the ladder, or what happened to me. Honestly, I can't,*' Ruth sighed, heavily. Recalled her relief when Ben, the consultant, had finally shooed the copper away. 'My God Sam, what the hell happened to me out there?'

'You still can't remember any of the details around your fall?'

'No, I can't, not a damn thing.'

'Well, I have to say, I'm not exactly sure myself.' Sam shook her head as though in disbelief. 'One minute you were climbing up the ladder toward me and the next, you were falling. Landed flat on your back on the beach, and knocked yourself out. I was terrified.'

Ruth attempted to give Sam a considered stare, but could not summon up the concentration required. Winced as a pain shot from one side of her head to the other, with the effort.

'All I can think,' Sam continued on, 'is that you must have slipped on one of the rungs. They were pretty wet.'

'Slipped?' *Is that it? I just slipped?*

'Yes, but honestly, I don't really know what happened. What with your fall, the tide rapidly coming in and everything else that happened afterwards, it's all become a bit a blur. And unlike you,' Sam chuckled quietly, 'I don't have a concussion or amnesia, to blame.'

'I wish I could remember,' Ruth mumbled, her words tripping over themselves. *What's wrong with me, I can barely get my words out?*

'In a way, I think you should be sort of glad, you can't remember. It was really scary down there, horrendous, in fact.'

'*You could have died out there.*' That was what the young policeman had said to Ruth, earlier. '*You were lucky you weren't on your own, when it happened.*'

'The police mentioned there was someone else…' Ruth had to pause to think, to find the words, 'down on the beach?'

'Yes, can you believe it? There was a dog walker down on beach, with us. We were so lucky he was there…'

As Ruth followed Sam's uncomfortable sentence through to its natural conclusion, her mouth became even dryer, parched. She licked her dry lips a couple of times. Felt some beads of perspiration, break out along her hairline. *Once darkness had fallen, no one would have been able to find us, or our bodies.*

Eventually, she rasped out, 'We were so stupid. We should never have gone down to that Godforsaken beach.'

Sam looked suddenly, uncomfortable. 'Well, we weren't the only ones down on the beach,' she shot out, defensively. 'He was there too, and with a dog, so it couldn't have been that dangerous.'

'But where did he come from?'

'Didn't that copper tell you?'

'I'm not sure?' Ruth struggled to remember. 'I think he may have done but I'm so drugged up, I can't think straight.'

'He was in a sort of cave thingy.'

Ruth frowned, hard. Tried to concentrate. Slowly began to remember that further along the beach, there was a disused lookout shelter carved into the cliff face, from the war. The lookout some way down from where they had been walking and slightly higher than the beach, it was not obviously noticeable. Unless, of course, you already knew it was there.

'He told the police, he'd gone in there to get out of the wind for a while, which is obviously why we hadn't seen him. When you fell, by the time I'd got back down the ladder to try and gauge how you were, this big hairy dog was standing over you. Really freaked me out, I can tell you. Then a couple of minutes later, he turned up. Seemed to appear from out of nowhere.'

'I was so tired and disorientated earlier, I forgot to ask the police if the dog walker saw what happened to me. Is he still around?'

'No, he's not. But the police said, he hadn't seen anything. Apparently, the only reason he came out of the cave thingy was because the tide had turned, and he wanted to get off the beach.'

Once the tide had come in, I would have been swept out to sea.

'So, who called the emergency services?'

No more than fish bait, I would have quickly disappeared, without a trace.

Sam gave Ruth an old fashioned look. 'I couldn't get a signal. Everything happened so quickly, and the tide was coming in so fast, thank God he was there and was able to get a signal on his phone. They were amazing, by the way, the emergency services.'

Ruth snuffed a yawn. Sam continued with a long narrative about what the emergency services had done for them both. She tried to listen, to keep her eyes open, but a cocktail of drugs still flowing through her system, she floated in and out of the scene. Took in very little of what Sam was relaying.

'Ruth? Are you awake?'

Ruth rallied herself. Made a determined effort not to drift off again. 'Yes, did you manage to get his contact details, you know, the stranger? Only once I get home, I'd like to thank him properly, and his dog,' she said wearily.

'No, I didn't, believe it or not. It's all been rather hectic, and confusing,' Sam replied, her tone, for some reason, sounding irritated.

'So you think, I slipped? That's all it was, a stupid mistake? An accident?'

'Yes, why? I don't see what else it could have been?' Sam said as she gave Ruth a suspicious look. Seemed to consider something, then urgently whispered, 'Ruth, you don't think...? Do you? You're not saying...?' Sam shook her head. Looked questionably at Ruth.

Their eyes locked for a second. Sam's message, delivered and received.

Ruth shuddered, and winced. She refused to go there.

Sam looked doubtful, unsure. Visibly contemplated. Studied someone in a nearby bed for a second or two, then quietly said, 'Ruth, after everything that's happened to you lately,' she paused, 'you know, what with Adam and everything... I'm sorry, but I have to ask...'

Please don't, Ruth thought. *I'm not sure I can go there, right now.*

'Did you deliberately let go of that ladder?'

Fighting the thought, but knowing what she had tried do to herself earlier, when standing on the top of the cliffs, and uncertain again, Ruth hesitated. Really, she did not want to think too closely about what Sam had insinuated, but the doubts crowding in, following each other like a swarm of bees, she was unable to leave it alone. Then, she became angry, really angry, furious with herself, with Sam, with *him*, with the world, with whole wretched business.

In mental agony, Ruth forcefully challenged herself.

Was Sam right?

Did I really try and kill myself today... twice?

Am I actually, insane?

Is Ben going to section me? Put me in a padded cell, in a straitjacket, and throw away the key?

Guilt, smashed her like a hammer.

Struggling to breath suddenly, Ruth took a minute. Watched an elderly woman in a tatty dressing gown and floppy slippers, slide her way on a Zimmer frame with grim determination, across the ward.

Her head thumping agonisingly, her memory coming and going and totally blank where she did not need it to be, she had to give up. Flopped back against her pillow, and gave a low moan as an excruciating pain shot up her spine.

I should have ignored Sam's phone call. I should have stayed at home, where I would have been miserable, but safe.

'Well, did you?' Sam pressed, under her breath. Her eyes furtively checking the neighbouring beds for eavesdroppers.

'Of course I didn't,' Ruth stated firmly, whilst inwardly fighting hysteria.

Breathing hard, anxious, uncomfortable, her back aching intolerably, Ruth struggled to sit more upright, and failed. Sam got up and helped her. Plumped up her pillows. Grabbed the beaker of water, then pressed it into Ruth's lightly trembling hands. Ruth took a greedy sip and passed it back. Her mouth was bone dry, but it was not for water.

'Ruth, you've gone white as a sheet? Should I call the nurse, or a doctor?' Sam asked, concern written all over her face.

'No, I'll be okay. It's just every time I move, it's really painful.'

'Yet the consultant reckons, you should be able to go home tomorrow.'

'Yes.'

'He also said, you're going to need some help at home and that you shouldn't be left on your own, at least not for the first few days.'

Wary of where the conversation was going, Ruth tried to quell a flash apprehension. *I cannot, have her living with me.*

'Just to make sure there are no unexpected repercussions, mainly from the bump to your head,' Sam continued.

'I'll be fine on my own,' Ruth stated. The level of her voice rising slightly, it echoed around her sore head and she could not help, but grimace.

'You think? You can't sit up in bed without some sort of assistance, and you can't even move a muscles without wincing. I also reckon you're going to feel a lot worse, by tomorrow morning. And without Adam…' Sam broke off, looked embarrassed as her cheeks pinked.

'Yes, I get where you're coming from. It's not like I have a husband at home to help me, anymore,' Ruth snapped out bitterly. Regretted the words as soon as they fled from out of her mouth. Even though Sam had raised the subject, she should not have agreed with her.

'No, but you do have a sister sitting right in front of you,' Sam stated, her voice calm but firm.

Ruth managed a thin smile, *Careful.* If she could mollify Sam, pretend she was more okay than she looked, then perhaps she could steer the inevitability of what was likely coming, in a *different* direction? *It was worth a try, wasn't it?*

'Look Ruth, it's no trouble for me to book a week off work,' Sam continued, smoothly. 'If you don't mind my borrowing your car, I can drive home tonight, pack a bag, and be back in time to collect you, tomorrow afternoon,' she said reasonably. Looked rather pleased with herself, with her plan.

Ruth's stomach dropped. *And there it was. The offer had been made, and it had been made so casually, it was barely even a kindness.*

Realising she had reached a pivotal point in her relationship with her sister, Ruth was suddenly undecided. Granted, she was in a poor physical state and needed help, but having Sam living-in, albeit for a few days, was the last thing she wanted. Feeling upset and uneasy, the whole, crazy nightmare of a situation leaving a nasty taste in her mouth, Ruth was at a total loss for words. *I can't think, but I have to think.*

'Ruth? Are you okay?'

Sam's gaze was so probing, Ruth felt compelled to tell her at least a partial truth. 'I'm sorry Sam. It's just my head's so fuzzy, I'm struggling to think straight.'

'My point exactly, the consultant was so right, you must have some help at home.'

Ignoring her pain, her confusion, Ruth thought, hard. Located what she thought would be plausible grounds for putting Sam off, without offending her. 'Look Sam, I appreciate your offer, really I do. But it doesn't seem fair that you should have to use a whole week of your precious annual leave, just for me. I can manage on my own, I'm sure.'

'I wouldn't hear of it,' Sam said, smiling broadly. 'In actual fact, I have too much annual leave at the moment. Only the other week, my boss reminded me, if I don't use up what's left of my annual leave by the end of February, I'm going to lose it.'

There was a beat of silence as Ruth anxiously plucked at the bed sheet. What more could she say? *You could just say no,* a voice from nowhere whispered into her brain.

Sam, suddenly looking visibly ill-at-ease, hastily said, 'Oh, sorry Ruth, I wasn't thinking. It's just that I've been so worried about you, and after everything the consultant said to me, I only wanted to help. But if you find the idea of me staying with you, too difficult after what happened between us… or you have someone else in mind to look after you, please, just say so. I'll understand.'

Bewildered, Ruth briefly closed her eyes.

Can I really trust her?

Why can't I shake off the feeling I'm being skilfully coerced?

Acknowledging she was in agony, that family were thin on the ground and that there were no friends to call on, Ruth was torn, wavering.

There's no way I'm going to be to manage at home, on my own.

'Ruth?' Sam prompted.

Ruth's heart sank. Capitulating to the inevitable, she conjured up a weak but grateful smile. Resignedly said, 'Thanks Sam, it's a lovely idea and very good of you to offer.'

'Great,' Sam nodded. 'I'm sure it'll be fun.'

Sam leaning across to the right hand side of Ruth's bed, she opened the doors to the hospital locker, retrieved Ruth's shoulder bag, and held it out to her. 'Are you able to look for your car keys yourself,' she signalled toward the medical paraphernalia puncturing Ruth's body, 'or should I find them for you?'

'Go ahead, knock yourself out,' Ruth said, with a sigh. Feeling weak and overwhelmingly weary, all of sudden.

Watching Sam scrummage around in the scuffed and badly water damaged handbag, extract an overstuffed brown leather purse, a matted hairbrush, a wad of screwed up tissues, a tiny silk bag covered in daubs of make-up, what looked like her mobile phone and last, the seemingly elusive set of keys, Ruth cringed with embarrassment. There was nothing like seeing your personal possessions, through the eyes of someone else.

'Oh Ruth, your poor phone,' Sam said, dropping Ruth's key fob into her own bag. 'It must have happened during the fall. Look, it's ruined.' Sam held up what was left of the mobile phone, so Ruth could get a clearer view, of just how trashed it was. 'Is there anyone I can call, for you?'

Useless piece of junk, Ruth thought bitterly, tiredly. Briefly gave thought to her mother and father-in-law as she gingerly closed her eyes against another shooting pain discharging itself through her throbbing head. *Should I ask Sam to ring them?* Decided, they would not be too keen on having to come all the way down from Hertfordshire. Then she thought of her brother-in-law, and she shivered inwardly. 'No, it's okay.'

'You sure?'

'Yes,' Ruth snapped out, no longer caring if Sam was offended, or not.

'Look, I think I ought to shoot off now,' Sam said. You look done in, it's starting to get pretty late and I've still got to rescue your car from the National Trust carpark.'

Ruth's gaze blank and uninterested, she yawned with fatigue. She needed sleep, lots of it. *Sam,* she said to herself, *could do what the hell she wanted.*

Sam getting up from her seat, Ruth's head nodded and her eyes closed as she drifted away again. Slipped into a deep sleep induced not by drugs, but by sheer exhaustion.

Chapter Thirteen

Outside Ruth's unlit house, looking up at its pitch black windows, the strong wind of earlier finally spent, Sam stood in the welcome silence and contemplated on whether to go in or not. Roughly calculating her flat was just over an hour away. Half an hour tops to pack her stuff, then the return journey. If she left now, she could be back here, before midnight. It would make for an extremely long day, and she was exhausted, but it would be worth it. Tonight, she would not sleep in her own flat, she would come back here and sleep in Ruth's house. Take full advantage of her sister's absence.

After the day I've had, I think I deserve a little fun.

Using Ruth's key fob to let herself into the garage, Sam strolled over to Adam's silver Jaguar F-Type Sports car, and smiled to herself. Chuckling at the vanity of the car's number plate - *XTC-1* - she depressed the central locking button, and slipped comfortably into the driver's seat. Switching on the ignition, revving the car's sizeable engine, Sam checked the fuel gauge and seeing it had almost a full tank, carefully manoeuvred the vehicle out of the garage. Accelerated away. Enjoyed the amazing sound of the car spitting and farting its way up the motorway. *Such a beautiful, powerful car, such fun!*

As she drove, Sam steered her thoughts back to the conversation she'd had with Ben, the A&E consultant. In the *Family Room*, he sat opposite her, his hands hanging loosely between his legs as he leant in toward her, Ben had asked her a number of pertinent questions. His questions mirroring those she had already been asked over and over, by the emergency services, Sam's answers had been practised and polished.

'No, I have no idea what caused Ruth's fall. One minute she was climbing up the ladder and the next, she was flat on her back on the beach, and out cold.'

Ben avidly listening to everything Sam had to say, he had then quietly asked, *'Is there anything troubling your sister, something that might have been keeping her awake at night?'*

Hesitantly divulging, what had happened to Adam, and that Ruth was still in the midst of grieving, Sam had allowed a couple of tears to fall. Then mentioned — because she had wanted to try the story out to see how it sounded — that under the strain of it all, Ruth was struggling to cope. That she could be depressed.

Ben's head nodding thoughtfully, he had gone on to ask if there was anything else, Sam thought he should know about?

Looking terribly worried, Sam had tentatively answered, *'I can't be certain, but I do have some concerns… I think she might be drinking, a bit too much. It's something, Ruth has a tendency to do, when things get too much, for her.'*

Nodding gravely, Ben had replied, *'So this is nothing new, then?'* This time, fashioning a guilty look as though betraying a trust, Sam had lightly shrugged her shoulders, and not responded.

Reassuringly patting her arm, Ben had strongly suggested Sam should keep a good eye on her sister. That she should encourage Ruth to see her own GP, as soon as possible. In the meantime, he would write to Ruth's GP and update him on her accident, her recent treatment, and his concerns, regarding her mental health.

Ben also recommended she should keep Ruth well away from the cliffs, or any other potentially *'high risk'* scenarios, for now. Then his beeper then going off, beckoning him to attend to his next patient, he hurried away in a flurry of white coat.

The scene was set.

Chapter Fourteen

As the overcast sky gave way to a cold, sleety rain, Ruth stared blankly out of the car window and wearily tried to gather her tangled thoughts. But the amnesia she had sustained, making it impossible for her to unravel them, no matter how hard she tried, they remained firmly knotted.

Sam drawing the car up in front of *Orchard House*, Ruth's spirits sank, even further. She had been dreading this moment. The thought of having to explain to Sam, why the whole house was in such a dismal state of domestic neglect, totally mortified her.

I'm useless. I should be ashamed of myself.

Purchased by Adam, just before they moved down from London to Kent, very quickly, he had knocked the tired and dilapidated building, into shape. Developing the house into a prized asset that represented everything he stood for and had worked so hard to obtain, it had swiftly become, his pride and joy. Whilst for Ruth, and though in the early days she had loved the very bones of they nineteenth century house — dust constantly seeping up through the wooden floorboards of the ground floor from the dirt foundations, seemingly alighting on everything and all over the house — it had slowly become a tiresome beast of burden, and a prison.

South-east facing, symmetrically double fronted with a detached double garage, *Orchard House* was a traditional build of red brick, under a Kent peg tiled roof. With three double-bedrooms and a family bathroom on the first floor. A large living room, a mirror image study, and an enormous open-plan kitchen-diner extension running across the full width of the back of property on the ground floor, the house was spacious and perfectly formed; big enough, for a family.

Positioned slap bang in the middle of a third of an acre of front and back gardens, accessed by a private u-shaped driveway, and surrounded by arable farmland on all sides, the house could not have been, more romantically situated.

Remote, but still within easy reach of the city of Canterbury to the North, Dover, and the undulating Dover Cliffs - a mere ten minute walk across the fields at the rear of the property — to the South, and Deal to the East, *Orchard Cottage* was isolated but peaceful. The house of Ruth's dreams, after her chaotic and tumultuous childhood, it had instantly wrapped its arms around her and for a while, she had felt secure, and safe.

'You okay?' Sam asked, snapping Ruth's attention back to the present as she stooped to face her through the open passenger car door.

'Yes, I'm fine. But wait, before you go in, I have to tell you something... about the house.'

Sam threw Ruth a puzzled look. 'What about the house, it's beautiful?'

Ruth inwardly cringed. *Wait till you get inside,* she thought with dismay.

'It's such a large house to manage all on my own,' Ruth hesitated, tried to find the rest of her words. Wished she had not been so rebellious and listened to Adam when he had tried to insist, she take on the services of a cleaner.

'Here, let me help you,' Sam ordered, brushing aside what Ruth had been about to say as she leaned into the car, grabbed a hold of her arms, and pulled.

'Hey,' Ruth objected, the moment for explanations suddenly disappearing as she concentrated on helping Sam, to assist her, out of the car, 'I'm not an invalid, you know.'

'Yes, I know,' Sam said, taking no notice as she continued to support Ruth's weight until she was fully out of the vehicle. 'Race you,' she giggled, throwing an exaggerated wink over her shoulder as she ran toward the house.

'Stop it,' Ruth begged, holding onto her aching sides. 'Please don't make me laugh, it hurts too much.'

In spite of herself, Ruth chuckled. For the first time since the accident, felt unexpectedly good. Wondered how she could have ever thought, Sam was so awful. Chose not to listen to a voice in her head, that insisted, *you know why*.

A few arduous and exhaustive minutes later, following Sam into her home as if it was her house, and she was the guest, Ruth deposited herself thankfully onto the living room sofa. Ignored a sneaking resentment of Sam's pretentious familiarity with the house as she pulled back the curtains, checked the radiator for warmth, plumped up the cushions.

It was good to be home, Ruth told her indignant self.

Switching from carer to hostess, Sam said she would fetch them both a drink. Hustled out of the living room door with a sense of importance, emanating from out of her.

Listening to Sam's footsteps moving toward the back of the house as she headed for the kitchen, feeling sore and tired from her minimal exertions, like an old crone, Ruth struggled to relax. Propped her feet up onto the coffee table in front of her, so she could ease more comfortably into the soft cushions Sam had put behind her back. Then experienced a swift pang of guilt as she heard *him* berating her for doing so. *It's my house, so I will put my feet where I damn well like*, she thought stubbornly.

A couple of minutes later, and Ruth was on the very edge of sleep. Knowing Sam would be back with her drink any minute and fighting to keep awake, for something to do, she forced her weary eyes to drift lazily around the room. The crystal droplets on the overhead chandelier catching her attention as they glistened and sparkled in the thin winter light filtering its way through the large bay window. Very slowly, it began to register, the decorative light had lost weeks worth of dust and cobwebs.

Snapping to attention, Ruth scanned the space in detail. Then quickly realised, someone had tidied up and cleaned. The whole room wrinkle-free, hoovered and smelling of furniture polish, everything around her positively glowed. *Just the way he,* Ruth thought with a start, *would have liked it.*

Gasping with shock, Ruth stiffly hauled herself up and out of the sofa. Unsteadily hobbled her way down a spotlessly clean and tidy hallway and on through, to an equally pristine kitchen.

For a couple of seconds, Ruth was scared she was going to cry with the horror of the violation. Her voice catching with emotion, she ejected out, 'Sam, what on earth have you done to my house?'

'Sit down, before you fall down,' Sam instructed gently as she grabbed a hold of Ruth's arm, pulled her toward the kitchen table, extracted a chair, and pushed her firmly down into it. 'There's no need to panic. All I've done is clean the place for you. And please don't look at me like that,' she retaliated condescendingly. 'Look, it's just that you've had such a rotten time these last few weeks, all I wanted to do, was to make the place look nice and welcoming for you,' she said nonchalantly, as she moved away.

Though revolted by her sister's equanimity, Ruth could not help herself. She watched obsessively as Sam pulled the cork on an elegantly embossed bottle of red wine, placed it on a wooden tray alongside of two sparkling goblets. Flicked her tongue over her suddenly, inordinately dry, lips.

Breaking her compulsive stare, noticing Sam move around the gleaming kitchen as though she knew it very well — *as though it is her own* - Ruth felt sick with anger, her craving. 'But, it looks like you've cleaned the whole damn house?' she whined, and hated herself for it.

'Yes,' Sam nodded, smiled benevolently. 'I have. Once I started, there seemed no point in stopping, but that's okay isn't it?'

Sam flicking her olive green eyes round the unsullied kitchen as though searching to see if anything was amiss, Ruth stared at her in disbelief. *This is not your house. You are trespassing where you do not belong,* she wanted to shout.

'But when, Sam? When did you find the time to do all of this?' Ruth demanded to know, sounding accusatory and ungracious.

'This morning,' Sam replied easily. Bustled around the kitchen like a housewife wanting to make her guests as comfortable as possible during their visit. Poured some wine into each glass, brought one of them to her lips, and had a little taste.

Ruth's mouth started to salivate. She folded her hands, across her chest. Distracted her thirst, by getting her thoughts back onto Sam. *She couldn't have cleaned the whole house in just a couple of hours, could she? Perhaps, she was just teasing me, earlier. Perhaps, she's only managed to clean the ground floor, and she's not been anywhere near, the bedrooms?*

'This morning?' Ruth questioned parrot fashion.

'Yes,' Sam nodded. 'I couldn't sleep, last night. Guilty conscience, I think. I couldn't stop myself from going over and over everything that had happened to us, *to you,* yesterday. I kept worrying about how it could all have turned out, so very different. Kept blaming myself, for pushing you into going down to the beach. In the end, I gave up trying to sleep. Decided I might as well get up, and come down here. The only problem being, I hadn't thought it through properly. Leaving London so early this morning, when I got to the hospital, it was still well outside of visiting hours. Not sure what to do with myself, I then realised, I still had your keys. So, I thought I might as well come over here first. You know, to unpack my own stuff and pick up a change of clothes for you,' she explained straightforwardly.

Puzzled, for a second or two, Ruth cast her eyes down to what she was wearing. For the first time, realised the clothes she had on were a totally different set to the ones she had left home in, yesterday. *Damn the concussion.*

'But then…' Sam hesitated, breaking into Ruth's thoughts as she continued to explain, 'when I saw the house needed a little help, well, I figured I might as well roll up my sleeves and get on with it. It's not as if, I didn't have the time, and please don't worry, it wasn't nearly as bad as it looked. Took me less than a couple of hours to get the whole house straightened out for you. Next to no time really.' She smiled sweetly.

She's said it again. She's just said, she's cleaned the whole house, not just the downstairs. Is this really happening, Ruth thought miserably? Felt a deep corrosive sense of shame flood through her.

The humiliation making Ruth feel clammy and nauseous, she momentarily closed her eyes. Then dropped her head as she began to feel dizzy and hot. Loathing the thought of Sam spending time in every single room in the house, unchaperoned, and in such an intimate way, Ruth felt sickeningly nervous at what her sister was sure, to have been noticed.

Dear God, she was desperate for a drink. Surreptitiously ran her eyes up and down the glasses of wine Sam had poured out, then the bottle; coveted them.

'You know, you're so lucky Ruth.'

Why does everyone keep telling me how lucky I am? I'm not lucky, I am miserable. Exhausted. Lost and broken.

'This house is so handsome, and it's in such a perfect location,' Sam continued on, sighing out with delight as she noticeably reflected on Ruth's home and all it had to offer.

Ruth sucked back a wave of anger. Made herself look around as she attempted to see the house through the eyes of her sister. Tried to fall back in love with her home again, but after all that had happened in it, failed miserably. Knew, in that moment that ultimately, it would be sold.

'There is just one thing though…' Sam hesitated as she keenly watched Ruth for her reaction, 'I'm afraid I didn't have enough time to clean up the lovely cream rug in your bedroom. So I've rolled it up and popped in the garage. You can decide later, what you want to do with it. I trust that's okay?'

Slammed with the memory of what had happened to the rug — the condemning wine stain she had chosen to ignore in her hurry to leave the house on Saturday morning — Ruth's cheeks burned. Determined not to explain herself, she simply replied, 'Thanks, that's fine.'

Sam nodded. Said a lot, by not saying anything.

Picking up the tray, Sam started to walk toward the kitchen door. Asked over her shoulder, 'Are you coming? I know it's early, but I thought we should celebrate your homecoming, in style.'

Maintaining a composure she did not feel, Ruth put on a straight calm face. Pretended as if everything was okay, as she thirstily trotted after Sam. Whilst inside, her gut was twisting. Her conflicted and troubled emotions on collision course, Ruth did not want the topic of the house that was no longer a home, to linger.

It will do my head in, put me in hell, if I keep thinking about where Sam has been and what she may have discovered.

Any normal person, she told herself, *would be grateful to their sister for being so incredibly kind, and thoughtful.*

Yeah, who are you kidding? Queried an inner voice. *All you really want to do, is throw yourself at her. You want to yell and scream, like a three year old having the worst, of all possible, tantrums.*

How dare she! How dare Sam have the nerve to take such liberties in someone else's home! Ruth silently yelled.

Shuffled down the hallway as fast as her bruised and battered body would allow, as she endeavoured to catch up with Sam.

Chapter Fifteen

Later that evening, sat on the sofa in the living room, Sam was preparing to relax. Wood crackling and popping comfortably in the log burner, scarves of smoke trailing up the flue, at last, she was beginning to wind down after the day's exertions. Ruth temporarily out of her hair, upstairs and in the tub soaking away her aches and pains with the last glass of wine in the bottle before bed, the house had become wonderfully cosy, peaceful.

Not quite comfortable, Sam undid the top button of her jeans, sighed out with what felt like, her expanding waistline. Then swivelling herself around, she placed a cushion behind her head and lay flat out on the sofa. Tucked her bare and blister free feet, under a tartan throw she had acquired from the airing cupboard, a couple of hours earlier.

Feeling as though she could do with a nap herself but her brain in overdrive, Sam knew there was no way she would be able to sleep, not just yet. Submitted with good grace, to the more pressing of her many thoughts.

No matter what Ruth said or more to the point, what she had not said, she had been so *mad* earlier; *so unappreciative.* Yet the dreadful state of the place when Sam had walked into it last night, there was no way, she could have ignored the situation. *The sign of a disordered mind?*

Getting off the train from London yesterday morning, *who knew,* Sam thought, gazing pensively up at the twinkling ceiling chandelier, *I would end up living in Ruth's home as though it's my own?* Yet all it had taken, was one carefully engineered mishap and although the outcome, she had to admit, had not turned out quite as planned, it would most definitely do… for now.

Briefly ruminating on Ruth's saviour, his sudden and almost miraculous appearance, *thank God,* Sam thought, *he and his monstrous dog popped out of their hidden cave, just when they did.* Ruth's fall, not quite as disastrous as she had hoped for, a few seconds later, and who knows what they might have witnessed?

Sam turned her head from one side to the next as she languidly flicked her eyes around the refreshed and sparkling room. Surrounded by all Ruth and Adam's things, the *stuff* that had made up their relationship and marriage, for the second time that day, she admired the well chosen furniture, the refined and soothing decor. Correctly guessed that most of it, would have been Adam's taste, his choice.

Antiques juxtaposed against high-end contemporary pieces, pops of colour provided by the original artwork on the walls, like the rest of the house, the living room oozed style and money.

The house, its situation, its opulent contents, so very different from the council houses and foster homes she and Ruth had been brought up in, Sam coveted, all of it. *How well, Ruth has done for herself,* she thought nastily.

In Ruth's two plus years of marriage, Sam had been invited down to the house, just twice. The first visit taking place a few weeks after the happy couple had moved in, when Ruth had been keen to show off the newly renovated house. The second, taking place a little under a year later when Ruth, complaining of feeling isolated and lonely with Adam away on yet another of his business trips, had rung Sam out of the blue; practically begged her to *pop* down for the day. On neither occasion, had Sam been asked to stay over. But then with their history, it was hardly surprising, she supposed.

Obtaining the keys to Ruth's house. Being in the property overnight and then again this morning, and unencumbered by her sister's claustrophobic presence, had brought Sam such a rush of emotions; glee, being the abiding one.

Euphoric, with the promise of unlimited access to all areas, and having had a super comfortable sleep in Ruth's spare room, this morning, Sam had got up super early. Given herself plenty of time, to luxuriate in slowly unveiling as many of Ruth's secrets, as she possibly could; approached each uncovered enigma, as a riddle that just had to be solved. In the process, Sam's understanding of the blueprint of her sister's life, her marriage, had been taken to a whole, other level.

Passing through each room in turn, cleaning and restoring as she went, Sam had suspended reality for a few hours. She had revelled in pretending the house and all its contents, belonged to her. Examining everything with zeal, she had opened wardrobes, cupboards, and drawers. She had studied photographs, post, and paperwork. Had been elated to unearth that Ruth's finances, were thriving. *Such a pity, she's set to die without issue.*

Discovering Ruth's journal wedged between the wall and the headboard of the marital bed, had been one of Sam's most awing moments. The handwritten notebook revealing Ruth's deepest secrets, and her darkest angst, recording how apprehensive she was for the ongoing health her marriage; how afraid she was of the real world; how terrified she was of the rage that persistently consumed her, it had provided an illuminating and at times, an almost breathtaking, read. Pouring through the journal, analysing the messy script, the jumbled and increasingly erratic thoughts, the diary above all else, had given excellent evidence as to the rapid decline of Ruth's mental health; her neurosis, and her paranoia. *A perfect find.*

Uncovering a poignant, breadcrumb trail of Adam's possessions scattered throughout the property — a tatty pair of sheepskin slippers still imprinted with his footprint, an olive green Barbour frayed around the collar and cuffs, a battered flat cap — had momentarily saddened, then astonished Sam. *Ruth was hardly sentimental.*

The biggest surprise though, had been reserved for the larger of the two guest bedrooms. A gold wristwatch, rimless glasses and a partially read novel, all neatly stacked on the beside table. A man's grey flannel robe, pyjamas, belts and ties, draped over a couple of hooks straddling the back of the bedroom door. A pine wardrobe housing a man's clothing; suits, shirts, casual trousers and jeans, all tidily hung up on wooden hangers. A matching chest of drawers containing a man's smalls, plus a number of folded jumpers and t-shirts; male toiletries, standing to attention across its top. A hint of aftershave in the weave of the bed sheets, it was almost as though Adam had just stepped out of the room and out of the house. That he had not died.

Feeling suddenly spooked, Sam shivered. She found it disturbing — *unhealthy, and weird* — that Ruth had not yet cleared the house, of her dead husband's possessions.

Ruth and Adam definitely not sleeping with each other, Sam briefly wondered how Ruth had explained her broken-down marriage, to the police?

Sam's favourite room, had to be Adam's bolt-hole. Located across the hallway from the living room, the library-cum-study was a mirror image in form and size. Decorated in muted tones of dove grey and white. Accommodating a partner desk and swivel chair placed in front of the large bay window, a black leather recliner angled under a chrome floor lamp in the rear left-hand corner, the room was sparsely furnished and serenely monastic. There was nothing random, or out of place. Seemingly the only luxury, rows and rows of scientific tomes and books housed in a floor to ceiling shelving unit that ran the full length of the back wall, it was a practical space.

Scrupulously clean, the room's simple austerity full of purpose, the tranquil space had left Sam with nothing to do but admire its minimal content. Walking back and forth across stripped floorboards that felt both warm and cool beneath her feet, sitting where he would have sat, she had taken time to savour the room. Allowing her gaze to lazily wander out onto the frost tipped fields that led to the cliffs, she had slowly realised, with no paperwork drifting over the green and gold leathered top of the desk, no computer, no printer, no phone, no pens or pencils in pots, and no photographs, there was nothing — other than the view — to distract the thoughts of its owner. A room for study and contemplation, it was steeped in Adam's presence. Sam had relaxed there, for quite some time.

During her hunt, Sam had found the affirmation she had been so keenly looking for. A number of empty wine bottles in the outside recycling bin, an open one on the kitchen table, one abandoned in the middle of a crimson stained rug, yet another hidden at the back of the wardrobe, all together, they had left Sam in no doubt... *Ruth was hitting the bottle, hard.*

A number of pills, sprinkled like tiny white snowflakes across Ruth's unmade marital bed, it appeared she was also taking Valium. Gathering up each and every one of the scattered tablets, then carefully depositing them back into their little brown container, Sam had returned the bottle to Ruth's beside table. Left them ready and waiting, for when Ruth next needed them.

Clearly, Ruth was unstable.

Alcohol, pills, a toxic combination. To anyone on the outside looking in, Ruth was blatantly a text book, *accident waiting to happen.*

Poor Ruth, Sam could almost feel sorry for her now.

But then again, we all have our crosses to bear.

Chapter Sixteen

Boulders of chalk, springing from the rock face as though plucked by unseen hands before crashing down to the shoreline, Ruth was teetering on the edge of a precipice. Fingers of ice cold spray reaching up to drag her down into the murky depths of the sea, she swayed, dangerously.

Shapes eerily moving beneath the surface of the water, the sea looked alive with creatures, *with possibilities*.

Her vision blurring as she stared down at the swirling water, Ruth felt increasingly weary, *drawn. It would be so easy…*

A hand, suddenly in the small of her back, she felt a massive push…

Struggling for air, Ruth awoke with gasp, and sat bolt upright in bed.

A phone ringing somewhere, she scanned the room in a panic. Terrified, she could feel her heart pounding.

Hearing the call being intercepted, Ruth held her breath.

Whoever you are, go away.

Footsteps running up the stairs, Ruth's bedroom door was thrown open.

A few strides, and Sam was across the room.

'It's Ed,' Sam whispered, her hand covering the receiver she held out to Ruth.

Still disorientated from the nightmare. Her head splitting from the concussion and a sleep that had done little to revive her, Ruth painfully shook her head, made it clear she did not want take the call.

Sam pushing the receiver into her hand anyway, mouthed back at her, 'It's too late.' Placed a mug of tea on the bedside table next to her, then left the room.

Ruth sighed. Left with no choice, she gingerly pulled herself up in bed, and sat straighter against the pillow. Then took a deep breath, and prepared herself.

The customary pleasantries swiftly over, Ruth haltingly told Ed about her fall but soon came to realise, she had massively underestimated his likely reaction. At first listening carefully to what she had to say, Ed then rapidly fired off round after round of head-splitting questions that felt like accusations.

Wishing, with every fibre of her being, she had kept her garrulous mouth shut, Ed's final response to her situation was immediate and firm. Treating her accident as though it were a grave and dire emergency, he abruptly informed her, he would be coming down to see her. Not once did he ask her for permission. Merely notified her in clipped tones, he would be down in time for dinner.

Then leaving her speechless, he hung up on her. No *goodbye* or anything, just hung up.

Three times Ruth tried to call him back, to cancel. But each time, his phone went to voicemail.

Bastard!

In a horrible daze. Furious with herself for being so pathetic, so naive, Ruth took a pill and crawled back under the quilt. Though Sam, it seemed, was having none of it. Again barging into the bedroom without knocking, Sam told Ruth she had run a bath for her. Then collecting up the phone, the now cold mug of tea she had brought up a few minutes earlier, said she would see Ruth downstairs in forty-five minutes, for breakfast.

Ruth's body stiff, aching, and blooming all over in a bouquet of wine and burgundy coloured bruises, she tentatively put a foot into the hot soapy water, winced in pain, then stepped in. Slowly, she sank into the bath. Allowed her face to slip right under for a few seconds. Briefly wondered, what it would feel like, to drown.

Feeling deliciously drowsy, Ruth closed her eyes but within seconds, her agitation of earlier, was back. She could not stop herself from revisiting the phone call. Obsessed on what she had, and had not said. Hated how Ed had interrogated her as though she had committed some sort of a crime. Despised how he had bullied her into submission, by absenting her from the decision making process. Eventually shook her head at herself; *I can't do this now, I have to relax.*

Despite the buoyancy of the water, it was an effort for Ruth to move her battered body. Her toes toyed with the chain of the plug, but she did not have the energy to climb out of the tub, not yet. Judging the water was cooling down, and that she was becoming chilled, Ruth knew that soon, she would have to get out, but maybe not quite yet.

Fifteen minutes later, out of the bath and in need of something fortifying, Ruth headed for the wardrobe. Found a half empty bottle of red wine at the back of it, and took a couple of long pulls. *At least Sam hasn't been poking around in my wardrobe.* Then took a Valium. Geared herself up for the effort it was going to require, to get dressed, to talk to Sam about her *news.*

Painfully crabbing her way down the stairs, Ruth tentatively shuffled along the hall, toward the kitchen. Sweating and out of breath, she hoped Sam was in a good mood as soon, she would have to be told about their extra dinner guest.

'Hey,' Sam said brightly as Ruth entered the kitchen. 'Nice bath?'
'Yes, thanks, it was just what I needed.'
'Good, I thought it might be. Coffee?'
Ruth sat gingerly down at the kitchen table. 'Yes, thanks.'

Sam placing a healthy bowl of porridge loaded with berries and seeds down in front of her, Ruth smiled gratefully, though really, she was not hungry.

'You look very pale,' Sam said.

So would you, if you'd been through what I've been through, Ruth thought truculently. 'Do I? I didn't sleep all that well, last night?'

'Really? I slept like a baby. How are you feeling now? Do you need some painkillers, yet?'

'Yes, please, I think I could do with a couple of paracetamol, but I'm not sure, I have any?'

'Yes, we do. I picked some up for you yesterday morning, just in case.'

Wow, she really does, think of everything.

Sam passed two tablets over to her. Ruth swallowed them down with a swig of coffee. 'Thanks.'

'I'm sorry about the phone call, Ruth. But being so early on a Monday morning, I thought I should answer it, in case it was important. And then Ed, well, he really was quite insistent, he talk to you. It was on the tip of my tongue to tell him you were unavailable, but he was so surprised to hear my voice, I didn't want to lie.'

'Yeah, I could have done without talking to him, this morning.'

'Why?'

'No particular reason, I just find he can be hard work at times, and I wasn't up for it.' Now, was her opportunity. Although it was no more than Ed deserved, she could hardly let him turn up unannounced. Jumped in, with both feet. 'By the way, we've got an extra dinner guest tonight.'

'What? Who?' Sam exclaimed, sounding supremely underwhelmed.

'Who do you think?'

'You do know, you don't have enough food in the house to feed another person? I haven't had a chance to shop, yet.'

Ruth had not got one clue about what provisions she did or did not have, but unable to remember the last time she had been to the supermarket, or even ordered an on-line delivery, she had to assume, Sam was right. For an answer, she shrugged her shoulders. What could she say?

'Great,' Sam sarcastically remarked. Leaned up against the kitchen counter top as she urgently started to compile a shopping list.

Sam's manner as distinctly off-hand, as her dialogue was cool and forced, Ruth was left in little doubt as to her sister's thoughts on the matter. Sam transparently blaming her for the unwelcome intrusion, and the resulting extra work and stress it would cause, Ruth found herself feeling absurdly guilty. *I didn't invite him.*

Silently cursing Ed again, then Sam for answering the damn phone in the first place, Ruth sighed out her irritation. Feeling washed out again, and hating the prospect of having to spend hours on her feet shopping and cooking, but determined not to give Sam any further reasons to gripe, she firmly stated, 'Look Sam, I don't feel anywhere near as bad as I look. I can go to Tesco, do the shopping, and cook the meal. I'm more than capable.'

'You reckon?' Sam snorted with derision. 'Look at you, you can barely twitch a muscle without wincing.'

'I'm just a bit sore that's all. I can manage.' Then, in spite of her bravado, fatigued all of sudden, Ruth collapsed back into her chair. Bit back a groan before Sam could hear it.

'No, you're not,' Sam disagreed, violently shook her head. 'And what about the concussion? The hospital clearly stated you should *not* be driving for the first few days, as it could be dangerous.'

'Dangerous? I don't remember them saying that.'

'Yes, of course, think about it. What if you were to have an accident?'

'But I won't have an accident.'

'Ruth, you have a diagnosed concussion with amnesia, and a body that's so battered and bruised you can barely move. I doubt you could do an emergency stop,' Sam argued. 'If you were to have an accident whilst driving, your insurance company would have a field day. Not to mention the fact you could kill yourself or worse, kill someone else.'

There was a sudden silence as they both inwardly balked at Sam's poor choice of words.

Seconds passed.

'Oh God Ruth, I'm sorry. I didn't mean that quite the way it came out,' Sam apologised profusely. 'Look,' she hastily continued, 'the whole purpose of my moving in here, was so I could take care of you. So why don't you get a book, go upstairs and get some rest, while I go to the supermarket? And I'll cook the dinner. I was being thoughtless and selfish, earlier. It's not a problem,' she insisted. 'Your news just took me a little by surprise, that's all.'

You're not the only who's been taken by surprise, Ruth thought bitterly.

Though it was on the tip of Ruth's tongue to explain, to point out that Ed had summoned himself to dinner, exhausted, she could no longer be bothered. Then Sam looked at her watch, made ready to leave, and Ruth's opportunity to explain everything, passed.

'Look, I'd better run. But do me a favour will you, go to bed,' Sam commanded.

Not having the energy to argue, Ruth nodded her head in tacit agreement. Watched Sam hurtle herself out of the kitchen like a mini tornado. Briefly held her breath as she listened to Sam's footsteps trot on down the hallway.

Hearing the front door open, then slam shut, Ruth instantly flicked her eyes to wine rack. Hankered for its contents.

Having slept away most of the afternoon, Ruth awoke to the sounds and smells of a house that was once again alive with activity. The silence to which she had become accustomed and so hated, now punctuated with the muted burble of pop music playing on a distant radio, and the softened noise of someone clattering around in the kitchen below.

Lonely, yet no longer alone, she thought ironically.

Gingerly pulling herself up in bed, the room chill, Ruth shivered. She grabbed at the tangled quilt, and pulled it up over her. Snuggled into its warmth.

Feeling exhausted but wired. Her mind both blunted yet bursting, Ruth's head was all over the place. On the one hand, she was finding it hard to summon up the necessary concentration she needed, to think. Whilst on the other, she had the strong feeling there was a critical fact teasing at the periphery of her brain; a detail she *should* be thinking about, or a memory she should be seizing.

Becoming more and more anxious as she struggled to remember. Wishing she could reach into her own skull and take apart her brain, Ruth's perplexed thought process was suddenly interrupted by yet another muffled clang seeping up through the floorboards. It was at that point, Ruth finally gave up.

Guessing Sam was in the throes of preparing dinner, Ruth half-heartedly toyed with the idea of going down and volunteering her services. But knowing Sam had her own way of doing things, and that she could be a hell of a control freak when she was stressed, she concluded it was best she stay put. Keep herself well out of the way, of her sister's capricious temper.

Ruth took a Valium, then napped for a little while longer.

Later, the house at peace again, all Ruth could hear was fingers of rain tapping against the windowpane. The clicks and gurgles of the radiator.

The room in darkness, guessing it had to be getting late, Ruth hauled her aching bones out of bed. Audibly groaned, with the effort.

Her mouth dry and tasting foul whilst her head thudded, Ruth knocked back a glass of water, then plonked herself down in front of the dressing table. Flicked on a table lamp.

Studying herself in the mirror, Ruth could see the image of a woman who looked far older than her twenty-four years. Felt as though she was fraying around the edges, disintegrating.

I hate my looks.

Finding her reflection too disturbing, fretting about it, Ruth was trying to decide if slapping on some make-up would make a difference? Peered closer into the mirror. *More wrinkles.* Every day, there seemed to be new ones. Dark bags under her eyes as large a suitcases. A face the colour of sour milk.

Daunted by the scale of the project, her heart palpitating, her limbs aching, Ruth turned away from the mirror. She needed a moment.

Picking up her coffee mug, Ruth drained the dregs of a bottle of red she had purloined from the wine rack earlier. Then she popped another pill. Almost instantly, felt the familiar, warm sleepy drunkenness spreading right through her tender body. Lazily figured out, she had far bigger things to worry about, than how good her face looked.

Ed's voice on the phone earlier, sounding so like *his*, disorientating her, Ruth had struggled to remain calm and centred. Always, she had to be in the right frame of mind to deal with her brother-in-law and right now, she was not even in the picture. Her brain muddled, her body weak and fragile from her accident, from what the last few weeks had put her through — *from what life has put me through* — the mere thought of Ed being anywhere near her, made Ruth squirm with a self-conscious embarrassment.

Tonight, she thought with a heavy sigh, *it is going to take a monstrous force of effort, to even be polite.*

Returning to her reflection, no longer certain she could pull the evening off, Ruth nervously chewed on her bottom lip. Slapping on make-up, choosing *something* to wear, making conversation, all seemed tremendously difficult tasks.

She desperately wanted to cry.

Like I have a lot of choice? He's coming.

Automatically rubbing moisturiser into her ashen face, her pale neck. Mechanically brushing her brittle hair, though with every stroke of the brush, like severe palsy, her hands shook, Ruth tried not to peer to hard at the hollowed eyed, spectral face, staring back at her.

Why can't my eyes be bright, my hair gleam, my cheeks be rosy, like Sam's? What's happening to me?

Tears of self-pity gathering at the corner of each eye, suddenly, Ruth clutched her stomach as she tried not to vomit.

The queasiness passing, Ruth could breath again.

Two-seconds later, terrible memories of the past forcing their way into Ruth's exhausted and befuddled brain, small beads of sweat popped out along her hairline.

Her heart flailing in her chest, Ruth flew from the bedroom.

Leaping across the landing into the bathroom, kicking the door shut behind her, Ruth finally gave in to the nausea.

Chapter Seventeen

An October gale blew leaves wildly across the fields. Twigs and small dead branches fell to the ground, whilst the trees bordering the fields, bent and swayed in a gusting, gale force wind.

Ruth, skirting the field that adjoined the back of the house, was headed toward the beckoning desolation of the cliffs. Weaving her way between the straining trees, she paid no mind to the maelstrom thrashing around her. Out in the world, yet detached from it, she moved blindly on with a momentum she did not dare question.

Thinking of Adam, recalling their first kiss, how he had brought his face down to hers. How his soft and responsive lips had so completely and passionately devoured her, Ruth stumbled. Kicked out angrily at the offending branch.

An elixir, Adam had exploded into the veins of Ruth's life like the worst of all drugs. Unable to rest until she was next with him, from the start, he had been an addiction. For the first time in her life, feeling deeply loved and extraordinarily beautiful, Ruth had not questioned the wisdom of it.

Adam seemingly just as hooked and powerless to ignore her, from their first meeting — *that first night* — he had shamelessly pursued her. Then determined to have her, he had ruthlessly swept all barriers, out of the way.

Both of them chucking caution to the wind, within a matter of days, almost hours, Adam had asked her to move in with him. Three months later, they had married.

Some would say their whirlwind romance, the collateral damage their relationship had left in its wake, it was doomed to failure. Yet up until recently, not once, had Ruth ever seen it that way.

Young, immature, barely into her twenties and moulded from a past she had chosen to forget, Ruth had been quite desperate, when they married. Adam, older by fifteen years, more experienced, successful and ostensibly in a hurry, it had seemed natural for him to take charge of her life. Brought up in foster homes from the age of eight, her only known relative and sibling absent for much of her childhood, all Ruth had ever wanted, was for someone to take care of her, to love her.

Yes, I willingly conspired with him. I encouraged his fantasies, in every way possible, but no more than any other woman would, in my situation.

Once married, Ruth had readily subsumed herself into Adam's established patterns. She had invested all her time and energy into doing everything she could, to make him happy. She loved him, so why wouldn't she?

Suddenly experiencing one those ghastly moments when life comes unerringly into focus, Ruth comprehended Adam had become her sole purpose, her whole reason for being. Now nothing without him, her life had become shallow and aimless.

I've been such a fool.

With hindsight, Ruth could see it would have been better to have taken a job when they first moved down to Kent. That way at least, she would have had a life of her own, not been so dependent on Adam; *or his attention.* But Adam, under the assumption that before long she would be pregnant, had told her he was earning more than enough for the both them. That she should not bother. That he liked her being free, to look after him.

If only, I had got pregnant.

Paying no mind to the arboreal debris swirling all around her, unshed tears pricking behind her eyes, Ruth kept her head down. Kept on walking.

Her gaze misting, Ruth began to think of the first few occasions Adam had not returned home on time. Thought of how he had begun to turn away from her bed, of how it felt to be so hopelessly disappointed in love.

Somewhere, at sometime, Ruth had heard it said that *falling* in love was a form of psychosis. A passing state that was not the same, as *being* in love. She feeling sick with love, obsessed by it, Ruth discerned she had obviously never got past the psychotic stage. Briefly pondered on what a psychiatrist might make of that, of her?

Ruth's thoughts whirling away from the incalculable state of her psychosis, she alighted on the equally uncomfortable condition of her troubled relationship with Adam's parents.

It had taken Ruth a while to suss out her in-laws but now she realised, they had never loved her, just the idea of her. The replacement parents she had tried to get close too, had only ever loved her for Adam's sake. If he had taken home someone else other than her, they would have loved that person in equal measure; *probably more*.

Certain, should the marriage be dissolved, her in-laws would not miss her, Ruth felt a hot knot of fury in the pit of her stomach. She guessed they would probably chalk up her transient passing in their son's life, as an unfortunate digression.

I have been such a fool, to think I could trust them, to think they actually cared.

Swallowing down a sob of pain as the rage tried to escape, Ruth attacked the leaves twisting around her feet. Booted them into oblivion. She did not care that it had started to rain.

Ruth's chaotic thoughts unable to settle, she next worried on the nuisance phone calls. Thought about the number of times of late, when she had answered the house phone, how no one would speak. Recalled how the silence would build and accumulate, whilst again and again, she would say, *'Hello? Hello? Who's there?'* How after a few more seconds the connection would be cut, leaving her looking down at the silent phone as though it had betrayed her.

Every time Ruth mentioned her concerns to Adam, he would tell her she was overreacting. Insisting they were just unwanted sales calls from an obscure office located somewhere abroad, like India, Adam would either laugh or get angry with her. He would tell her she was making the proverbial, *mountain out of a molehill.*

Ultimately, the final outcome was always the same, Ruth would be left feeling stupid, and humiliated. Like she had imagined it.

The thought of Adam, perhaps having a mistress, Ruth felt sick; partly from anger, and partly from the dread of him knowing she had caught him out. Baulking at what would likely happen, should she find and present Adam with some indisputable proof of his dirty secret, Ruth had been forced to consider the wisdom, of actually doing so. *But if there is something to find, I have to know.*

Over the last couple of days, Ruth had scoured the house, the garage, the garden shed and even the log store, looking for evidence of her suspicions. Delving into every single one of Adam's trouser and jacket pockets, searching every drawer and cupboard in the house, looking under all beds, including their mattresses, she had thoroughly examined each and every item found. Skimming through the reams of paperwork (financial and credit card statements, receipts, utility bills, phone bills...) she had kept going, until her eyes, exhausted from lack of sleep, had finally blurred over.

Three days ago, with Adam about to leave for his latest business trip, she had even stolen his mobile. Like a thief in the night, she had crept down stairs, and hidden in a corner of the kitchen. Crouched on the floor in a dark and dusty corner, she had mercilessly interrogated the phone's content; emails, texts, photos, call log, every single app she could open, and get into. Yet her comprehensive search, had proven fruitless. *Nada! Nothing!*

Frustrated and disappointed, Ruth could only assume it was luck, cunning, or both, that had kept Adam's bitter betrayal, hidden from her. The whole, drawn-out process serving nothing but to leave Ruth in tears, and still full of doubt.

In her desperation, Ruth had turned to the oracle. With *google's* help, she had spent hours researching the signs of a cheating husband and it had not taken her long, to establish Adam's behaviour, fitted the profile.

Increasingly secretive and distant, Adam had started to find any excuse to avoid spending time with her. Regularly disappearing from the house, and sometimes for hours on end, he would say, *'I need a run.'* Or, *'I have to see a colleague about an experiment we're in the middle of conducting.'* Or, *'There's a patient partaking in one of my studies, who needs urgent help.'*

Then when he was at home, he would spend hours closeted away in his study. He would not look up at her when she took him in some refreshments, and when she sat down in his favourite recliner, so she could have his company, he would clearly signal he wanted to be alone. Then if she ignored his cue, he would retaliate with a simmering silence. Passive-aggressive, he would keep his gaze firmly directed on his paperwork, or his laptop. Keep his discourse, to the absolute minimum.

Recently, his more frequent business trips were being extended either side, by a day or two. His work day frequently eroding into the evening, and the previously sacrosanct weekend, it was as if he was gradually sliding away from her.

Worse, he had stopped initiating the casual touches. Those brief displays of intimacy, that were used to let her know she was loved and treasured. Now, frequently moody and irritable, at any given opportunity, he would sling hurtful remarks her way. Only a few days ago, he had told her she had the most appalling dress sense. Casually looking up from an article in the newspaper, he had pointed to the picture of an actress with too much make-up and not enough clothes, stated how beautiful she looked. Then, and as though it were a perfectly reasonable question to ask, he had demanded to know why she no longer made an effort. Hurt, she had become instantly defensive, and the bickering had descended into a full blown argument. *'He was selfish, and neglectful. She was a slovenly drunk, an embarrassment he could no longer trust.'*

Seemingly every one of Adam's comments of late, negative and utterly wearing, was it any wonder, Ruth thought, she was becoming paranoid?

Google also confirmed that a cheating husband would typically loose his sex drive, *at least with the wife.*

Bemoaning how demanding his work had become these last few weeks, Adam had begun to turn to her less often in bed. They had not made love in weeks and most days, he preferred to go to bed early and he slept, heavily.

Now striding out along the cliff paths, muttering to herself as though insane, Ruth could not help but imagine his mistress.

Was she beautiful, more curvaceous?
Did she know he was married and if so, why didn't she care?
Would she give him the child he so obsessively craved?
What, ultimately, did the bitch want from him?

Ruth's mind protested and rebelled. As terrible and vivid as her thoughts were, she could not bear to picture her life without him. Adam might be making her miserable but she loved him, and he was all she had.

But neither could she lie to herself, any longer. Even without any proof, instinctively knowing the tenor of their marriage had changed, an intolerable pain darkened Ruth's eyes.

Feeling a deep level of insecurity, it shocked Ruth to realise, envisaging Adam dead, was nowhere near as dreadful as imagining him abandoning her.

Chapter Eighteen

Throwing open the front door, the cold air flooding in, Sam greeted Ruth's brother-in-law with a wide and carefully composed smile. Her displeasure at his arrival, off-set by being able to open the front door of Ruth's house as though it were her own, and the fact that his visit would be fleeting.

'Hi Ed, please, come on in,' Sam said brightly.

'Sam, good to see you again,' Ed replied, sounding equally as warm, his grey-blue eyes resting on Sam's face, with a quick interest. Darting in to drop a chilled and slightly wet kiss onto Sam's hot cheek, he said, 'You know, I can't remember the last time we saw each other?'

Though hating the moist kiss, as well as the pungent waft of an astringent smelling aftershave unpleasantly hitting the back of her nose, Sam politely smiled through it. 'Not that long ago,' she answered. 'I was at Adam's funeral,' she reminded him.

'Ah yes, of course,' Ed nodded to himself. Looked mildly embarrassed as he acknowledged his obvious, faux pas. 'Sorry, there was just so much going on that day, I barely registered a lot of what was happening, who I saw.'

Receiving what she hoped was an unintentional insult, with good grace, Sam bestowed him with a weak smile. Then pressing herself flat against the wall, she carefully made way for Ed's thin frame to brush past her. Pushed closed the heavy front door behind him, with a thud.

Both now standing part way down the hall, Ed gingerly transferred a bunch of flowers and a bottle of wine across from one hand to the other as he awkwardly divested himself of his outer clothing. 'Sorry Sam, hands full and all that,' he pointed out, his head nodding by way of an explanation toward the gifts he was carrying.

Sam unexpectedly finding herself on the receiving end of a heavy navy jacket, a preppy scarf, a pair of black driving gloves and a grey woolly hat that left Ed's tousled black hair looking unattractively windblown, she tensed. 'You should have said, I could have taken those for you,' Sam said, smiling sweetly back at him as she threw her eyes toward the items he was carrying. 'Then you could have hung these up for yourself,' she continued on, whilst pointedly dipping her head down at the bundling of outer clothing now laying heavily across her arms.

Met with a supercilious smile, Sam thoughtfully began to size Ed up. She strongly disliked small men with rat-faced features, and conceited eyes. She also hated the sort of public school accent that was so affected, it was tantamount to a joke. So unalike, she was finding it hard to believe, Ed and Adam were brothers.

Anticipating the evening ahead was likely to prove as tiresome as Ed was, Sam sighed quietly to herself. *Four or five hours tops, and it'll all be over,* she silently consoled herself.

Ed shuffling from one foot to the other, his impatience was obvious. Becoming irritated by his restlessness, by what she could only assume was his keenness to get to her sister, Sam stepped in front of him. Then using her body as a barrier, she blocked his ability to move any further up the corridor. Began to hang up his clothes. Took her time about it.

'So how is she then, our patient?' Ed asked. Threw his head toward the end of the hallway as he restlessly waited for Sam to finish her task.

Ed's pompous demeanour and proprietary attitude, grated on Sam, Consequently, she snapped out a little more tartly than she intended. 'No different to when you last spoke to her.' Noticing Ed flinch at the unexpected sharpness of her tone, Sam reminded herself it would not do to get him riled or worse, suspicious. Modified her voice. 'Obviously, she's bruised and sore, and she has a thumping headache most of the time. But according to the hospital, that's all quite normal considering what's happened to her.'

'Hmm,' Ed nodded. Looked a mixture of thoughtful and agitated as he watched Sam's every move.

Is it that time already, Sam asked herself? Was it time to introduce Ed to the story she had been so carefully weaving? In the grand scheme of things, Ed's response to what she had to say was unimportant, but it would be good to practice it again. To see if it still sounded right. It would also help to set the tenor for evening, and she might not get another chance later. Sam made her decision.

'But, it's not her body I'm worried about,' Sam said, conjuring up an anxious look. 'I think...' she paused, 'Ruth might be having a nervous breakdown.'

Snapping to attention, Ed instantly shot Sam an alarmed look. 'A nervous breakdown?'

'Yes,' Sam nodded. 'I think she's in a bit of a state.'

'How do you mean?'

'I think she's depressed.'

'Depressed?' Ed repeated. Looked slightly confused, then agitated as his jaw clenched.

'Yes,' Sam nodded, keeping her voice low, conspiratorial.

'I'm sorry, but I'm not sure I follow you?' Ed's earlier puzzlement, now seemingly replaced with annoyance, he was scrutinising every inch of Sam's face.

He's observant, Sam realised. *I'll have to watch this one.*

'Ruth's grieving, so if she's down in the dumps, I would say, it's hardly to be unexpected,' Ed said more to himself than to Sam. He paused. Thought. 'Unless of course, there's something else you're not telling me?'

For effect, Sam sighed, heavily. Bit her lip as though she was about to betray a deep, dark secret. 'I'm sorry Ed, but I don't think Ruth *is* just down in the dumps, I think she's…' Left the sentence hanging as though struggling to work out what to say next.

'What? What is it? Just spit it out,' Ed commanded.

'I think she's unstable. I know the concussion could go some way toward explaining her lack of concentration, but it doesn't explain why she keeps on bursting into tears at the drop of a hat. Or why she keeps mumbling incoherently to herself, when she thinks I'm not listening. She's also really jumpy and nervy.'

Ed pulling his weedy frame up to its full height, Sam suddenly found him leaning over her as he crowded uninvited into her personal space. Ed then firmly gripping the top of her arm, in spite of herself, Sam tensed, uneasily. She had always loathed, unsolicited physical contact and she hated bullies. Though in this particular instance, she was more exasperated, than intimidated.

What the hell is going on with him, and why is he so hostile toward me? He doesn't know me very well. I'm Ruth's concerned sister and yet he's treating me as though I'm the enemy?

Shaking off Ed's hand, Sam pushed herself back into the wall and his mouth silently moving as though he was about to speak, she waited. *This had better be good.*

'Sorry, Sam, I didn't mean to grab your arm like that. I'm just finding what you're saying upsetting, and difficult to get my head around.'

Sam maintained a strained silence. Pretended to be lost for words. She wanted him to feel bad, to doubt himself.

'For God's sake Sam, what is it? Why do I get the feeling there's more you're not telling me?' Ed breathed out.

Ed's tone forceful, almost threatening and so close his garlic tainted breath was wafting unpleasantly down and into her face, Sam inwardly cringed. Looking up into two greyish-blue eyes boring into her own, from behind the tortoiseshell frame of a pair of unfashionable glasses, Sam briefly held fast to his peculiar gaze. Then sidestepping to the left, she pointedly moved herself out, from under him.

He blushed.

'Ed, when I got here on Sunday, the house was in such a mess. I don't think Ruth can have cleaned it, for quite some time.' Ed's glance, looking suddenly skittish and evasive, Sam could not leave it. 'What?' She demanded.

'Yes,' he agreed. 'Apparently the house had been getting into a bit of mess, even before Adam died. He complained to mother about it, on numerous occasions. He also said that Ruth point blank refused, to get a cleaner in. And although it was more dusty than dirty, the three of us, my parents and I, even had to give the place a spring clean, a couple of days before the funeral.'

Excellent, Sam thought. *There were other witnesses she could call on if needed, to corroborate to Ruth's declining mental health.*

'Ed, when I first met up with Ruth on Saturday morning, she looked terrible. She's obviously not been taking care of herself, and she's so thin. Even now, she barely eats. And if I didn't run a bath for her, I'm not sure she would even bother to wash.'

Ed looked shocked.

'But what I really find unnerving, is the talking to herself. Sometimes, she will even break into hysterical laughter.' Sam said slowly, building a note of extreme worry into her voice.

Ed tensed. Moved to stand over her again but this time, he kept his bunched hands, firmly by his sides. 'Okay, but let's not forget, she's been to hell and back. She's been through a sudden bereavement, and she's had a massive shock.'

Ed's voice rising to match his visible irritation, Sam sighed, heavily. If she didn't reign him in a bit, Ruth was bound to hear and that she thought, would most definitely, not do.

'Ed, I do have something else to tell you, and I'm talking to you now, here in the hallway, because I may not get another chance later. But please, you have to lower your voice,' Sam said, in hushed tones. 'Ruth mustn't hear us.'

Rocking bumptiously on the soles of his feet, Ed glowered down at her. 'Look Sam, whatever it is that's bugging you, just tell me. I can't be doing with all this cloak and dagger stuff,' he whispered crossly.

A noise in the distance, and both their heads swivelled abruptly up the corridor.

Relieved to see the kitchen door was still firmly closed, Sam rapidly thought through what she wanted to say next. *It was time to get on with it.* She could not afford for Ruth to come out of the kitchen, looking for them.

Ed striking her as the sort of man who would speak first and without thinking, Sam knew she had no choice but to water down, what she had been going to say. Instead of telling Ed about Ruth's suicidal flirtation with the cliff edge, she would imply Ruth had deliberately let go of the ladder. Still provocative but hopefully, not quite so contentious.

'Okay, I don't think Ruth's fall from the ladder, was an accident.'

Ed hissed unattractively through his teeth.

'But,' Sam continued on, 'I would strongly recommend you don't challenge Ruth about it. Only if you do, and she's as unstable as I think she might be, I dread to think where it all might lead.'

All sorts of muscles twitched and moved in Ed's face as he visibly acknowledged the seriousness of what Sam had divulged. Then, in an instant, his face smoothed away again.

Straightening up, Ed pulled himself away from Sam. Crinkling his eyes, he flashed her a brilliant smile as though she had said nothing, of any importance. 'So, where is she now, our little invalid?'

Confused by the sudden change in tempo, Sam could not help herself. She threw Ed a puzzled, questioning look. Silently asked, *What's going on? Don't you believe me?*

But Ed remained unnervingly silent as he waited for Sam to answer to his query.

'She's in the kitchen.'

Stepping out of Ed's way, Sam watched him lope off down the hallway in search of her sister.

What just happened?

Seriously hoping she had not missed something important, or said too much, Sam reassured herself that even if she had, it did not matter as very soon, none of it would matter.

Hurried up the corridor herself.

Chapter Nineteen

'Oh please Ruth, don't stand on ceremony for my benefit,' Ed quipped, striding across to the kitchen table where Ruth was sat.

Flashing Ed a somewhat nervous smile, Ruth visibly shrank back into her seat as he leaned down and in, to place a fleeting kiss to the side of her cheek. 'Good journey down?' she asked.

Ruth's tone dull and indifferent, she is obviously finding it an effort to be polite, Sam thought. Mind, she wasn't surprised. Ruth confessing earlier that Ed had invited himself down for dinner, Sam could hardly blame her for feeling the way she did.

'Yes, it was fine,' Ed nodded. 'I had a clean run down for a change.' Ruth's response to his arrival less than warm and welcoming, Ed pulled himself upright again. Almost sulkily dumped the bottle of wine and flowers he had brought with him, down onto the table top in front of Ruth. 'Here, these are for you,' he proclaimed.

The cutlery she had so carefully laid out earlier that afternoon, scattering to either side of his offerings, Sam frowned fleetingly.

'Thanks, but really, you shouldn't have,' Ruth stated flatly. Cast Ed's gifts a barely cursory glance as she nervously picked at an invisible spot, on her jeans.

Watching the awkward interactions play out between the pair, Sam's brows briefly knitted. *There's something else going on here. An undercurrent, I can't quite put my finger on yet.*

'Here,' Sam said to Ruth, 'why don't I take those for you.' Then not waiting for Ruth to answer, she swept up the flowers, took them over to the kitchen sink and ran the tap. Sighed out with a carefully disguised irritation as she briefly recalled the damp patch, the flowers had left on her newly washed and ironed tablecloth.

'These are lovely, Ed,' Sam commented conversationally over her shoulder, into the strained silence that had descended on the two in-laws. 'Ruth, can you point me in the direction of a vase, please?'

'Top cupboard, first one to the left of you,' Ruth answered softly, her eyes glistening wetly.

Sam turned sideways on to Ruth and Ed, so she could surreptitiously watch the two of them as she worked. Quickly trimming the stems, stripping off the lower leaves, she filled the crystal vase with water, then swiftly cleared the debris left by her ministrations. Fleetingly thought about how much she hated chrysanthemums; *ugly, hideous things*. The flower heads an awkward mix of bitter yellow and lurid pink, they had definitely not been bought from a florists. The sort of blooms one would pick up cheaply, she guessed Ed had probably bought from a petrol station forecourt. The flowers already stinking, smelling like cats pee, *first thing tomorrow,* Sam promised herself, *I will bin them.*

'So?' Ed asked, stepping closer to Ruth again, flapping his hands up and down her stiffened form as he either ignored or missed, her visible discomfort.

'So, what?' Ruth said tightly.

'So, how are you?'

'I'm okay. I don't know why you would come all this way, just for my benefit.' Bit down on her bottom lip as she nervously avoided any direct eye contact with him.

'Yeah, well, it's not every day you end up being rescued in such a dramatic fashion and anyway, I needed to see for you for myself.'

'Well, as you can see, I'm fine.' Ruth said tartly.

'Yes, but there is one thing I don't understand, why didn't you call me?' Ed asked, his tone polite but demanding as he turned and walked away from where Ruth was sitting. Leant himself up against the kitchen wall, then nonchalantly crossed his arms in front of his narrow chest.

'What do you mean?' Ruth hissed back, her tone scathing all of a sudden.

Looking put out, Ed frowned back at her. 'Isn't it obvious? If I hadn't have rung you this morning, I would have been none the wiser.'

'So?'

'Ruth!' Ed exclaimed, sounding both disappointed and exasperated. 'Since Adam's death, I feel responsible for you. So as far as I'm concerned, if you weren't capable of ringing me yourself, the least you could have done was ask someone from the hospital, or even Sam, to call me?'

The already tense air between the two in-laws feeling suddenly supercharged, Sam wondered if a full-scale row was brewing? Hoped Ed would be able to keep his mouth shut about what they had discussed in the hallway, earlier.

Ruth snorted rudely. Replied, sarcastically. 'Well, let me see, why didn't I call *you*? Was it because my mobile was smashed to pieces during the fall? Or was it because I was only in the hospital for one night and at the time, I wasn't exactly thinking straight. You know, what with the concussion and all.' She broke off, for thought. 'Oh, or was it because I'm a fully grown woman who is *not*, and has *never* been, *your* responsibility,' she emphasised.

Ed looked momentarily crestfallen. Then retaliated, in kind. 'Ruth, whilst I fully accept you're a grown woman, I also think you're being incredibly unfair. As your brother-in-law, I'm family. So if something as serious as this happens to you, why on earth wouldn't you have the decency to call me?' he demanded, his voice rising with his agitation. 'Even if it's only to say, you're okay?'

He is so mad, but then so is Ruth. But why? What is it with these two? Sam mused. Thought for a couple of seconds. Then remembered something she had read in Ruth's journal, and smiled to herself.

'For pity's sake, Ed! Why can't you just leave me alone!' Ruth burst out angrily. Rubbed the middle finger of her right hand vertically across her brow a rapid number of times.

Almost as though, Sam thought, *she wished she could rub him out too.*

'Tell me, Ruth,' Ed began to ask, with a nasty little grin on his face, 'have you remembered what caused your fall yet?'

Ruth threw Ed a puzzled look. Then she turned a suspicious gaze Sam's way. Sat bolt upright in her chair, then winced in pain. 'What did you say?' She growled at Ed.

Now he's gone too far, Sam thought with exasperation.

Ruth's eyes flashing dangerously at Ed, then her way, Sam knew her feisty sister was preparing to do battle and who knew, where that would lead? Not wanting the present topic to escalate, or to have to answer any awkward questions herself, Sam diplomatically interceded. 'Sorry to interrupt folks, but dinner is more than ready and if I don't serve it up soon, it's going to spoil.'

Picking up the vase of flowers, Sam's smile never wavered. Ed looking sheepish, he turned away from Ruth's anger, and suddenly wanted to help Sam carry the *heavy* flower vase. Sam politely brushed him off. Slowly walking over to the kitchen table, she placed the arrangement of chrysanthemums down in the centre, herself. Instantly hated, the way they somehow transformed her carefully laid out table, into something ludicrous.

Looking as though he was somewhat embarrassed at being summarily dismissed by both women, Ed retreated with his tail between his legs. Took to propping up the wall again. Yet blatantly looking for a suitable way to defuse some of the friction he had so obviously, been responsible for causing. To no one in particular, he quietly said, 'I'm starving. What are we having?'

Undependable and quite the chameleon, Sam thought with contempt. Told herself how right she had been earlier, not to trust him with the full version of her story.

Snatching up the bottle of wine Ed had dumped on the table and reorganising the splayed cutlery, Sam ignored his question and allowed herself a couple of seconds, to admire her earlier handiwork. She had spent a significant amount of her precious time setting up everything that afternoon. Digging out Ruth's best china and her cut crystal glasses, she had polished the silver cutlery to within an inch of their lives. Excluding the monstrous chrysanthemums, Sam was proud of the display she had created and you never got a second chance, to make a good first impression.

'Don't ask me, ask Sam,' Ruth answered truculently. 'She's the one who had been slaving away all afternoon to prepare all this, for you.' Ruth dutifully waved a hand toward Sam's meticulous tableware.

'Well, credit where credit's due, then,' Ed nodded. 'The table looks great, Sam. You've obviously gone to a lot of trouble.'

'No, not really,' Sam lied.

Ed cocked an ear. 'You've even put on some music. Who can I hear playing in the background, is it Michael Jackson?'

'Yes, he's one of my favourite artists,' Sam replied.

'He was one of Adam's too,' said Ed, looking suddenly wistful.

Sam nodded. 'That explains the extensive CD collection I found in Adam's study. This album was in amongst them, and I just couldn't resist. I was sure you wouldn't mind, Ruth. You don't do you?' Sam asked her sister. Held back a duplicitous smile.

Ruth shrugged her shoulders. Caustically said, 'No, why should I mind if you poke around in all my stuff, help yourself to all my things?'

Oh dear, I've obviously hit a nerve, Sam thought, with just as much sarcasm. Smiled inwardly to herself. 'Sorry Ruth, you sound offended but I genuinely thought, you wouldn't mind,' she lied easily.

Ruth gave a phlegmatic shrug of her shoulders. Mumbled something unintelligible that Sam chose to ignore.

'If I had known just how much trouble you were going to go too, I would have spent more time on my appearance,' Ed bantered, seemingly seeking to deflect some of Ruth's crass behaviour over the CD. 'Perhaps even put on my best bib and tucker for you both.'

Smiling good-naturedly, pretending to enjoy the joke, Sam seriously doubted Ed had the aplomb to wear anything quite so sophisticated or as formal, as a dress suit. Now wearing a pair of polyester slacks in a boring charcoal grey, a white polyester-cotton work shirt under an equally boring, grey acrylic sweater that was fraying at the one of cuffs, Ed looked dated, cheap, and not even remotely well dressed.

'Thanks, I think,' Sam quipped back. 'It's been a lot of fun to be able to do something like this for a change and I'm not too ashamed to say, I've totally enjoyed myself. Ed, why don't you take a seat?' She prompted him.

Ed pulling himself away from the wall to join Ruth at the kitchen table, Sam gave herself a minute as she mentally compared the two brothers, with each other.

Adam just shy of six foot tall and principally possessing his father's athletic stature and aspect, he had always had about him, the suave air of an academic. Lean and strong with short blond hair and piercing ice blue eyes, behind rimless glasses, he had been good-looking in a serious sort of a way.

Favouring his diminutive mother in appearance though not her effortless style, Ed had the sort of rat-faced features Sam had always hated; thin lips, hollow cheeks, eyes the colour of dishwater behind the tortoiseshell frames, a knife-like nose, and all topped by a thatch of scruffy dark hair. Under average height, with limbs that were gawky and angular, thin wrists at the top of pale hands, and narrow shoulders that supported a smallish head on a slim and delicate-looking neck, he was a far less beguiling prospect than his younger sibling.

Ed pulled out the chair at the head of the table, the one nearest to Ruth and what would have been, Sam suspected, his dead brother's seat. Noticing Ruth's face turn a paler shade of white as she took in the significance of Ed's seemingly heedless insensitivity toward her feelings — *no stranger to the house, Ed must have known* — Sam knew she had presumed correctly. But nothing was said.

Guessing Ruth must have run out of steam and that it was now safe to plate up, Sam briskly turned her back on them both. Then smartly returning to the kitchen counter top, she began to pull together everything she would need to serve up their meals. The two fractious in-laws haltingly talking in frosted tones about the extent of Ruth's injuries and judiciously avoiding, it seemed, any of the events that had led up to them, Sam allowed herself to become lost in thought. Mindlessly got on with her task.

Today, Sam had hoped to take much easier but Ruth's shock announcement that Ed was coming to dinner, had immediately put paid to that. Now, after doing the shopping, the cleaning, the cooking, the whole damn shebang on her own, she was feeling quite tired. Knew that later, she would be exhausted.

Ed's unanticipated arrival also necessitating a deviation from plan Sam had neither expected nor prepared for, she had spent a vast majority of the day, rethinking everything; also tiring. Having gone over and over in her head, her original strategy for today and tomorrow, Sam had eventually decided there was no reason for her to be concerned, by Ed's arrival. *Every cloud had a silver lining.* Admittedly, Ed's interruption had presented an unwelcome interval but more importantly, it had not caused a delay. In another twenty-four hours, still, it would all be over. In fact, if Ed did but know it, he had unwittingly provided Sam with the perfect excuse she had been looking for. He would become her reason for getting Ruth so quickly, out and up onto those cliffs again. All she had to be careful of, was not triggering Ruth's memory into recalling what really happened to her, on the ladder. *All I now need to do, is keep a cool head and play the evening out.*

Sam felt no real compunction about what was to happen to Ed. Unfortunate, maybe, but he had only himself blame. *Collateral damage, isn't that what they call it?*

The phrase, '*Two birds, one stone.*' Sprang to mind, and Sam softly chuckled to herself. Thought how apt the idiom was.

'Ed would you mind pouring out the wine?' Sam asked as she delivered a plate of home-made steak-and-kidney pie with organic carrots, green beans and sweet potato mash to each of her seated guests, in turn. 'Gravy and mustard are already on the table, so please, dive in and help yourself.'

The last supper, Sam thought, with irony. Had to stop herself from grinning like an idiot.

Ed doing as he had been asked, Sam covered her glass momentarily with her hand. Politely refused the wine as she helped herself to a glass of iced water instead. She needed a clear head, for later.

Michael Jackson softly banging on in the background, about talking with a *man in the mirror*, for the next few minutes, a silence descended as they ate; Ed and Sam with relish, Ruth slowly.

'So you were able to get away from school easily enough this afternoon?' Sam asked Ed, some minutes later. 'Sorry, that was presumptuous of me. I take it you are still teaching aren't you?'

'Yes, for my sins,' Ed confirmed.

Sam gave herself a metaphorical pat on the back for correctly remembering Ed's profession. *I bet he has no clue about what I do for a living.* 'Where do you teach? Is it a local school?'

'I teach at Mallory High, in Beckenham. So yes, it's not too far from where I live.'

'Nice,' Sam nodded. 'What age do you teach?'

'Year Eleven; fifteen and sixteen year olds, I teach them carpentry.'

'Do you enjoy it?'

'Yes, it can be challenging at times, but I like working with kids.'

'Right,' Sam nodded, 'rather you than me,' she offered with feeling.

Ed barked out a laugh. 'Yes, well, each to their own as they say. It has its perks, like today, at least I was able to get away fairly early. Just means, I'll be marking homework into the wee small hours, later tonight.'

Sam chuckled politely.

'*Poor you,*' Ruth ejected sarcastically, from the sidelines. Her words stated with emphasis, she mock toasted the two of them before gulping down an enormous slug of wine, with ease.

In the room, the air went thick and heavy.

Way to go, sis. Keep knocking it back, you look seriously thirsty, Sam thought.

Visibly embarrassed, Ed squirmed on his seat. Behind his glasses, his insipid coloured eyes blinked rapidly a few times as he flashed Ruth a troubled look.

'You all right, sweetie?' Sam asked Ruth, as though concerned.

'Of course I am. Why the hell shouldn't I be?' Ruth snapped back rudely. Took another slurp of wine. Replenished her own glass. Ignored everyone else's.

'So, where are you living now?' Ed asked Sam, casting Ruth a twisted little smile as he seemingly, cut her out of the conversation.

The air around the three of them, again tensed.

Sam picked up her water glass, took a dainty sip. Pleasured in the awkward silence, for a second or two.

'At the moment, I'm living in Hackney.'

'Oh, what's it like?'

'Hackney or the flat?'

'Both, I suppose.' Ed pick up his wine, swirled it around his glass, took a generous sip and savoured it.

'Hackney's all right, if you like noise, pollution and being around far too many people.'

Ed nodded his head as though in agreement with her. 'It's as okay as anywhere else in London, I guess. It's not a lot different, where I am. You mentioned, you live in a flat?'

'Yeah, it's really a studio flat.'

'Oh, what one of those open-plan things?'

'No, it's not a bedsit. There's a separate bedroom and bathroom, but it does have an open plan lounge-diner-kitchen.'

Ed briefly pulled a face. One that said, *poor you.* 'Garden?'

'No, a garden doesn't fit my rental budget, I'm afraid.'

'Furnished or unfurnished?'

'Part furnished, part unfurnished.'

'Sounds okay,' Ed said. Rather condescendingly, Sam thought. 'Have you ever thought of buying?'

Of course I have, Sam bridled inwardly. Composed herself. 'Yes, occasionally,' she calmly replied. 'But I'm not ready to buy, yet. I find the thought of owning a property, far too limiting.'

'How do you mean?'

'Well, at the moment, I can vacate the flat at a month's notice. So I enjoy the freedom of knowing that should something better come along, I can leave easily.'

Sam twisted her water glass round in her hands, reflectively. Thought about how from the age of sixteen, and up until a few months ago, she had been uncomfortably house-sharing with a number of other, similarly broke and starving individuals; creative types mainly. How paying out over fifty percent of her salary on rent each month, she had found it impossible to save enough money to afford even for a small holiday, never mind the deposit she would need to get a mortgage. Not that she was prepared to admit any of that to Ed. Or to Ruth, for that matter.

'Buying's a much better investment,' Ed pointed out pompously. Wagged his school teacher finger at Sam in a way that was not only annoying, but insulting.

'Maybe so, but as I said earlier, I'm not ready to be tied down by bricks and mortar, just yet.' *Time to move the conversation,* Sam thought, *before the topic gets really personal.* 'Anyway, what about you? You said you lived not too far from the school?'

'I live in Catford. It's a ten minute walk from the town centre, and just off of the main road that takes you into Bromley.'

'Cool,' Sam nodded. Flicked the envy away. 'House or flat?' She asked courteously. Could not be less interested, but Ruth still mutely silent, anything to keep the conversation going.

'A Victorian mid-terrace. Not big, just two bedrooms, bathroom, kitchen, lounge-diner. I suppose, in a way, I was lucky.'

'How do you mean?'

'Well, following the divorce, there was just enough money left for me to get in and buy the place, before all the house prices went crazy and permanently priced me out the London market. You know, I don't envy your situation,' Ed continued on, apparently determined to ram his point home. 'If you don't own your own property these days, it can be extortionate trying to rent in London. Never mind finding somewhere that's half decent enough, to live in.'

Sam reflected resentfully on how right Ed was. Thought how she had never been priced *in* to the London housing market, or anywhere else for that matter. How, her finances so tight, within a couple more months, she wasn't sure where she would be living. Sighed out, with feeling. Ed throwing her a prospective look, Sam warned herself to be careful as now, was not the time to divulge. Nodded her head in Ed's direction. Then said, 'Yes, you *were* lucky.'

'You know, I've been thinking of selling up,' Ruth interjected from the sideline.

Sam concentrated on keeping her face neutral. Took a distracting forkful of food as she waited for Ed to speak. Guessed from the disturbed and astonished look on his face, he would be asking all the necessary questions.

'Seriously?'

'Yes,' Ruth affirmed. Vigorously nodded her head with a grimace. Hiccuped into her almost empty glass.

'Sorry Ruth, but I don't get it? Why on earth would you want to leave this lovely old place?' Ed demanded to know as he threw his hands out expansively. 'Adam put his heart and soul into making this into a beautiful home, for the two of you.'

Ruth looked into her glass as though it were a crystal ball that held all the answers. 'Yes, well, there's your problem, right there.' She nodded. Screwed up her eyes with pain.

'I still don't understand?'

Ruth shuddered. 'There are too many memories here, for me to want to stay.' As Ruth spoke, her eyes never left Ed's.

Ed, looking uncomfortable, broke Ruth's gaze and took a sip of wine. Said nothing further.

There it was again, that weird undercurrent, Sam thought.

'Everywhere I look, he's there. He's in every room, in every chair. He's in my bed… and I can't stand it. Without him, this house feels too big, too empty, and too remote. All wrong.' A couple tears fell onto Ruth's reddened cheeks.

Sam, maintaining her silence, curiously watched a gamut of emotions rip across Ed's face; puzzled, pensive, and then sad. He hesitated, for just a beat.

'What you've described sounds awful, Ruth. If you do decide to move, you must let me know and I promise, I'll help you in any way I can.'

Yeah, I bet you will, Sam thought nastily. Although Ed appeared solicitous, Sam guessed that really, he was far from it. She had not missed the glimmer of suppressed excitement flicker across his duplicitous face. Thought how transparent he was as she watched him flick from grieving for his brother, to licking his lips in an almost greedy anticipation. Ed wanted Ruth to move. He could not wait for her to sell up.

'Perhaps,' Ed continued, 'you could even consider moving closer to London again? At least then, you would be closer to family. Yours and mine,' he finished, pointing his finger toward Sam as if to make his point.

Watching the panic fly across Ruth's face, her mouth tremble as tears sprang into her eyes, Sam could almost have laughed out loud. *This is going to be so, so easy.*

The main meal finished, Sam cleared away the debris. Noticed Ruth unsurprisingly but rather rudely, after all her effort, had only picked at hers. Neatly stacking everything on top of the kitchen counter, Sam decided she would deal with the mess, later. She would use the unfinished task as an excuse to get some much needed, alone time.

As the meal had worn painfully on, Sam had become increasingly exhausted by the two of them. Ed, a man of seemingly infinite butterfly interests, clearly had a point of view on everything, whilst Ruth, stubborn and determined to be difficult, apparently had an opinion, on nothing. Even though Sam had thrown question after question into the air in an attempt to get the continually one-sided and stilted conversation going again, very few of them, had worked. The charged atmosphere between Ruth and Ed palpable, and at times, most unpleasant, Sam had felt imprisoned by the unfinished business that lurked between the two of them.

Now feeling worn out by the evening's challenges, Sam would be relieved when the whole sorry meal, was over. She particularly looked forward to getting them out of her kitchen, and at least for a short while, out of her sight.

Unscrewing the bottle of cheap plonk Ed had brought with him, Sam placed it on the end of the table nearest to Ruth. Returned to the kitchen counter top, collected up the dessert bowls and placed one of each, in front of the two of them. 'Cream?' she asked Ed, waving the jug toward him as he inspected his pudding.

'Hmm, what with that massive dinner and now this,' Ed said, gesturing toward a pudding bowl full of red berry pie, 'you just have to be trying to fatten me up.' Slapped at his hollow belly, through his jumper.

'I hardly think so,' said Sam politely. Watched him proceed to pour a huge dollop of double-thick cream on top of his dessert. Idly wondered how his major arteries were doing? Encouraged him to take some more.

'This,' Ed pointed to his thin frame, 'is down to years of working in a job where you're constantly running around after kids, and never seem to find the time to eat. I can tell you, being a teacher makes for the best diet in the world.'

'Ah, so that's the secret,' Ruth said, her words slurring together as she cast a rueful eye down over her own physique. 'To get into shape, I need to get myself back out and into the workplace again.'

Even though Ruth's petite frame was clad in the most unbecoming pair of loose black jeans and an awful baggy jumper in a depressing shade of grey, still, Sam struggled to see her point. A mess, Ruth might, but she was not overweight, had never been overweight. A wash, cut and colour for her greasy and unkempt hair. A decent diet, minus the alcohol and pills, to clear up her skin. A couple of weeks of good sleep, make-up and some new clothes, and Ruth would look as fabulous as she had done, the day she met Adam. But then, Ruth was always hopeless. Took a pride in being hopeless, in acting like a victim. Used it as an effective way to gain the attention, she constantly craved. Ruth was, Sam mused spitefully, the kind of woman who made a man feel manly and protective, endowed with a virile power. Yet her apparent *need* for the support of a man, well nothing could be further from the truth.

'I see nothing wrong with your figure,' Ed threw out suddenly, to Ruth.

Ed's face immediately blushing a hot scarlet, along with the way he shifted in his seat, Sam gathered the compliment had unintentionally slipped out. She could not resist the urge to embarrass him further. 'You don't say,' she said mischievously. Watched with a wicked pleasure as for a moment, Ed did not know where to put himself.

The intended recipient of the compliment ignoring him as she scooped up a huge spoonful of pudding that was also drowning in cream, and shoved into her mouth, Sam smiled to herself. It seemed Ruth now regretted the attention she had so schemingly drawn to herself. *That would teach her.*

'You look nice as well,' Ed said hastily, gesticulating toward Sam's form as he tried to self-consciously recover his mistake.

Sam looked down at what she was wearing. A loose silk blouse in the most gorgeous shade of green that set off her chestnut hair and the colour of her eyes, to perfection. Skin tight navy jeans that did wonders for a pair of shapely legs. Dainty gold ballet pumps and a discreet amount of gold jewellery to top it all off. She could not agree more. 'Thank you,' she acknowledged. Gave Ed a winning smile.

Having finished serving, Sam took her seat at the table again. Watched Ed and Ruth hide their embarrassed faces in their desserts, as a silence descended.

'More wine, Ed?' Sam asked, a few minutes later.

'No, thanks,' Ed said, shaking his head at Sam as he hovered a hand over his glass, 'I'm meant to be driving, remember. This pie is delicious.' Waved a cream laden spoon Sam's way. 'Is it home-made?'

'Yes.'

'Wonderful.'

'Thanks.'

'Don't you want any?'

'No, as lovely as it is, I unfortunately, know what went into making it.'

A pair of jade green eyes flashed doubtfully Sam's way. 'What do you mean?' Ruth asked. Suspiciously looked down at her half-eaten pie.

Realising that Ruth had just made an uncomfortable memory leap, Sam chuckled inwardly. 'I just meant the pie is full of carbs and sugar,' she said innocently. 'Much too fattening, and sweet,' she pronounced, a secretive little smiling pulling at the corners of her mouth as she threw Ruth, a wicked little wink.

'So you get to watch the both of us indulge instead,' Ed said, oblivious to the unspoken communication being shared between the two sisters. Scooping up a second helping of cream, he then laughed out loud as though what he had just said and done, was somehow hilarious.

'Precisely,' Sam exclaimed. Watched on with a quiet amusement as Ruth, acting as though her appetite had suddenly been lost, pushed what little was left of her pudding, firmly away from her. 'When you're both finished, and only if Ruth agrees, I was going to suggest we vacate to the living room to have our coffees? Get ourselves comfortable.'

Ruth threw Sam an old fashioned look. Rudely muttered something under her breath, about Sam being the hostess with the mostest.

'Is that okay with you, Ruth?' Sam repeated, pretending to be puzzled and a little hurt, at what she thought she had heard. *Ruth could be such a bitch, at times.*

'Whatever you say,' Ruth said as she grabbed at the bottle of wine Sam had placed so conveniently to hand. Helped herself to another glass of wine, then smacked her lips with pleasure as it obviously hit the desired spot.

Ed looking aghast at Ruth's rudeness, at the ease at which she was knocking back the booze, Sam smiled to herself. *Ruth's in for a bumpy ride.*

Chapter Twenty

Situated on an old flood plain, approximately two miles from the nearest village, was the UK subsidiary of the international pharmaceutical company that Adam worked for. The first building erected in the sixties, the site had grown exponentially since its inception. Repeatedly modernised over the years, it now provided a number of purpose built facilities that included a manufacturing plant, research laboratories, business and administration offices, multiple cafeterias, a gym, and even a general store that sold the company merchandise to its staff. The site interwoven with private roads, paths and landscaped gardens that spanned a total area of just under a hundred acres of reclaimed land, the premises housed a population of around six thousand. Now, it was now the size of an exclusive, small town.

 Security high, the site surrounded by a high wrought iron fence with metal barbs on the top and hundreds of strategically placed surveillance cameras, there were manned guard posts at every entrance and exit turnstile. Excluding the *Visitor Centre* and its adjacent car park, no member of the general public could get anywhere near one of the company buildings, without a micro-chipped security pass.

 Just before eight pm, Ruth pulled into a vacant bay in the visitor car park and stopped the car. Stationed directly opposite the now practically empty, staff car park Adam always used, she soon spotted his unmissable, Jaguar.

 Adam returning from a five night business trip to the Company headquarters in New York, his plane, Ruth knew, should have landed at

Heathrow some three hours earlier. Anytime now, a company limo would be dropping him off back at the site, to collect his car.

Knowing she was unexpected, Ruth was especially anxious.

I can't stay in the car. I have to move, to think.

She got out the car. Started to pace up and down the narrow strip of public road that separated the two car parks. Looked up at the blinking cameras a couple of times, wondered who was on the other end of them, watching her.

The cold starting to seep through Ruth's coat, her minimal clothing, she shivered. Drew her coat tighter around herself.

Before leaving the house, Ruth had taken care to make every effort with her appearance. She had put on make-up, fussed with her hair, and then she had changed into the sort of outfit, she thought Adam would appreciate; a dark red dress, black stockings, a pair of high-heeled black shoes she knew he had always liked, and a black wool coat. Not exactly the appropriate type of clothing for what was a supremely cold, November evening, but she was out to impress.

The odd flake of snow falling from an inky sky that was liberally punctuated with stars, Ruth watched the waxing moon cast its silvery glow across the frosted car park as it dodged free of some clouds. Briefly thought how beautiful the night sky looked. Hoped Adam would think the same, of her.

Ruth's breath clouding around her frozen face, again, she trembled; though whether it was with cold or nerves, she could not be sure. Feeling as though she was in the eye of a hurricane, she hoped with all her heart, the pleasure of seeing Adam's surprise would be all she needed, to keep her still and safe.

Unable to face Adam at home, Ruth had wanted to see him here, on neutral territory. She was determined to tell him just how much she missed him when he was away, and how much she loved him.

Ruth closed her eyes and for a couple of seconds, she imagined herself lying in their bed, Adam spooning into her back. She felt herself reach out for him, then move against him. She felt him respond.

Hah, who are you kidding? Chided an unwelcome voice, in Ruth's head. *If you and Adam were in bed together, it would not be like that at all. You would not make love. You would argue. Adam would resist your affection by picking a fight over something trivial. Then seething with hostility, he would seek any excuse to goad you into marital warfare.*

Ruth snapped open her eyes, and shook her head. Flicked the painful thoughts away. She could not think like that, not now.

Where is he? Why isn't he here yet?

Adam's late arrival amplifying the tension, the longer she had to wait, the more anxious Ruth became.

Will he be able to tell?

Ruth drew her coat tighter around herself again. Sternly told herself, nothing profound had happened.

But what if he can tell, just by looking at me?

Ruth tried to pretend she had not made the biggest mistake of her life, but overcome with her guilt, it seemed her brain had other ideas. Forced her to ask, *will he see it in my eyes, or will he hear it in my voice? How will he tell?*

One night, Ruth assured herself, *that's all it was.*

Shame made Ruth blush.

A night fuelled by loneliness and desperation, she had fought back at despair with the power of uninhibited sex. It had simply been a coupling borne of some primal need; *a screw*. Quickly over, and best forgotten.

If only I had not succumbed to that additional glass of wine, I might have seen what was happening, averted everything that had followed.

The remorse made her feel sick.

Becoming defensive of her actions, Ruth reminded herself she had done no more to Adam, than he had done to her.

Everybody does it once in their marriage. Don't they?

Then if that were really true, why, afterwards, had she rushed into the hottest shower she could bear? Scoured off every trace.

What if he did notice? What then?

Stop! Ruth yelled at herself. *Enough, already!*

Fighting to compose herself, Ruth mentally thought through her options; tell the truth, or lie?

She could take Adam home and then over dinner, she could tell him the truth, readily admit to her indiscretion. An adulterer himself, surely he, of all people, would understand and make an exception? Knowing he was not the only one in the marriage who had behaved badly, who knows, he might even be relieved, Ruth thought? They could then start afresh. Put the craziness of the last few months behind them, and be a lot happier and stronger for it.

Ruth shook her head at herself, again, who was she kidding? If she were to tell Adam the truth, it would finish her marriage. No matter how conscience-stricken she was, it was time to err on the side of caution. She needed to keep her dirty little secret to herself. To do otherwise, would be playing right into Adam's hands. Giving him exactly the excuse he had been looking for, to get rid of her.

Suddenly, the limo arrived.

Ruth immediately felt nauseous. Her stomach tied up in painful knots, it ached incessantly. Taking a deep, slow breath, she walked toward the car, then stopped, waited for it to draw up alongside of her.

'Ruth? What on earth?' Adam said through the open window, his tone disbelieving, taut.

'Surprise,' Ruth said, feeling absurdly foolish.

Adam's face wearing a look of dismay as if he wished her to be anywhere else but in front of him, Ruth tried not to feel hurt.

As Ruth stood awkwardly to one side, the chauffeur got out, grabbed Adam's suitcase from the boot and placed it by her feet. He then let Adam out of the limo, and gratefully touched his cap as money surreptitiously passed hands.

The limo sliding away, husband and wife were left standing in the dark, in the cold.

Ruth tried again. 'Hi, how are you? I've really missed you,' she said with conviction. For good measure, pasted a big welcoming smile onto her face. Sounded more confident than she felt.

A drop of melting snow falling onto Adam's face, Ruth automatically moved forward to wipe it away. Took the opportunity to press a kiss to the side of his cheek, noticed his breath smelt like toothpaste. As she went in for a hug, Adam froze, left a cloud of musky scent hanging in the air as he icily disengaged himself. Moved away.

In that moment, the questions flooded in.

Why, at this time of the day, does he smell of toothpaste?

Did he slip a mint into his mouth as soon as he saw me waiting for him, and if so, why? He rarely sucks them at home.

There is scent is lingering on his face, his neck, and it certainly isn't mine?

From an early age, Ruth had learnt the invaluable lesson that all too often, people are not who you think they are. They do inexplicable, and hurtful things. *Sometimes they lie. Sometimes, they have an affair. But trust,* Ruth reminded herself, *goes both ways.*

Her stomach churning, Ruth fought to control her suspicions, her anger.

Attempting to put herself in Adam's shoes, she convinced herself the animosity that crackled between them, was caused by her, not him.

I surprised him, took him off his stride.

I should have told him I was coming.
He's had a long flight and he's tired.
He's not thinking straight.

Ruth moved toward him again, tucked her hands around his stiffened arm. 'I'm sorry Adam, I've surprised you, and I know how much you hate surprises. Why don't we start again?'

Yet still, Adam looked irritated, even angry. There was no warmth in his eyes, no smile of reassurance. 'No,' he said, 'I do not like surprises.'

Crushed by his callousness, Ruth let go of him. Her eyes brimming with tears, she watched helplessly as he abruptly walked away, wheeled the roller case toward his car.

She decided to follow him.

'Why Adam? Why aren't you pleased to see me?' Ruth attacked his retreating back. Then immediately felt terrible. Again, she reminded herself, it was not his fault she had turned up unannounced. At the very least, she should have rung him, warned him of her intentions. Yet up until a couples of hours ago, she had not known herself.

Ignoring her question, Adam waved his company pass at the imposing carpark security turnstile. There was a staccato click, and he put his hand on the revolving gate, which turned freely. Weaved his case through, and Ruth could go no further. She watched him walk toward his car, then stash the case into the boot. Hastily returned herself to the point from where they had started. Lined herself up a couple of metres distance from his car. The high, wrought iron security fence, acting as a barrier between them.

Adam turned to face her. Walked a couple of paces toward her. 'I'm confused,' he said through the fence, 'since when have you ever come to meet me at work and to be perfectly honest, why on earth would you?'

His question asked with a thinly veiled exasperation, Ruth shrank inside herself. Stared blankly back at him. *What do I say?*

'It's not as if we can share each other's company on the drive home as now, we have two cars to deal with.'

Ruth had not thought of that, and heat flooded her cheeks. *I've been so stupid.* Relieved, that under the cover of darkness, Adam could not see her visible embarrassment, feeling witless and defensive, Ruth retaliated badly. 'Tell me Adam, who did you take to New York with you? Oh, and I think before you answer that one, you should think very carefully as like a bitch in heat, she's left her scent all over you.'

Adam's face was pinched and ghoulish, under the harsh beam of the artificial security lights. His eyes watering in the cold, he glared at Ruth in disbelief. 'Really, Ruth? You want to do this now?'

Ruth closed her eyes for a moment. A wave of melancholy washing over her, it was as if Adam's angry response had just erased her last remaining hope that her marriage would survive. 'Yes, I do!' Ruth yelled back at him. 'I can't stand, whatever *this* is, any longer. I have to know what is happening to us?'

Adam looked incredulous, at a loss for words.

Ruth drew a short breath, but she could not let it go. She had to keep trying. 'Adam, you've been away for five nights, and yet you're not even pleased to see me. Aren't I enough for you, anymore?' she pleaded, her eyes wild with fear, with guilt.

He seemed surprised by her accusations, as, in truth, was she. He rapidly blinked. 'Ruth, it's freezing cold and it's getting late. You're right, I have been away for five nights, but I've also worked six days in a row. Now I'm tired, jet lagged and we are in the middle of my work's car park. It's hardly the time, or the place, don't you think?'

Though the words sounded mollifying, spoken coldly and through tight lips, Ruth knew they were anything other than that. Adam was furious with her.

'You know, I've not even got home yet and already, you're attacking me with your wild fancies.' Sounding and looking extremely agitated, Adam shook his head at her.

'I just wanted to surprise you,' Ruth wheedled, hated herself for her weakness, her desperate need for him to want her as much as she wanted him.

Adam looked at Ruth, dubiously. Stepped closer to her. 'How much have you been drinking today? Are you even safe to be driving a car?' He challenged back rudely.

Adam's face suddenly pushed in close to hers as he tried to catch a smell of her breath through the wrought iron fence, Ruth recoiled from him. Her bottom lip quivering, she started to cry. Regretted wearing the high heels as she tripped unsteadily along the tarmac, and away from his disapproval. Made for the sanctity of her own car.

I will not answer his unfair accusations. I am better than that.

Why has he changed so much?

I hate him.

Chapter Twenty-One

Pushing back against the sofa, Ruth stretched as luxuriously as her battered and aching body would allow. Her energy levels descending, like a couple of fading batteries, she wished she could go to bed. Three full on days and in spite of sleeping away almost two of them, still, she was exhausted. Right now, all she wanted to do was to crawl upstairs and shut out the world.

Tilting the glass of red wine she had just poured out for herself, Ruth watched it slowly swirl. Then taking a large swig, felt it satisfyingly hit her bloodstream. Hoped, it would give her just the boost she needed, to get through what remained of the evening.

Wearily lying her head back against the cushion behind her, firelight dancing across her closed eyelids, *one more day*, Ruth promised herself, and she would ask Sam to leave. She had had enough of feeling like stranger in her own home. Thought how ironic it was that having spent the last few months craving for company, she would now give anything, to be on her own again.

'Hey, you okay over there?'

Ruth jumped. Ed's voice booming out from the depths of the armchair adjacent to the inglenook, he had been so silent she had forgotten he was there. *Do I really have to speak to him? Can't I just ignore him and then perhaps, he might go away.*

Recalling how Ed had taken any opportunity he could during dinner, to paw at her; a hand sneakily brushing her arm; fingers slyly caressing hers as he had handed her a condiment — Ruth instinctively recoiled. She did not want his attention and yet even now, and without looking, she could feel his eyes intently examining her, roaming all over her face, her body.

Certain Ed had been scrutinising her every move since they entered the living room, Ruth suddenly grew hot. Could almost read his thoughts as she felt a familiar sense of panic starting to build. *Not now!* But her chest tightening, and almost to the point where she was frightened she would stop breathing, Ruth had to force herself to take a couple of deep inhalations. Knowing Ed would notice, and unable to stand the thought of him being anywhere near her, Ruth prayed he would not get up and out of his chair, to help her.

'Ruth, what's the matter? Are you okay?'

Breath!

'I'm fine,' Ruth snapped out a little breathlessly.

Why can't you leave me alone, you creep?

If Ed had heard the contempt in Ruth's voice, he did not show it. Chattily, he said, 'That was a great meal your sister cooked for us.'

'Yes,' Ruth nodded, with a punchy little laugh. Sam, the perfect model housewife mastering the kitchen as if it were her own. Then waiting on them hand and foot, demonstrating a subservience of manner that had successfully managed to leave Ruth feeling sorely lacking and most definitely, intimidated.

'If I didn't know you better, I'd say you sound peeved,' Ed commented discerningly. 'Is everything all right between you two?'

How dare he presume to know me.

'Yes, of course, why shouldn't it be?' Ruth replied sourly. Gave a hollow, phoney, uncomfortable laugh.

'Good.'

Although Ed seemingly shrugged off her response as if it was of no importance, once again, Ruth found herself on the receiving end of a penetrating stare. Wished he would leave her alone and in peace. That he would go home.

The buzz from the alcohol already starting to fade, Ruth lifted her glass and took another greedy swig. Drank to alleviate her awkwardness.

'Ruth, why have you been so elusive these last couple of weeks?'

'*Have I?*' Ruth carefully enunciated.

'Yes, you know you have. You haven't answered a single one of my phone calls. Nor have you responded to any of my text messages.'

'I'm sorry. I hadn't realised you were so *desperate*, to speak to me.'

'Oh come on, Ruth, play nice,' Ed reproved. 'You know, if you hadn't have spoken to me this morning, I was seriously thinking about turning up on your doorstep. If only to make sure, you were still alive and kicking,' he stated, delivering his criticism with a light tempering chuckle.

Ruth kept her eyes focused firmly forward. Stared into the flaming heart of the mesmerising fire as she deliberated on an appropriate answer to his barely disguised castigation. *Just like Sam, he takes too many liberties. He acts like he owns me or something,* Ruth thought with bitter vehemence.

In the end, her brain too dulled to think clearly enough to come up with a clever answer, Ruth shrugged her tensed up shoulders. Realised the way she was feeling at the moment, it would be easier to give him at least a partial truth. 'These last couple of weeks, it's all just got a little harder, and I haven't wanted to talk to anyone.' *And especially not you,* she did not add.

'I'm sorry to hear that. And yet…' Ed paused. 'You've obviously been able to talk to Sam, otherwise she wouldn't have come to visit, on Saturday.'

She's my sister, you moron, what do you expect?

Listening to Ed whinging on like an aggrieved and spoilt brat, Ruth dare to glare at him. The assertiveness of the alcohol giving her the courage to bite back, with an abrupt laugh, she challenged, 'Christ Ed, don't tell me you're jealous of my little sister?'

Ed scowled back at her. Shook his head as though he could not quite believe what he was hearing. 'Don't be so ridiculous, Ruth. Of course I'm not jealous of Sam. I'm glad you've been able to talk to *someone*, at least. It's just that I never thought you two were particularly close, you know, after what happened...' he broke off. Looked a trifle embarrassed as his prominent Adam's apple, worked overtime.

Ruth said nothing. Left him to stew.

'Well, anyway, you've had such an awful time these last few weeks, and as I tried to explain earlier, whether you like it or not, you are family and I, no *we*, the oldies and I, feel a responsibility toward you. And isn't that, as they say, what families are for?'

Discomforted. Feeling stuck, like she was trapped in quicksand by Ed's reasoning, but instinctively suspicious of it, Ruth bit anxiously down on her bottom lip. She had no idea how to respond to what he had said. But if there was one thing Ruth was certain of, it was that when it comes to the working dynamics of a family, she had very little in the way of example, experience or understanding, to go on.

Unable to trust Ed's motives, Ruth suddenly found herself despising him, and despising herself. Wished she were miles away from him, miles away from Sam, and miles away from the whole awful mess that had become her life. Had never felt so utterly alone.

'I just wish,' Ed pushed relentlessly on,' you would find some time to talk to *me*, as well as Sam. You know, since Adam died, you've barely said a word to me. You've not talked to me or the parents about how you're feeling, or how you're coping. You've rejected all our offers to help you around the house, to sort out his things. Consequently, we've all been seriously worried about you and it seems, after everything that happened to you down on that beach... The mere thought you might have...' Ed gave Ruth a knowing stare. 'Well, let's just say, it seems we've been right, to have been worried about you.'

Each word of what Ed had just intimated, hit Ruth like a thunderbolt. The room seeming suddenly smaller, Ed's proximity to her much closer, she mentally thrashed around for something to say, but she could not think straight.

Descending into silence, Ruth pushed her concussed, alcohol and pill infused brain to make some rapid sense of what she thought she had just heard.

Until this morning, Ed had known nothing about the accident, and he had been in school all day. So whatever it was, he now thought he knew, that information could only have come from one source. At some point during the evening, he and Sam had talked. *But why? Why would Sam suggest to Ed, I tried to kill myself? What does she stand to gain, from saying something as terrible as that?*

A torrent of questions now swirling in her mind, Ruth had the sudden, and *crazy* notion, her sister might be out to do her some harm. *Am I in danger, serious danger?*

Deeply disturbed by what she was thinking, unable to cope with it, Ruth swiped the thought away.

I can't think like that, I just can't. It's just too depressing, too paranoid. She's my sister, why would she want to harm me?

'Ruth?' Ed queried, breaking into her angst. 'Did you hear me?'

Ruth was stone-faced. 'Yes, and I don't know what it is you think you know about the accident, or where you got your information from, but all I did was slip?'

'Are you sure about that?'

'Yes, who the hell have you been talking to?'

Ed ignored the question. 'Look Ruth, all I'm trying to say is, it's not as if you've had much in the way of support these last few weeks. So if you want to talk, now's your chance. I'm here, and I'm listening.'

'I don't need you to bloody listen,' Ruth ejected stubbornly. 'All things considered, I think I'm doing fine,' she replied with an undisguised sarcasm as she critically examined his pale face, his thin and pale lips. For the first time, noticed how his hair, hanging limp and shaggy around his ears, the back of his neck, was in desperate need of a trim. How his gross, unfashionable glasses, kept slipping down his prominent nose. How, other than his voice, there was absolutely nothing about Ed that reminded her of *him*. Was astonished to think she could ever have thought, anything different.

'Oh, Ruth,' Ed sounded exasperated as he regarded her with disappointment. 'I just can't win with you, can I? And I think you keep forgetting, Adam was not just your husband, he was also a cherished son, and a brother? So, you know what, you don't have the monopoly on grief. None of this has exactly been a walk in the park for my parents, or for me.'

Feeling suitably chastised, a pang of shame flamed Ruth's face. A vein throbbing painfully in her forehead, she felt herself turn red, hot. Wished she could disappear.

Yet then, unable to help to herself, she ejected a bitter laugh, and defiantly threw out, 'Well, at least you haven't had the police crawling all over you. They've been asking me the most God awful questions.' *Now, who was behaving like an indignant child?*

'Okay, so, why don't you tell me about it?'

Ed leaning right forward and crossing his arms, and to Ruth's ears, sounding condescending, she was wishing she had kept her garrulous mouth shut.

'Ruth, answer me,' Ed ordered, as he closely watched her face.

Automatically responding to the command in Ed's tone, in spite of herself, Ruth found herself saying, 'They wanted to know about the intimate side of our marriage.'

'Like?'

'They wanted to know why Adam was sleeping in the spare room, and whether we had a good marriage, or not.'

For the first time, Ed looked suddenly uncomfortable, nervous even. 'And what did you say?' he asked, with a certain amount of intensity.

'What could I say?' Ruth stopped. Took in a deep breath and for a moment, held the building tension. *Serves him right.*

'Ruth?'

'I told them our marriage was no different to any other.'

'What's that supposed to mean?'

'It means, I told them our marriage had its ups and downs but that in the main, we were happy. That Adam sometimes slept in the spare room, when I was having trouble sleeping.'

Ed nodded. Looked suddenly relieved, and sat back into his chair again. 'That all sounds pretty reasonable to me. A lot of couples have periods where they sleep separately, for one reason or another. I'm sure you have nothing to worry about.'

'You think?' Ruth asked, suddenly desperate for some reassurance.

'Yes, they asked me and the oldies a load of questions as well; about him, you, your marriage, and whether Adam had any enemies. All pretty standard stuff, bearing in mind what happened to him.'

'The police asked *your* parents about *my* marriage?' Ruth exclaimed, in her surprise. Fought with the distinctly uncomfortable memory of the police scouring through every room in the house and especially, the guest bedroom. Of them asking a number of pertinent questions, she would rather not have answered.

'Yes, but again, I really don't see your problem?'

Ruth squeezed her eyes tight shut. Recalled her mother-in-law's surreptitious antipathy toward her these past few months. Thought about the suspicion Jenny could stir up should she so choose; *the chaos she could wreak.* Ruth's heart now beating furiously in her chest as she strained to keep back the anxiety, the fear from her voice, she demanded to know, 'And what did they say?'

'They said it was fine, of course. What else would they say?' Ed, looking perplexed, was watching Ruth closely again.

Ruth gave a sad, dark little laugh. *He obviously has no idea of the depth of his mother's hostility toward me.* 'What, even your mother?'

Needing a top up, Ruth refilled her glass. Sipped it greedily.

'Yes, of course, why would she say anything different?'

Ruth nervously chewed her bottom lip. Surprisingly, Ed's response seemed to imply his mother had not made him aware of some of the relationship issues, she had been witness too. *Oh well,* Ruth thought belligerently, *time to burst his little bubble.*

'As soon as your mother knew we could never have a child of our own and that it was all my fault, her attitude toward me changed, and it was certainly not for the better. In fact, I would go as far to say, she hates me.'

Ed studied her, hard. 'Really? Oh come on Ruth, now you're just being paranoid. My mother likes everyone.'

Ruth visibly balked at the word *paranoid*. Her voice hardened. '*Paranoid*? Am I? Am I really?'

Ed looked at her dubiously. 'Of course you are. My dad loves you, and so does mum. She's just not quite so good at showing it.'

Ruth dispatched a sceptical look. *How could he be so stupid, so thick?*

'Look, it's me who has been cast into the role of the black sheep in this family, not you,' Ed lightly joked as he made reference to the scandalous affair that had ultimately led to him being dumped by his wife.

Ruth did not laugh with him. Nor could she be bothered to reply. Instead, she took another large slug of wine. Saw Ed's mouth stiffen and his eyes narrow; *the exact same way his had.* Guessed what was coming and braced herself for it.

'You're drinking too much,' Ed criticised bluntly. Sat up in his chair, then pushed his face forward toward hers as he sought to get a better look at her eyes. 'And what else are you taking? Your pupils, are huge.'

Ruth ignored his rebuke, and the question.

Battling to quell her humiliation, she became filled with a deep sense of despair.

What is it about me that yells it's okay to question everything I do, everything I say? To bully me? I drink no more than anyone else and yes, I know I should not be mixing alcohol with pills but if I want to sleep at night, to be able to function during the day, it's not exactly like I have a lot of choice.

Suddenly feeling the need to defend herself as her temper flared, Ruth went on the attack. 'You do know, he was having an affair?' She blurted out, without thinking.

Ed sat bolt upright in his chair. 'What?' He shook his head in disbelief. 'Adam, having an affair? No, I don't think so. He wasn't the type.'

Ruth snorted. 'You're seriously telling me, you didn't know?'

'No, I didn't know, and I don't believe it either, not for a single second.' Ed pushed his slipping glasses back up his nose.

'Well, I'm telling you, you couldn't be more wrong about him.' Giggling inappropriately at Ed's look of shocked indignation, Ruth lifted her glass in a mock toast, and accompanied it with the most ridiculous wink. 'Yeah, apparently, you're not the only one in the family unable to keep it in his pants.' She sniggered crudely.

The blood drained from Ed's face.

Chapter Twenty-Two

A wave of musky scent heralding Sam's imminent arrival, Ruth's misplaced sense of mirth, instantly shrivelled up and died.

'Don't mind me,' Sam said with a smile as she entered into the room.

Putting a laden tray down in the centre of the coffee table, Sam precisely placed a pre-filled mug of coffee before Ruth and then Ed, in turn. Encouraged them to help themselves to cream and sugar with a flourish of her hand.

'Ed, perhaps you could be an angel and see to the fire, for me?' Sam asked, looking toward the inglenook as she studied a fire which had calmed to glowing embers. 'I did build it up earlier but it looks like it needs some more logs and the basket's empty. Do you know where to find them?'

'Of course I do,' Ed snapped out edgily. Got up out of his chair, grabbed the log basket from the inglenook, then huffed and puffed his way out of the room. Made it quite clear, he was more than reluctant to complete the task. That he was in a bad mood about something.

'Wow, what on earth was that all about?' Sam asked Ruth, lifting a well arched eyebrow at her. 'What did I do?'

Not caring that Ed's hostility was rooted in exasperation with her and her *apparent* excesses, Ruth shrugged her answer. In the space of less than half an hour, she had oscillated back and forth between hatred and anger and now she was feeling exhausted, depressed. If Sam thought Ed's truculence was anything to do with her, so be it, Ruth thought.

'You seem really on edge tonight, is everything okay?' Sam asked.

Draining what little was left of her wine, Ruth began to experience that pleasant slippage that was then accompanied by the dangerous sense that in ten or twenty minutes, she might say almost anything. *Either that or pass out.* Recalled what she had already blurted out to Ed, and a cold wind blew through her. She shivered. *When will I ever learn?*

'You're also looking really tired.' Sam commented.

'Nothing a year of sleep wouldn't fix,' Ruth mumbled, laying her head back against the cushion behind her. Closed her eyes, for a minute.

'Ed's quite an intense character and I would imagine, once he gets going, he's not the easiest person in the world to talk to or even to be around, for that matter,' Sam stated, blatantly not put off by Ruth's silent retreat. 'Would you like me to try and get rid of him for you?' she asked, sounding unabashed by her derogatory tone.

Ruth thought. Even though she would have liked nothing better than for Sam to find a reasonable excuse to eject Ed from the house, she slowly shook her head. 'No, it's okay. He's still got marking to do, so I would imagine he'll be off soon, anyway.' If Ruth's voice had sounded calm, it was not how she felt. She did not want her brother-in-law here, anymore than she wanted her sister in the house, but she'd had more than enough friction for one night. Craving peace, she could not face another angry exchange.

'Okay, if you're sure.' Sam said as she turned her attention back to coffee table. Added a drop of cream to the blue mug in front of Ruth. Removed the cellophane from the box of after dinner mints.

Ed returned from the log store. Breathing hard, he was straining under the weight of the full basket held firmly between his arms. Dropped the vessel down into its usual place on the hearthstone, before ignoring Ruth and saying to Sam, 'It's freezing out there, and did you know it's started to snow?'

'Really?' said Sam. 'I had no idea.'

'Yes, it's only a light flurry at the moment, but it is most definitely snowing,' Ed answered as he grabbed up a couple of logs, opened the burner door and built up the fire until it hissed and popped. Hot flames of jagged yellow and red teeth providing a false, cheery glow.

'Snow, how lovely,' Sam said as she took Ruth's empty wine glass from her hands, replaced it with the blue mug of coffee. Held the opened box of mints in front of Ruth's face. 'You never know Ed, you might be stuck here for the night.'

Ruth felt the colour rush to her face. *She is joking right?* Had to damp down an immediate spark of anger before it could escape.

Ed got up from seeing to the fire. His face florid from the exertion, he flopped down into the adjacent armchair. 'Nice thought, but I've still got a ton of work to get through before school in the morning. So unless there's a white-out in the next hour or so, I'll be going home tonight.'

Reaching across to pick up the red mug she had set down on the coffee table in front of Ed's chair earlier, Sam passed it over to him. 'Here, there's cream and sugar on the coffee table so please, help yourself,' she reminded.

'Thanks.'

'You know what, thinking about it, why *don't* you stay here for the night,' Sam suggested? 'You could always leave here a bit earlier in the morning, to get the marking done. It would be no trouble for us. Oh and by us, I really mean *me*, to make up a bed for you, would it Ruth?'

Has she lost her mind? Stunned into silence for a couple of seconds, unable to quite believe her ears, Ruth sent Sam a questioning, *what the hell are you playing at,* look. Only five minutes ago, Sam had been offering to get rid of Ed for her. Now she was hell-bent on giving Ed the spare room, and not any room. The only spare room in the house, was *his* room; *the room she knows full well, I haven't got round to clearing yet.*

Sam smiled innocently at Ruth. Returned a puzzled, *I don't know what your problem is?*

'Ed can't stay here tonight,' Ruth rushed out, unable to help herself. 'If it's snowing now and it gets any worse, the country roads around here are likely to become impassable, by morning.'

Shuffling awkwardly in his seat, Ed gave a nervous little laugh. Looked both embarrassed and dispirited by Ruth's outburst, her glaring inhospitality.

Sam, switching her gaze back and forth between Ed and Ruth, and apparently oblivious to the upset she had caused, nibbled calmly on a mint.

'It's okay Ruth, you don't have to concern yourself. I have absolutely no intention of staying here tonight,' Ed said, his voice reassuring, though his tone was condescending and doing little to mask his annoyance.

Thank God. Uncertain how to respond without making the situation even more awkward, Ruth wisely held her silence.

'Sam, how come you're not having a coffee?' Ed said. Flashed Sam an all inclusive smile that left Ruth feeling effectively ostracised, and cringing with humiliation. 'Ah, no, let me guess, you can't have a coffee because it's too fattening?' he quipped, laughing at his own joke as he pointedly added a good helping of cream into his mug, followed by two lumps of sugar. Irritatingly clinked his teaspoon round and round the inside of the mug as he vigorously stirred his drink. Blew on it, then took a tentative sip.

Smiling broadly, Sam lightly patted her stomach. 'Very funny, but no, of course not, I'm just so full from dinner I don't think I've got room for anything else.'

Ed nodded.

'Tell me Ruth, have you heard anymore from the police yet, about Adam's case?' Sam asked suddenly.

The loaded question Sam had so casually asked, so unexpected, Ruth felt her pulse quicken. Shell-shocked, she blinked furiously as her mouth went dry and sour. Her heart thudded. *Why is she being so evil to me, so vile?* Three whole days in each others company and yet this was the first time, Sam had broached the manner of *his* death, head-on.

Panicking, shaking on the inside as well as the outside, the ever-present tremble in Ruth's hands visibly escalated along with her thoughts. Then clumsily spilling a little of the hot coffee directly into her lap, emitting a hiss of pain, Ruth catapulted out of her seat. Every aching muscle in her body screaming from her convulsive actions, she almost collapsed. Took a few distracting moments as she jerkily brushed herself down. Gingerly sat back down.

An uncomfortable silence hung in the air.

Think Ruth, you have to think, she pleaded with herself.

'Are you okay, Ruth?' Sam queried. 'Only, I didn't mean to startle you. You don't mind my asking you about Adam, do you?'

Of course I mind.

'Ruth?'

'How much do you already know?' Was all Ruth could find to say.

'I only know what little the police have told me, and what I've read in the papers.'

Ruth recalled how she had stopped reading the local newspapers or watching the local news, weeks ago. Fought with an impulse to get up and walk out of the room as she tried not to recall the horrific memories of that morning. Briefly closed her eyes against all the rage and misery, still churning in her broken heart.

'Which is what?' Ed asked, inadvertently saving the day as he stifled a yawn behind his hand.

Sam shot Ed a cursory glance as if he were some minor irritation. Addressed her response to Ruth. 'The police said, Adam was killed by a hit-and-run driver, early in the morning, whilst he was out for a run.'

Ruth forced down some coffee. Wanted to vomit. Stared miserably into the fire. Said nothing, still.

'Yes, that's about the size of it,' Ed answered as though the conversation was between he and Sam, instead of Ruth and Sam.

'The papers reported that Adam died at the scene before the emergency services were called, and that the police still haven't located the car, or the driver. Is that still the case? Haven't any witnesses come forward yet?'

Ruth maintained her wretched silence and again, Ed filled the gap.

'No, there are no witnesses, and there is no evidence. So the police still have nothing to go on.' Ed took a long pull on his coffee. Sank even further down into the depths of his chair. His face was pensive, sad.

'I just find it so hard to believe,' Sam said in a conversational tone. Though her gaze as she looked over to Ruth was hard, stoney, 'that Adam could have woken up in the morning, thinking it was going to be just another day and then *wham*, suddenly, it was game over.'

Silence, as all three of them, contemplated what Sam had said.

Her eyes glittering in the firelight, Sam leant forward in her seat, picked up the box of mints and offered one to a yawning Ed. Turned back to face Ruth and casually held them out to her as though she had not just said one of the most terrible things in the world.

Sam had spoken his name too easily. She had spoken of *him* as though it was she who had been close to him, instead of her. Suddenly, Ruth was extremely cold. She waved for the mints to be taken away, for Sam to go away.

Sam withdrew the mints. 'Everything all right?' she asked, her tone almost appeasing, but not quite.

No, Ruth wanted to scream! *Everything is not all right! Not all right, at all!*

Feeling like she was losing her mind. Ed and Sam, now both watching her with their concerned and curious stares, Ruth felt like a bug trapped under a microscope; helplessly pinned down as she was slowly and painfully being picked apart, dissected.

She shuddered.

Still, she could not find her voice.

'Ever since we got on this topic, you've been really quiet Ruth. Oh God, I'm sorry, I wasn't thinking. You don't want to talk about it, do you?' Sam looked expectantly across at Ruth and when she didn't get a response, studied her for a long moment. 'It's just that I find, sometimes, I can't sleep at night trying to work out why on earth someone would want to kill Adam? Who could possibly hate him, that much?'

In spite of herself, Ruth whispered a soft moan. *Why is she doing this to me? What is she trying to imply?*

'There is no *why,*' Ed jumped in straight away. 'What happened to Adam, was not planned, it was a hit-and-run. Just some bastard driver, not concentrating, some freak of a human being who driving irresponsibly, carelessly ploughed into my brother and then like a coward, drove away from the mess,' he said through gritted teeth. Seethed with emotion.

Slammed with a vivid memory of the coroner's description of the catastrophic pelvic injuries *he* had sustained. Of the horror of knowing *he* would have died alone and in agony, the tears Ruth had been holding back, began to freely fall.

Sam reached over and put her hand on Ruth's. Instinctively, Ruth started to pull her hand away, but Sam held on to it, firmly. Bestowed Ruth with a warm smile of sympathy that did not quite reach her eyes.

'Ruth, we don't have to talk about this,' Sam said.

So why did we? Ruth thought bitterly.

For a couple of minutes, there was an intensifying silence.

Ed, sinking deeper and deeper into his chair, yawned heavily, then took another mouthful of coffee. Heaved a massive sigh as though trying to rouse himself. 'Sam, from what you've said, I assume you were interviewed by the police, as well as us?'

Knowing she needed to pay attention, Ruth swiped away her tears. Winced as she carefully sat straighter in her seat. Had to withdraw her hand to do so and this time, Sam let it go.

'Yes, I was. Being a close family relative, I presume they wanted to cover all their bases. That said,' Sam paused, 'they did seem to ask an awful lot of questions and some of which, if I'm honest, did seem a bit odd.'

Concentrate, Ruth commanded her heavy eyes, her sluggish brain.

'Like what?' Ed asked.

'Well, they asked the obvious ones, about my relationship with Adam, with Ruth, you know, the usual stuff. But then they started to ask so many questions about Ruth and our upbringing, it started to feel a bit weird. I suppose though, in the eyes of the police, we're all suspects until proven otherwise.'

'*Our upbringing?*' Ruth ejected without thinking. Could have bit off her tongue as Ed instantly threw her an interested look.

Sam's steady, inscrutable gaze, never wavered. 'Yes, but I'm sure they would have asked you the exact same questions?'

Ruth did not answer. Pulling her gaze away from Sam's, she studied her hands, which were gripping the mug so fiercely, they ached.

Damn! Ruth was angry with herself. She had overreacted. What did it matter if the police asked Sam about the past? Sam would not say anything more, than was already on public record.

'Why are you so worried about your past?' Ed asked Ruth, before clapping a hand over his mouth to stifle yet another yawn, from escaping. 'You can't help being orphaned, or fostered.'

The sisters exchanged a glance of veiled complicity. A glance that implied they would keep their secret, their past, to themselves.

There was a short silence, then Sam changed the subject. 'Ed, please can you thank your father for being so kind as to give me all the details I needed, to attend Adam's funeral. It was very kind of him to think of me.'

Ah, so that's how she learnt of the funeral arrangements, Ruth thought sourly. Bitterly recalled how her father and mother-in-law had taken over everything, to do with Adam's funeral.

Yawning his head off again, it seemed all Ed could provide by way of an acknowledgement of Sam's request, was a brief wave of his hand in her direction.

In physical, and emotional pain, her head swimming from concussion, stress and tiredness, Ruth was now seriously struggling to keep it together. Could feel herself detaching, floating away like a helium balloon. 'Stop,' she whispered.

'Sorry, but just one more thing before we let the topic of Adam's case drop, is it still open?' Sam asked, directing her question to Ruth again.

Ruth's throat tightened. She coughed, to clear it but her breath catching in her throat, she was mute. Trying not to cry, she felt wretched as she concentrated on bringing herself back down, and into the room again.

'Yes, but it's in the process of being closed.' Ed answered, through a couple of gaping yawns.

For the first time, Sam's previously tranquil composure, slightly slipped and behind the carefully composed mask, Ruth thought she saw a look of strain and upset. Surprised, Ruth's previous unease deepened as she hunted for the origins of Sam's distress. *No, after all this time, surely not?*

'But I don't understand? Ruth, I'm sure I overheard you say to Ed earlier, you thought Adam was having an affair?'

So, Sam had been listening, eavesdropping. Cold air swirled through Ruth's veins. What she had said to Ed about Adam having an affair, had been an aberration borne from frustration and anger. She should have kept her mouth shut.

Overwhelmed by the direction in which the conversation was suddenly going, Ruth wracked her brains for what to say. If she managed to get through this tortuous evening in one piece, she did not want to have to explain anything, to anyone, ever again.

'Only if I *am* right, how come the case is being closed so soon? Don't the police want to investigate the affair, further?' Sam prodded determinedly.

'Sam,' Ed cut in suddenly, his glasses slipping down his beak-like nose as he struggled to galvanise himself from the pit of his chair, 'don't you think Ruth is entitled to at least some privacy?'

'I think, if Ruth was prepared to tell *you* what was going on, then I don't see why she wouldn't tell me? After all, you are only the brother-in-law,' Sam caustically pointed out. Then granted Ed a small smile as though to take the sting out of her words. 'Ruth, what made you think Adam was having an affair, and do the police know?' Sam said, her voice calmly insistent.

Merciless.

Ruth looked to Ed for help, but visibly wrestling to keep his eyes open, the fight apparently sapped out of him, he collapsed back down into his seat. Left Ruth to fight her own battles as unbelievably, his mouth fell open, and a soft snore escaped.

Chapter Twenty-Three

Stood by the living room window, peering out from behind the curtains, Ruth was looking over a garden that was white with frost. Pitch dark outside, in the harsh winter moonlight, ice crystals shimmied on the grass like a spangled shawl.

Nervously listening for his car, waiting to hear the scrunch of the Jaguar's heavy wheels on the gravel driveway, Ruth was feeling both lonely and alone. Feeling as though she was becoming an outsider in her own home. Disconnected from her husband and seemingly unable to relate to him, strangers, tears pricked at the back of Ruth's eyes. *All I've wanted, is to belong.*

Today, Ruth had decided she would no longer collude with her husband. She would not sneak compliantly away to a solitary bed before he had even crossed the threshold of their front doorstep, and pretend to be asleep. No, tonight, and no matter how late it got, Ruth intended to wait up for Adam. She planned to surprise him with all her hard work and then she would encourage him to spend some time with her, regardless of how tired he might be.

Distracted from her vigil by the sudden snap of a log burning hotly in the fire, Ruth briefly looked back at the room. She had spent hours slavishly putting up decorations. A six foot Nordic pine delivered to the house that morning, now taking pride of place to the left-hand side of the inglenook and covered in brightly coloured bulbs threaded between equally colourful glass ornaments; balls, angels, and bells. The room scented with wood smoke, fresh pine and candle wax, it looked and smelt, of all things Christmassy.

This is everything I ever wanted, so why aren't I happy?

Thinking about Christmas and all it exemplified, Ruth became saddened by it. Most of her childhood spent living in the homes of strangers, Christmas had always proven to be an especially difficult time of the year. This holiday, out of all of the public holidays to be marked and endured, had always signified a period of abject loneliness, and absence. It was a time of year that had come to represent a negative reminder of the family she had once loved, then lost.

The last couple of years, Christmas Eve, Christmas Day and Boxing Day celebrated still in someone else's home, it had been spent at Adam's parents house. But this year, Ruth was determined to ask Adam if they could stay home. For once, selfishly keep the holiday, purely for themselves.

Their relationship feeling more and more as though it was inexorably reaching a crisis point, and terrified by it, Ruth was desperate to use the time being at home for Christmas would afford. Use the holiday as a last-ditch attempt, to work on decompressing the pressure cooker of their unstable marriage. Somehow, Ruth was determined to find a way to reconnect with Adam, before it became too late.

I miss my husband and everyone deserves a second chance, don't they?

Ruth sighed. At the edges of her brain was a familiar, dull headache.

She twitched back the curtains.

How much longer?

Thirty-three minutes later, Adam's car was at last drawing up into the driveway, and Ruth hastily removed herself from the window before he could see her. Walked across to the sofa, sat down and contained her trembling hands. Listened, intently.

Ruth heard the sound of Adam's key in the lock, the door being quietly opened and shut, his coat being hung up on one of the wall pegs, his wallet and keys being placed into the bowl on the console table. Then he was coming up the hallway, his stockinged feet lightly shushing up the flagstone corridor, toward her.

Adam pausing as he approached the open doorway to the living room, Ruth held her breath. Then realised she was bathed in a sweat that was triggered by the familiar hopeless panic. Felt her chest tighten.

He's going to leave me, I know it. She snapped the thought away.

Ruth swallowed hard. Found some courage. 'Adam!' she called out. Made it obvious she wanted to speak with him. 'I'm in here.'

Walking into the threshold of living room, his arms hanging loosely down by his sides but his fists clenched, Adam looked tense and unhappy. Ruth inwardly cringed. It broke her heart to see him that way and she hated to think, she might be the cause of it.

'Hi, did you have a good day?' Ruth asked brightly and with a confidence, she did not feel. Gave him her best and most radiant smile. 'Look what I've been doing,' she said with false cheer, throwing her arms out expansively. Desperate for him to notice what she had done for him, the effort she had put in.

Adam blinked rapidly. Cast his eyes around the room as he took in the decorations, the tree. He paled. Looked suddenly sheepish, then furtive.

Ignoring Adam's shifty look, Ruth appealed, 'Well, what do you think?' Hearing the whine in her voice, Ruth hated herself for it. *Why do I always sound so needy?*

'I think,' said Adam, looking down at his wristwatch, 'it's really late.'

Ruth ached to get up and go to Adam. She wanted to put her arms around him, to tell him she loved him but before she could move, thought again about her feelings of abandonment, of his blatant lack of respect toward her, toward meeting her needs. Then allowing herself to acknowledge her crushing disappointment at his negative response to her labours, repentance gave way to grievance. 'The least you could do,' she bossily exploded, 'is comment on how nice the decorations look! I've been working on them all day, for you!'

Hearing the shrillness in her voice, how appalling it sounded, Ruth inwardly cringed. But she was sick of being miserable, of walking on eggshells, and of thinking nothing she did was ever good enough for him. *Why should I, always be the one to back off?*

'Look Ruth, I'm far too tired for any of your usual histrionics.'

Furious, Ruth watched Adam look around the room again. Knew that this time, he was looking for something specific.

'I haven't had a single drink, all day,' Ruth stated flatly, whilst inside, she was silently screaming. Watched her already compromised power, dwindle even further.

'Really?' Adam said, his hands bunched into fists as though preparing to do battle.

'Yes,' Ruth almost shouted. Strived to keep the resentment from out of her voice as Adam looked across at her, with an undisguised incredulity.

Why is it, when we really need to talk, the ones we love always seem furthest away?

'So what is it, you *really* want?' Adam asked brusquely as his jaw clenched defensively.

'Adam, please, sit down.' Ruth implored. Bit back the threatening tears as she patted the cushioned sofa seat next her. 'All I *want*, is a nice evening with you before we go to bed.' Then without thinking, said, 'I'll fix us a drink.' Could have bitten her own tongue off.

Adam threw her a withering look. 'Seriously, Ruth? You want *me* to have a drink, with *you*? Are you crazy?'

Ruth felt anger flare inside her, and hastily damped it down. True to her word, she had not touched a drop all day. Had only got through the day, the perpetual thirst, by keeping herself constantly busy. She had not even stopped to eat. Felt unfairly judged.

'No, that isn't what I meant,' Ruth said hastily as she tried to fix her blunder. 'All I wanted, was to offer *you* a drink,' she emphasised. 'I promise you, I don't want a drink. Honest I don't.' She could hear the pleading in her own voice, and was humiliated by it. Desperately looked for a way out, a change of topic. 'Adam, please, I really do need to talk to you.'

There was a brief silence.

'What about?' He demanded to know.

Ruth worriedly bit down on her bottom lip. Looked for the words she needed. Though she only wanted to talk to him about where they should spend their Christmas, was shocked to hear her treacherous mouth say, 'Our marriage.'

Silence.

A Freudian slip? The enormity of what she had unwittingly said, flooding Ruth's already over-anxious brain, the ever present cold and sickening buzz of panic residing deep inside of her, rose up and sucker punched her full in the stomach. For a full minute, Ruth could not breath. A conversation like that, who knew where it could lead, where it would end?

Ruth did not want to talk about their marriage, really, she didn't. She would find it too hard to put into words, the sense that she was losing him, the sense that he was moving away from her, into a place she could neither see, nor locate; *a place where anything might happen.*

Adam moved further into the room, and in spite of the cold weather, Ruth could see a film of perspiration coating his face. Watched him remove his jacket and sling it over the back of the sofa. Saw his shirt, damp with patches of perspiration at the armpits, was clinging to his torso; *a man under pressure?*

Dropping himself loosely down into the wing chair adjacent to the inglenook, Adam pushed his hands through his hair in that familiar gesture, Ruth so loved. Under his eyes, there were the shadows of tiredness.

'Okay, but if we're going to talk about our marriage, perhaps you could apprise *me* on a few things, first?' Adam said, his tone eerily lifeless as he stared coldly at Ruth.

Alarmed. Adam's words carefully enunciated with a spine-chilling menace, Ruth's chest again tightened as it began to heave and fall. The air scouring her parched throat, she gawped stupidly back at him. *What does he mean?*

Suddenly achingly aware of what Adam might be about to say, to ask, Ruth's brain turned jelly. Slid all over the place as she tried to get some semblance of control over her slippery thoughts.

This cannot be happening.

The stakes were so high, Ruth could not speak.

Jumping into the ominous silence, Adam said, 'I'll tell you what, why don't I help you out? Perhaps we could start with you telling me about the pregnancy?'

Ruth gulped. 'The pregnancy?'

'Yes, you know, the pregnancy you used to coerce me into asking you to marry you.'

Coerced? Had he forgotten, already, how in love they had been?

'Then, perhaps,' he laughed hideously, 'we'll revisit the miscarriage that so conveniently happened, less than a week after our wedding.'

Ruth gasped as if she had been walloped. Not once, in all the months that had passed since the meeting with the fertility consultant, had Adam ever mentioned her pregnancy or the subsequent miscarriage.

Convincing herself he loved her as much as she did him, and that he had tacitly forgiven her for her mistake, she had stupidly maintained the unspoken lie, pushed away the truth.

Horrified by what Adam was voicing, Ruth could no longer bear to look at him. Briefly closed her eyes against the explanation that had been demanded of her, his condemning stare.

'Well?'

Ruth's hands twisted over and over in her lap. White-faced, she weakly said, 'I'm sorry, but I'm not sure I know you mean?'

Adam snorted. Looked at her with open dislike, with repulsion. 'You know *exactly*, what I mean.'

Ruth shook her head at herself, at him. It was useless, Adam was leaving her with no choice. She had to try and explain. 'Adam, I am so sorry.'

'Is that it? After all this time, is that all you've got to say for yourself? You're sorry?'

A whorl of fear spiralled through Ruth.

This is it, this is really happening.

Afraid of Adam's steely need to confront her, the awful realisation that it was probably just a fraction of what was yet to come, Ruth became suddenly light-headed. She wanted to faint. Putting her arms protectively across her stomach, she leant forward and expelled a heavy breath.

But Adam took no notice of Ruth's discomfort, and again he ruthlessly demanded, 'Well?'

'It was a mistake. I m-made a dreadful mistake,' Ruth finally managed to stutter out.

'Really?' Adam ejected a mock laugh. Reeled back in his chair with the absurdity of what she had just said. 'You're seriously trying to tell me you made a mistake? Hah, and there I was thinking that telling a lie was a deliberate and conscious act.'

Ruth shrank as if he had made to strike her. 'No,' she insisted, 'I did *not* lie.' Heard her voice imploring him to believe her. 'I thought I was pregnant, I honestly did but then all of a sudden, I wasn't. And by the time I realised I had got it all so terribly wrong, we were already married. And then I felt I was in too deep to tell you the truth. I was frightened.'

Adam frowned. 'So, on the one hand you claim you didn't lie to me, and yet you're also saying, you were too frightened to tell me the truth. Seriously Ruth, can you hear yourself?'

Realising she had unwittingly sabotaged herself, Ruth blinked, furiously. *Why do I do that? Why do I always end up undermining myself?*

Because it takes a clever person to lie, and you're just stupid, said the daemon in Ruth's head.

Adam stared at Ruth, his face incredulous. Shook his head at her. 'You must take me for such a fool?'

Ruth glanced wildly around the room. Felt herself blanch as the blood receded from her face.

There was heavy pause.

Adams voice grew suddenly quiet and somber. 'When, Ruth, when will you stop lying? You've had so many chances to tell me the truth and yet not once, have you come even close to attempting to do so.'

'Please, Adam,' she pleaded, her voice trembling.

'No!' Adam exclaimed. Shook his head at her. 'No matter what way I look at it, you *deliberately* set out to deceive me. Christ, you even showed me a positive pregnancy test and the fool that I was, I trusted you. Happily believed you.'

Ruth did not answer. She could not bear to think about what she had done. Squeezed her eyes tight shut as she failed to gather up her traumatised thoughts.

'Tell me Ruth, how did you do it?' Adam's face was bleak. 'Did you buy a fake tester on-line, or did you pee on the stick when you were on your period? Come on Ruth, enlighten me. Tell me how such a deliberate act to deceive, can simply be a mistake?'

The silence that followed was an answer more honest than anything Ruth could have said.

'And then, you put me through of pain of thinking you'd lost our baby. Again Ruth, how could you? How could you do that to me?'

'I'm so sorry,' Ruth beseeched him.

'But what I really can't forgive,' Adam continued on as if Ruth had not spoken,' is that you knew how much I wanted children. How excited I was when you told me we'd slipped up so soon into our relationship. That you were pregnant, when…'

They were both silent for a moment.

How do I make this better? Ruth scrabbled for the words. 'Adam, I loved you so much and I really thought, after we were married, it would only be a matter of time.'

'Really? My God, and still you're lying!' Adam growled loudly. 'I'm a scientist, Ruth. Surely you of all people must have realised that after we got the results of our fertility tests, I would have followed up on them?'

Ruth briefly closed her eyes, inhaled deeply. *In, out. In, out.*

'And yours,' Adam sneered, 'made for an especially interesting read.'

Ruth's veins turned to ice. She knew what was coming, and was horror-struck by it. Dropped her gaze from his overtly hostile stare.

'It appears, you've had an abortion at some point in your life,' Adam threw out. Paused. 'Consequently, your uterus is now full of scar tissue, and you also have an unhealthy endometrial lining. What with that, and the fact that the scar tissue from the abortion has also become a physical barrier to any sperm entering the upper uterus, meaning any ovulated eggs are left unfertilised, no embryo, would ever be able to implant. The bottom line being, your abortion has made it impossible, for you to ever become pregnant.'

Ruth wildly shook her head at Adam. 'But I never knew any of that.'

'You're seriously expecting me to believe, you didn't know you'd had an abortion?'

Tell him, a voice in Ruth's head screamed! *Tell him what really happened to you!* But no matter how much she wanted to, Ruth could not go back there.

'Yes, I knew I'd had an abortion but what I didn't know, was that it had left me barren,' Ruth whispered, her voice breaking with emotion, her face wet with tears. She wanted to curl up and die. Felt it would be a blessed relief, and that it was no more than she deserved.

Adam shook his head at her. Despite his obvious anger, he looked desperately sad. 'But why, Ruth? Knowing how strongly I felt about you, about having a child, why would you be so cruel as to trick me into marrying you. Why didn't you just trust me? Tell me the truth about the abortion from the very start, then perhaps, we could have worked something out?'

Ruth's heart was breaking. How could she tell him, about what she had never been able to admit to herself, to anyone? How could she explain, that to revisit that bit of her past, would be tantamount to emotional suicide?

'Because, from the very first time I met you, I worshipped you and from that point onwards, I could not envisage a life without you,' Ruth implored. 'Please believe m-me,' she stammered, 'when I say that in spite of the abortion, I truly believed I could still have a child with you. I'm sorry. I'm so sorry I lied to you.'

Adam waited a moment before replying. Seemed to gather his reserves, then coldly said, 'I'm sorry as well, but I'm done. If you're capable of faking a pregnancy, a miscarriage, of tricking me into marrying you, of lying to me about your abortion, then what the hell else, are you capable of?'

Ruth did not answer. Could not answer.

I am not a bad person.

'As far as I'm concerned, our relationship has been built on nothing but lies. Our marriage,' he paused, 'is a joke. It should *never*,' he stressed, 'have happened.'

'Adam, let's at least try. Now you know everything there is to know, don't you think we have a chance to fix this?'

Adam shook his head. 'You know, right now Ruth, I can't even look at you.'

Ruth shrank from the ice in his blue eyes. Had never been more insecure. Her heart palpitating out of her chest, she could no longer breathe. Felt dizzy and faint again, the sensation of tumbling. To revive herself, bit her tongue and drew blood. Stricken, she began to sob.

'Oh, please,' Adam said heartlessly, 'can't you for once, just spare me the waterworks. You are a deeply disturbed individual, Ruth. Damaged, and I don't mean just physically. You're a compulsive liar. You're delusional. And, you're an alcoholic. You need professional help. Psychiatric help. Can't you see that?'

Adam looking brutally triumphant in that moment, his face morphing into that of the bully who's child had been so callously terminated, Ruth gasped. Dreadful memories of the past, pitilessly poking at the simmering embers of the anger residing deep within her belly, her desecrated womb, suddenly, all the pent up rage burst into flames. 'You fucking hypocrite!' Ruth yelled. 'You dare to call me a liar, when you're just as bad! You're the one who's been having the affair, these past months! Christ, you've even got me thinking I'm going mad, crazy, and all because of you and your lies!' she exploded.

Recoiling into his chair as though shocked at the level of her unexpected fury, this time, it was Adam who looked distinctly uneasy. 'Ruth, I have no idea what the hell you're talking about?' He denied. 'Of course I haven't been having an affair. Work has been so busy, when in the hell, would I ever have had the time?' he hollered back. Threw up his hands, in exasperation.

But Ruth did not believe him. She had seen his discomfort, the flash of guilt as his cheeks burned red. Could not understand why, after everything that had been divulged, he would continue to lie about it?

A vein throbbed in Ruth's forehead as for the first time, she fully grasped how much trouble he had taken to get to the bottom of her fertility problems. How much advance planning he must have done, to get the evidence. How much time he must have spent plotting and manipulating, since. How much patience and discipline he must have exerted over himself in waiting for a night, like tonight. *How much, he must hate me.*

'That's it,' Adam stated with a finality. 'I can't do this any more. Our marriage, *is* over.'

Now Adam had said the words she had been dreading, the words they had been dancing around for months, Ruth saw the relief flood into his face, the relaxed set of his shoulders. He expressed no remorse, and no self-hatred for what he had done to her.

Devastated by his callousness. Overwhelmed by her torment. Ruth exploded with fury. Screamed at the top of her lungs as she lunged from out of her seat.

Adam also sprang to his feet as Ruth flew at him. His fists clenched, he put his arms up to protect himself from the savage blows she aimed at his chest, his head. Grabbed her hands as she went to claw at his face.

Ruth swore. Words she had not used for years were flying crazily from out of her mouth. 'I'll kill you, you fucking bastard! I'll fucking kill you!'

Adam violently pushed Ruth away from him.

She staggered and fell.

On her knees before him, Ruth's frenzy gave way to a terrible keening as dreadful racking sobs poured out of her. The broken child inside of her grieving for the loss of its parents, for the loss of itself…

'Please, Adam. Please,' she begged him. 'Don't leave me. I can't cope without you. I need you. I am nothing without you. If you leave me, I'll kill myself. I swear, I will.'

Adam looked down on her. Briefly hesitated with indecision. Then he turned. Walked away.

Chapter Twenty-Four

Ed's snores escaping from a slack mouth, Sam smiled to herself. *Poor bastard, already, he was dead to the world.*

'Ruth, Did you hear me?' Sam asked. Her question met with a vacuous stare, she tried again. 'Ruth, why did you think Adam was having an affair?'

Ruth staring into the fire, she looked as though she was deliberating something important. As if, she might be steeling herself to confront something deep and dark, something unpleasant. Gave herself a little shake.

'Ruth, I asked you a question. Why won't you answer me?'

'It was everything and nothing,' Ruth stated flatly, though her speech was slurred. Appeared drained and worse for wear.

At last, she speaks. The excessive drinking, the antidepressants, the slovenly behaviour, Sam could only imagine what Adam must have had to put up with those last few months before he died. Felt sorry for him. 'Sorry, but you're going to have to explain that one for me.' But her question yet again met with an oppressive silence. *What's with the sudden reticence,* Sam thought irritably? 'Ruth, did you hear me?'

Visibly shivering, Ruth looked wildly around the room as though waking up from a nightmare.

Dear God, this was hard work. Becoming increasingly exasperated, barely managing to restrain herself from grabbing a hold of Ruth and giving her a damn good shake, Sam snapped out, 'How Ruth? How did you know Adam was having an affair? It's obvious the police didn't find anything, so it has to have been you. What was it, Ruth? What did you find?'

'No, it wasn't the police,' Ruth said quietly, staring right through Sam as though she were somewhere else entirely.

'Okay…' Sam said, unsurprised the police had not found anything. Adam, the obsessively detailed scientist, was fastidious to a fault and she very much doubted, he would have left any trace of an affair.

'And they tried. Really tried.'

'What?'

Ruth threw Sam a curious look. One that seemed to say, *What's it to you?* Thought for a moment. Then said, 'The police scrutinised everything. They analysed our finances, our mobiles, our diaries, our home computer, his office, and even *his* work equipment. Piece by piece, they systematically took apart out lives. Minutely examined every bit of crap they could damn well get their hands on. They even inferred we hadn't… we hadn't been sleeping together,' she mumbled out.

'But if the spare room is anything to go by, you hadn't been sleeping together.'

Ruth glared at Sam.

'But not sleeping together, does not constitute an affair,' Sam pointed out.

'Yet, he was.'

'Okay.' Sam nodded, satisfied she had got to her final answer. 'So what, Ruth? What was it that *you* found, that made you so certain Adam was cheating on you?'

Ruth nervously cleared her throat. Shook her head. Looked Sam straight in the eye, then bitterly said, 'Nothing, I found nothing.'

So, it was as she had suspected all along, there was no *tangible* proof of Adam ever having had an affair. 'So to summarise, the police found nothing, and you found nothing?'

Ruth flung Sam a look of withering scorn, then smacked her in the face with it. 'Just what is it, about my saying that *nothing* was found, you don't seem to understand?' She spat out nastily.

Sam sucked in a deep breath. Surprised to see her hands trembling a little, she willed herself to calm down. Now was not the time to cave-in to her emotions. First, she needed more information. Had to have it, in fact.

'So all you have on Adam, is a feeling. A wife's intuition?' she clarified.

'Yes,' Ruth said reluctantly. Slowly nodded her head. 'Tell me, how did you know?' Ruth suddenly demanded of Sam.

Reeling with surprise, Sam's mouth fell open. *I must have misheard,* she thought. 'What did you say?'

'I said, how did *you* know?' Ruth asked, her voice sounding brittle. Upset.

Ruth's question not one she had anticipated, Sam felt a hot rush of panic, then anger. *How dare she, so callous?*

The ensuing silence was uncomfortable, and ominous.

'Why, Ruth? Why would you be so cruel as to ask me, of all people, a question such as that?'

'Because I thought *you*,' Ruth quietly answered, 'would know the answer.'

'And what makes you think, I'll tell you the truth?' Sam challenged, unable to keep the disdain from out of her voice.

Ruth shiftily dropped her gaze as though embarrassed. 'Because you're my sister and because…' she had the grace to hesitate, 'I thought, we had been able to put the past behind us.'

The gall of her, or was it spite?

'I don't think you've any idea just how hard it's been for me this last year,' Ruth continued on colourlessly. 'For months, I felt as though I was going mad. That I was living with a split personality, a stranger.'

Sam remained silent. She did not want to give Ruth the pleasure of sympathising with her plight. Waited for her to continue. To implicate herself.

'From one minute to the next, I never knew how he was going to be toward me. Sometimes he would be his normal, cheerful self, the charming man I knew and loved. Then, out of the blue, he would turn on me, and be just awful. Do anything he could, to make my life a misery.'

Ruth sounding bitter and wretched with hurt as she wallowed in a sea of self-pity, Sam gloated inwardly. *Who would have thought, love could be so poisonous, so painful?*

'I'm positive he was cheating on me. I just know it, in here,' Ruth insisted. Stabbed a finger toward her heart as the ever present tears, streamed down her stricken face. 'And it's been driving me mad. I can't sleep, or think about anything else. Dead or not, I have to know if he was cheating on me and I think,' she blurted out, 'you can help?'

Ruth so drunk her almost incomprehensible words were running and bumping into each other like dodgem cars, Sam's concentration lapsed momentarily, as she stopped listening.

Sam was thinking back. Thinking back to a time when she had been happy, and content. A time when she had stopped worrying about the past and the present and for once in her life, had been looking forward to a future feeling cherished and safe, with the only man she had ever loved.

Losing her parents so young, growing up in foster homes and deprived of her older sibling for much of those years, Sam had always known her existence did not come with any guarantees. But *why*, she painfully asked herself, *did life have to be so depressingly unfair?*

'Sam, you're not listening to me?' Ruth accused.

Not that drunk then, Sam thought bitterly. Pushed the nails of her fingers deep into the palms of her hand and so hard, they left an imprint.

Looking directly into Ruth's miserable face, Sam quietly said, 'Nothing, that's what changed, nothing. There were no signs. Nothing was different. One day Adam was with me and the next, he belonged to you.'

Ruth had the grace to look uncomfortable, and Sam took some pleasure from it. Realised with contempt, just how easily her beloved sister had forgotten the chaos she had caused; *the intolerable pain*. Hated her, for her shallowness.

'I'm sorry, Sam. It was insensitive of me to ask you a question like that.'

Yes, it damn well was, Sam thought resentfully.

'Tell me, Ruth, is anyone else aware of your suspicions? A friend, perhaps?'

Met with yet another unhelpful silence, Sam tenaciously hung onto her cool. Waited for Ruth's pill and alcohol soaked brain to catch up, to work out why, the question might be of some relevance.

'No, of course I haven't. Why on earth would I do something as stupid as that?'

Sam sighed. 'I can't help you if you lie to me, Ruth. Don't forget, I overheard you earlier this evening, telling Ed. So who else have you told?'

'When you were eavesdropping, you mean,' Ruth said spitefully, her previous attempt at contrition, long gone already.

'Look Ruth, having the police get wind of what you've been thinking about in relation to Adam having an affair, will only encourage them to snoop even deeper into every aspect of your life. Perhaps ask even more pertinent questions, about your past, for example.'

'What?'

A genuine look of horror flashing across Ruth's tear soaked face at the thought of the police determinedly digging into her past, Sam knew she had hit a nerve. Pressed ruthlessly on. 'So, I'll ask you again, is Ed the only other person you've told?'

'Yes,' Ruth said. Looked mutinous.

This time, Sam believed her. Nodded more to herself than to Ruth, as she contained the feeling of relief that flooded through her. Now she had got to the bottom of all the questions she had needed to ask in relation to the affair, it was time to move the conversation, swiftly on.

'Ruth, I know you believe Adam was having an affair, but if he wasn't, why else, might he behave so badly toward you?'

Ruth threw her a malicious, threatening look. 'I don't know, you tell me?'

'Oh, come on Ruth, this is me you're talking to.'

'So, what? Now you're telling me, it was all my own fault? That is what you're thinking, isn't it?' Ruth confronted.

'Well, you did trick him into marrying you? Perhaps he found out about the…?'

'Leave it Sam, just leave it,' Ruth interrupted. 'I may have been desperate enough to try and talk to you about some of this stuff last year but believe me, I've learnt my lesson.'

'How do you mean?'

'You were awful to me on that day,' Ruth said, pausing mid-whinge, 'I turned to you for support, and yet all you did was vilify me.'

'After everything you'd done to us, to me, can you blame me?' Sam retorted.

Ruth stared blankly back at her. 'What do you mean, *us*? You mean, you and Adam?'

Is she really that damaged, that twisted, she has no clue as to what I'm really talking about? Sam thought, with disbelief.

'No,' Sam said, shaking her head with exasperation. 'I meant you and me, and the damage you did to *our* relationship. We're sisters and yet that didn't stop you from stealing Adam from me. And then, as if that wasn't enough, when I try and help you to sort out some of the mess you've got yourself into, just because you didn't like what I had to say, you viciously cut me out of your life and even though, I wasn't exactly in the best place myself, at the time. How Ruth, how could you do that to me?'

There was a heavy beat of silence.

'I didn't set out to hurt you,' Ruth hiccuped out.

Yeah, sure you didn't, Sam thought bitterly. *That's why you lashed out at me. Left me with a black eye.*

'Really? How can you honestly say that? If you hadn't have been so scared you were going to be found out by that fertility specialist Adam was dragging you to see, I'm not sure, you would have even bothered to see me that day. You used me.'

'That is ridiculous.'

'Is it? Up until then, you hadn't spoken to me properly, in months.'

'I was newly married,' Ruth bleated. 'With a new husband and a new house to take care of. I was busy. I didn't deliberately set out to exclude you from my life and anyway, I did invite you down. You came down, a few times.'

'No,' Sam shook her head vehemently. 'You invited me down twice and in between, you ignored all my phone calls, my text messages. You hung me out to dry as though I was no longer of any importance to you. To me, it felt as though you intentionally cut me out of your life. Yet it wasn't because of anything I had done to you, it was because of what you had done to me. It was your bad behaviour, your embarrassment, and your shame that drove a wedge between us, not mine.'

'No,' Ruth shook her head. 'You've got it all wrong.'

'Have I? Have I really? You're the one who took something precious from me, your own sister, and yet I'm the one who's been ruthlessly punished for it. I was in a desperate state when we last met, and yet you chose to ignore all of that. You were so indifferent. How Ruth?

How could you treat me, of all people, so insensitively, so badly?' *And after everything we've been through together.*

Ruth shook her head. 'You have to understand, it's all been such a terrible muddle, for such a long time. I've been so confused, and lonely. I just can't think straight.'

Excuses, excuses. Yet again, it was all about her, all about Ruth. Shivering with the memory of how close she had come to being penniless, to being homeless, Sam could not believe Ruth's self-centredness.

'Ruth, what I still don't understand, is why you wouldn't be honest with Adam about your past? He was hardly a monster, and he was supposed to have been in love with you,' Sam said, trying to hold back the scorn from her voice, and failing.

Ruth blanched as white as a sheet of paper. 'I could never do that. Anyway, it's not the past,' she shook her head, 'that's the problem.'

Sam was dumbfounded. How could Ruth seriously believe, after everything that had happened to her, that none of what was happening now, had anything to do with the past?

'And it is not up for discussion, not with you and not with anyone else,' Ruth stated fiercely.

'But what about the police, Ruth? Surely they discussed what happened, with you?'

Ruth wavered for an instant. 'No, why, should they?'

Sam shook her head, she did not believe her. 'No, of course they didn't. It never came up, so they didn't have to talk to you about it, did they?' Sam mocked. 'Well, they sure as hell discussed it with me.'

Ruth looked briefly petrified. Then disappeared into herself again.

'Look Ruth, no matter what you say or how often you lie about it, you don't fool me, Ruth. I'm your sister, remember. I know you and I know *exactly*, what you're capable of.'

'Do you?' Ruth ejected. Shot Sam a menacing look.

No, I don't, Sam thought with a flash of honest appreciation. But coldly determined, she ignored Ruth's flagrant intimidation and pressed on. 'After that horrendous backstreet abortion and how messed up it must have left your insides, surely you must have realised the chances of you ever getting pregnant again, were going to be slim to none. So why did you lie to him, Ruth? Why would you be so manipulative as to tell Adam you were carrying his child, when you so obviously weren't? Was it because of me? Did you take Adam away to hurt me? Were you jealous of my happiness, is that what was really going on?'

'Huh! Don't flatter yourself,' Ruth spat out, her eyes flashing with anger.

From past experience, Sam had been waiting for Ruth's loquacious tongue, after the copious amounts of wine she had drunk, to loosen and spill everything. Trusted that when Ruth finally did, she could deal with the consequences, but Ruth now glowering threateningly, Sam felt an unexpected bolt of apprehension. Feeling like she was hanging onto the edge of a cliff by her fingertips, Sam tried to relax and let go. Hoped, she would not go into free-fall.

Sitting back into the sofa as an arm automatically strayed across her abdomen, protectively rubbed a hand back and forth a couple of times, Sam consciously held the difficult silence. Ignoring Ruth's menace, she gazed into the fire. Briefly allowed herself to become lost in her own thoughts.

Possibly no more than twelve or thirteen at the time, Sam's recollections of the circumstances around Ruth's *disappearance*, were vague and distant. That period in her life hazily out of focus, Sam could barely remember Ruth being taken to a *friend's* for the night. But the one crystal clear memory she did have, was of Ruth being brought home later the next day, looking as though she had been to the depths of hell and back. Ruth incredibly young at the time, maybe it was true what she had said? Perhaps she genuinely, had not understood the longer terms consequences of the abortion she had been forced to endure?

'When *he* took an interest in me,' said Ruth suddenly, breaking into Sam's thoughts, 'I could not believe my luck at first…' she trailed off, thinking. 'It was, I suppose, the old cliché, I couldn't quite believe that someone like *him* would be interested in someone like *me*. After years of feeling numb, of feeling isolated and separate from the world, he made me feel important and cared for, safe. And no one, had ever done that for me before.' Ruth shook her head at the memory.

'So you decided it would be okay for you to take him from your own sister, from me. Then keep him, by tricking him into marrying you? How could you?' Sam cried out, in spite of herself.

'You have to understand, I loved him.'

Do I, do I really?

'We were so in love.'

As if that was enough.

'I *am* sorry, Sam,' Ruth repeated quietly as a real look of shame, flooded her face. 'It was never my intention to hurt you, but I just couldn't help myself. He was the first man, I ever felt I could truly trust, love.'

A distant rage whipped through Sam's body, and she shuddered with the effort of containing it. Her expression hardened. 'Seriously, Ruth? You expect me to believe you could not help yourself? The way you talk, anyone would assume you had no choice?'

'I didn't. But I would never deliberately set out to hurt my own sister, surely you can see that. It was just one of those things. Neither of us meant for it to happen.'

Could she hear herself?

Sam shook her head. 'No, I can't see that.'

'Then for the moment, we'll just have to agree to disagree.'

For a moment, Sam thought she had misheard. 'Pardon?'

'I said, we'll have to agree to disagree,' Ruth repeated, her manner now offhand, glib.

Furious at Ruth's flippancy, Sam could feel the rage surging in her blood. She could feel it pumping and heaving inside her. Her brain churning, she was struggling to keep control. Ruth's arrogance, her complete lack of empathy, her immorality, all of it, was leaving Sam shaking with outrage and although the growing tension between them was becoming more than worrisome, she was unable to help herself.

'Okay, well based on that premise, wouldn't it also be fair to say that if Adam *was* being unfaithful to you that perhaps he too, felt he had no choice in the matter?' Sam retaliated bitterly. 'That maybe, just like you, he couldn't help himself? I mean, let's face it, he'd already cheated once, so why not again?'

Ruth's face morphing to stone, her eyes hardened to chips of jade as she sat bolt upright in her sat. Looked as though at any moment, she would lunge at Sam, kill her.

Sam withdrew into her seat. A voice inside her head screamed:
Run!
Get away!

But she could not leave it alone. She had to finish what she had started.

I am so close, I can feel it.

Containing her trembling hands firmly in her lap. Making a concerted effort to hold back a couple of stray tears, threatening to fall. Determined not to let Ruth see just how frightened she was of her, Sam quietly said, 'You were never going to get away with it, Ruth. It's no wonder you were so scared of having to see a fertility specialist. I said it a year ago and I'll say it again, Adam was no fool and I think you were *mad*, to trick him into marrying you.' *And cruel,* she did not add. 'He must have been so upset, so angry, when he found out. And he *did* find out, didn't he?'

'Mad?' Ruth yelled angrily, her eyes blazing with ferociousness. 'You have the nerve to call *me* mad after everything I have done for you? How dare you sit in judgement me!' She spat out. 'You know nothing.'

I know more than you think, Sam thought. Gripped anxiously onto her owns hands as she recoiled from her sister's fury, from Ruth's desire to avoid, at all costs, having to accept any accountability for being the architect of her own downfall. But if she were to survive the evening, she would need to take some heat out of the situation, at least for now. 'I'm sorry Ruth, that came out badly,' she mollified.

Instantly, Ruth smiled at Sam. Behaved as though she had won a very important point. Sam, becoming less and less comfortable with Ruth's increasingly volatile behaviour, pretended not to notice, not to care. Taking Ruth's empty coffee mug from her, she pressed a replacement glass of alcohol into her sister's hands. Watched with relief as Ruth smacking her lips, took a large swig.

Ruth, an alcoholic, it was a thought that both saddened and amused Sam. *Life can be so complicated,* she thought with a faint ironical smile.

'You know,' Ruth said unexpectedly, 'I'm not sorry.'

'Pardon?' Sam said, momentarily confused as she hastily tried to work out in what direction, the conversation had suddenly deviated.

'I'm not sorry about what happened to *him*...' Ruth stressed quietly as she deliberately let the sentence tail off. Regressed somewhere private, dark.

Was this it, was Ruth finally going to confess? 'Who, Ruth? Who are you talking about?'

'*Him*...' Ruth repeated.

Regardless of the lack of a name, all of a sudden, Sam knew exactly who it was, Ruth was talking about. Felt her stomach clench at the thought of the horrors that had been inflicted. Blinked the tears from her eyes.

'You know, not once, did I plan on killing *him*,' Ruth stated thoughtfully, a flinty look in her eyes.

Still in shock, Sam stole a quick glance at her sister. Felt a tremor of terror and disappointment; *this is not the admission I had hoped for.*

Realising that Ruth was, for the first time ever, openly admitting to the part she played in a murder that had taken place all those years ago, when they were still children, Sam's unease, instantly deepened. She hesitated. Thought carefully about what she wanted to ask, and how to ask it. 'Okay, but why his wife, Ruth? Why did you kill his wife, instead of him?' Sam queried, cautiously.

Although Ruth was undeniably still drunk, Sam could see she no longer wore her usual affectation of unbridled anxiousness. An air of cold maturity now about Ruth's person, the change was scarily unnerving, made her appear significantly older and menacingly more powerful. Reminded Sam of a year ago, when Ruth had lost it and so viciously attacked her. Left her shocked and bruised, before walking away and never looking back.

'Because I wanted him to pay for what he had done to me. And because I *loathed* her,' Ruth said with an open dislike.

Watching a cold and bitter smile tug up the corners of Ruth's thinly cruel mouth, Sam's carefully controlled composure momentarily slipped as the ground buckled and roiled.

Wood snapped in the burner, startling as a gunshot.

Shadows flickered.

Snow hissed against the window panes.

Get a grip! She cautioned herself.

'Sorry,' Sam said, shaking her head, 'but I don't quite understand?'

'Don't you see?' Ruth frowned at her. Winced, then sat tall in her seat as her face hardened even further. 'Killing him would have been too easy but murdering his wife, well that made it personal?' She explained easily. Looked quite unmoved by the savagery of what she was saying. 'That *bitch* knew exactly what was going on but not once, did she try and stop it… him.'

Anger and spite, Sam thought as her blood ran cold with an unexpected dread. Not wanting to think, on oh so many levels, about what Ruth had suffered through, about what she had suffered through, Sam's face drained to white. But unlike Ruth, she forced herself to confront the memories, the horror.

She and Ruth had experienced things happen to them that were *never* supposed to happen to children. Crimes of the most horrendous abuse that neither of them had ever been able to talk about, or even to this very day, mention.

Recalling the fear encountered from having to live with such a monstrous couple, Sam queasily remembered her initial feelings as being ones of elation. After years of separation, then being told she was going to be living with her sister again, she had been so thrilled, ecstatic even. But the exhilaration had been short lived. Replaced, with a petrifying terror.

Night after night Sam had kept her eyes tightly closed. Pressed her face into the pillow, whilst pretending she had heard nothing. But the plasterboard walls between their bedrooms thin and unsound-proofed, she had heard, everything.

'Don't my hands feel good? I'm going to make you so very happy. If tell anyone, I'll deny everything, then I'll take it out on your sister.'

Almost as though she had heard her thinking, Ruth nodded at Sam. Quietly said, 'Yes, that *bastard* ruined my childhood. But at least he didn't get to ruin yours. *I* made sure of that.'

If only she knew, Sam thought painfully as she shrank back from the coldness in Ruth's dead eyes. Bitterly remembered their foster mother calling her, 'A *lying bitch,'* when she had tried to tell her what was happening to Ruth.

'So now you see why, I had to do it. He had to pay, and so did she.'

Calling to mind, a vivid image of their foster mother writhing in agony on the floor, Sam felt her stomach contract. The woman's evening meal laced with weedkiller, she had met a painful and appalling end; *a fitting end?*

The murder planned and executed with an adult precision, not once, had the police suspected a teenage schoolgirl of being the orchestrator of such a crime. In the end, it was the victim's husband, Karl Burrell, who had been arrested and convicted for the crime.

A heinous abuser who had prayed on an innocent young girl, got her pregnant, then put her through a backstreet abortion, Burrell had ruined Ruth's life before it had even properly begun. Set in course a sequence of events that had coloured all Ruth's choices — *and mine* — from that point forward, forever redrawn the pattern of her life, her character. Her experience from that time not only life-altering but life-shattering, for years, Ruth had been teetering on the very edge of insanity. *Some events, some people,* Sam thought, *exert an influence far beyond their due.*

'So don't you *dare* sit there in judgement of me,' Ruth said harshly, forbiddingly.

Sam flinched as if Ruth had slapped her.

'The truth as they say, is always a matter of circumstance. If it wasn't for me, you would have been next. You must know that?'

Sam slowly nodded her head. Agreed wholeheartedly with Ruth's vicious summation, but what else could she do? Not only was Ruth one hundred percent right but having a dangerous temper, and one that could kill, Sam was more than aware of what she was capable of.

The sister's locked eyes. Ruth looking in control, powerful — *unhinged* — Sam suddenly felt sick.

It was Sam, who looked away first.

Chapter Twenty-Five

The central heating not yet on, it was chilly in the bedroom. Out of bed and pacing, Ruth shivered against the coolness of the night. The bedside light off and dark outside, it was much too early to be awake. Hearing what sounded like someone throwing up in the bathroom, Ruth guessed Sam was up as well. Continued with her pacing.

Ruth could not sleep because she had recently surfaced from another nightmare. What her night terror had been about, she could not remember. But it had left her with the strong notion, there was something terribly wrong. Something she probably needed to remember but could not and it was annoying her, keeping her awake.

'Ruth, you up?' Came a muffled voice from behind the bedroom door.

Ruth stopped treading the floorboards, walked toward the door and cracked it open, poked her head around it. 'Yes, what's the problem?' Sam, fully dressed in spite of the stupidly early hour, she looked pale in the glare of the landing light. 'Are you okay? I thought I heard you being sick.'

'Yes, I'm fine, a bit of a tummy bug maybe,' Sam said dismissively. 'But I do need to talk to you about something. As you're awake, can you get dressed and come downstairs please.'

Sam's question rhetorical, and more of a command than a plea, Ruth's stomach lurched. *What now?* Reluctantly, she nodded her head. 'Okay, I'll see you in a couple of minutes, I just need to throw some clothes on.'

Closing the door, reaching up a hand to flick on the overhead light, Ruth looked down at herself and realised with some surprise, she was already partially dressed in her jeans and t-shirt. That she must have gone to bed like it.

Hurrying to throw on a jumper, to pull on some socks, Ruth felt a dark and slightly sticky substance down the front of her top, and her right trouser leg. Then noticed some weird red stains on the quilt cover. Assumed she must have spilt some wine on the bed, perhaps dropped some of Ruth's red berry pie down herself. Shrugged, dismissively.

Snatching back the curtains, Ruth glanced out of the bedroom window and under the light of the waning moon, could see that a thin blanket of white was draping everything. The snow covered countryside looking cleansed and calm, she only wished she could say the same for herself.

Will I ever feel normal again? Feel clean? Ruth did not think so.

The powerful outside floods suddenly flicking on, the lawn, the shrubbery and the orchard, were all drenched in a brilliant white light. Somewhat nervously looking for the trigger, Ruth spotted the movement of a fox slinking through the garden. Watched the wily animal sneak through the side fence and off into the field beyond. Relaxed, somewhat.

The dawn still some way off, Ruth guessed it would eventually look as colourful as the contusions spreading out across her torso, the back of her arms and thighs, her bottom. She sighed, heavily. Aching all over, stretching her back and legs to ease the soreness, she began to realise she wanted fresh air. Knew, if she were to prevent herself from completely seizing up, she needed to move. Decided that later that morning, once the sun was up, she would go out for a short walk. Perhaps just around the garden, or even the edge of the neighbouring field. See how she felt.

Then I will tackle Sam, about leaving.

Worrying on what Sam could possibly want from her, in what was essentially, still the middle of the night, Ruth had the distinct feeling there was something she should be feeling ashamed about. *But what?*

Suddenly feeling the all too familiar sensation of acid beginning to burn a hole in her stomach, the rising nausea, Ruth dry heaved. Hastily clapped a hand to her mouth. *I will not be sick.* Grabbed a glass of water from the bedside table, and drank thirstily.

Her head now spinning, aching intolerably and screaming with a sensory overload borne from an uneasy combination of prescription drugs, alcohol and concussion, Ruth grappled with herself. She had a strong feeling she needed to think, to remember. But her trembling hands clenching into fists, found herself desperate to ingest something that would take away the pain or as a minimum, take the edge off.

Just one steadying drink and I will be fine.

Realising she was already scheming of ways to get a drink, Ruth cursed her weakness.

Concentration now seemingly a permanent challenge, it had not escaped Ruth's notice that the spaces between her thoughts, had been stealthily lengthening. What with that, and the realisation her memory of what had occurred yesterday, the previous evening, fell somewhere between being indistinct to non-existent, Ruth was hesitant to surrender quite so easily to her usual vices, at least not without *some* consideration.

Having no recollection of what time she had gone to bed. Her wits, Ruth guessed, dulled by wine and exhaustion, she had little to no impression of what the three of them had discussed. Fretted on what her gossiping tongue, might have let slip.

Is that it? Is that why Sam is so keen to talk to me? Have I unwittingly confessed to something I can no longer recall? Have I finally incriminated myself, or am I simply worrying over nothing?

There was a part of Ruth that hoped the latter was the truth, but her instinct told her differently. Now experiencing an unexplained, low level throb of anxiety accompanied by an awful feeling in her gut that something was wrong, terribly wrong, guilt flushed her cheeks.

'I do not need a drink,' Ruth muttered into the empty room.

Ignoring a yearning to search all her usual hiding places for the alcohol she so gravely needed to quench her thirst, to numb the pain, Ruth ruthlessly questioned herself. *What is it? What is it, I'm hiding from myself? What have I done?* But she could not remember.

Restraining an equally overwhelming urge to swallow down a couple of pills — *followed by a wine chaser* — Ruth grabbed at the bottle of Valium that had been taunting her. Opened up the dressing table drawer, and flung them to the back of it. *Out of sight, out of mind*, she hoped.

This was not the first time Ruth had vowed to kick her cravings. Three times over the last year, she had tried to give up the alcohol but each time, she had slid back. The slightest crack somewhere, and her demons resurfaced. Then she was left with no choice, she just had to obliterate them. A couple of times, she had even tried to give up the pills but without them, sleep was impossible. Even with them, her sleep punctuated with nightmares. Unrefreshed, she would wake trying to squirm away from her past, from a repeated intuition she was on the edge of a disaster, that she was about to fall off the cliff for the very last time. Make that final descent before hitting rock bottom.

He, she realised with a bitter regret, had been so right. She did need help, professional help. Because no matter how hard she pretended everything was going to be okay, inside, she was going crazy.

Eight minutes after Sam had knocked on her bedroom door, Ruth was downstairs and in the kitchen. And although the time of morning was a dead giveaway, from Sam's silence, her weird frenetic energy as she manically whisked a cloth around the kitchen surfaces, loaded the dishwasher, then grabbed the chrysanthemums from out of the crystal vase and with their stems dripping across the flagstone floor, thrust them into the bin, Ruth could tell right away, something was dreadfully wrong.

But Ruth wasn't quite up to asking what was amiss, not just yet. Sore and thirsty, she was half-heartedly trying to divert her attention from her cravings through the consumption of at least *something* that was liquid. Sipped carefully at the mug of hot coffee Sam had plonked down in front of her, before she skittered away again.

A couple of minutes later, Sam's behaviour seriously beginning to freak her out, Ruth could stand it no longer. She just had to ask. 'Sam, what is it? What on earth's wrong with you? I've been down here ten minutes already and yet, you're ignoring me?'

Stopping what she was doing, Sam put the last dish in the dishwasher and closed it. She dried her hands on a tea towel, carefully threaded it through the drawer pull, then slowly turned to face Ruth. Watched her with those saurian coloured eyes that gave away nothing, yet noticed, everything.

'You obviously didn't stop by the living room on your way to the kitchen, did you?' Sam said.

'No, I didn't. Why?'

'So, you haven't seen him yet?'

'Seen who?' For a minute, Ruth was confused. *Who else is in the house?*

'Ed.'

Surprised, Ruth shook her head. 'No, I thought he went home last night?' Her heart beating fast, Ruth felt a sudden instinct for caution.

'No, he didn't go home. It seems he stayed here, last night.'

'What?'

'Look, I suggest you go to the living room, and see for yourself.' Sam said, her tone authoritative.

'The living room?' *Why is he in the living room and not a bedroom?* Ruth asked herself. Bewildered, the hair on the back of Ruth's neck, unexpectedly stood up.

'Yes,' Sam said.

It was with a feeling of dread that Ruth did as she was told. Her face milk-white, she got up from the table and left the kitchen. Slowly and quietly padded her way along the cold flagstone corridor. Then stopping just in front of the living room door, put her ear to it and listened, intently.

Heard nothing, but a deathly silence.

Inexplicably nervous, Ruth hugged herself and shivered. Wished she could rid herself of an unexplained feeling of trepidation. Taking a deep anticipatory breath, she slowly twisted the door knob and pushed it open. The curtains closed, the chill room in darkness, Ruth flicked on the overhead light and hung back. Allowed her eyes to adjust.

From her vantage point in the doorway, Ruth could make out very little. Ed's face tucked behind the wing of the armchair, all she could really see of him was his outstretched legs, his forelimbs hanging loosely either side of the chair arms.

Is he still asleep? Ruth asked herself. *Is that all Sam is fussing about, that he hasn't gone home yet? She wants me to wake him up, to deal with him?*

'Ed?' Ruth whispered.

There was no response.

Ruth's heart jumped inexplicably into her mouth, 'Ed?' she whispered again, though more loudly this time.

There was a creepy, almost terrifying stillness to the room.

Ruth hesitated, wondering what to do. 'This is crazy,' she said loudly but shakily. Then with nerves that were strung taught to snapping, walked slowly and crab-like, toward Ed.

Noticed there was a coppery, iron tang in the air. *Where have I smelt that before?*

Tremulous, Ruth looked down on her brother-in-law.

Her eyes wide, a white noise inside her head, Ruth's hands fisted at her sides as she backed straight into the sofa. Then like a terrified dog, she whimpered.

Chapter Twenty-Six

Within what felt like hours of her first spine-chilling scream, Sam arrived. Grabbed her by the arm and hauled her out of the room. Dragged her back up the pitch black hallway to the kitchen, like an errant child about to be whipped for its sins.

'So m-much blood, so m-much blood,' was all Ruth could stutter out as Sam pushed her down onto the same kitchen chair, she had only a few minutes earlier, vacated.

'Yes,' Sam replied. Calmly filled the kettle with water, flicked it on. Grabbed milk from the fridge, spooned coffee into a couple of mugs.

Ruth hid in silence. She could not stop shaking. Hugged her own body as she pitched herself back and forwards on the chair.

His face. His poor, poor face. Such savagery!

A mug was placed in front of Ruth. Steam curled up and into her face. Broke the spell that had bound her mouth, her words from issuing forth. 'Oh God, oh God, oh God,' Ruth gibbered out. She could not believe it. She could not believe what had happened, what she had seen. 'Why, Sam? Why?'

'Why, what?' Sam asked as she sat down across the table from Ruth. Took a sip of her own drink. Never once, took her eyes off of her sister.

'Why is he dead? My God Sam, what happened? Why did you kill him?'

'What?' Sam exploded with incredulity. 'You're asking *me*, why *I* killed Ed?'

Ruth did not speak. Could not speak. Felt an unexplained dread bubbling like acid in her stomach.

'It wasn't me, Ruth. *I* didn't kill Ed?' Sam's tone was emphatic, cold.

It took a few slow seconds for Ruth to register what Sam was inferring, and then an icy breath whispered up her frozen spine. 'No, that's not possible,' she said. 'You can't think it was me, I would have remembered?' *I would, wouldn't I?* But Ruth could not be sure. Could not remember anything much of what happened the previous evening.

'I think...' Sam paused, her face tight, ashen, 'Ed would beg to differ.'

Ruth reeled. Grabbed a hold of the table edge to prevent herself from oozing off of the chair, dripping like wax, onto the floor. She did not believe Sam, would not believe her. Yet a cold, dark, oily fear welled up inside of her.

Sam's lying, she has to be.

'If I did it, where's all the blood? Why aren't I covered in blood?' Ruth demanded to know, fighting back more tears.

Sam pointedly flicked her eyes over Sam's jeans, her top. Said nothing.

Looking down at herself, seeing the sticky residue on her t-shirt, her jeans, recalling the red stains on her quilt, Ruth's face bleached white. 'It can't be, can it?'

'How should I know?' Sam said, with a phlegmatic shrug of her shoulders.

There was a deafening silence.

Minutes later, her whole body still twitching and convulsing as though she had suffered an electric shock, Ruth fearfully said, 'I don't believe you, Sam. Why? Why on earth would I kill Ed?'

Sam regarded her coolly. 'I don't know *why* you would kill him, or even when you did it as I went bed soon after you both passed out on me. But what I do know, is that you were having an affair with him.'

Her horror at Ed's murder, momentarily eclipsed by what Sam had just accused her of, Ruth needed all her strength to fight back more tears, along with the urge to be sick.

'Well, you were, weren't you?' Sam confronted, a strange, twisted little smile playing across her mouth. 'So maybe… it has something to do with that?'

Ruth drew in a startled breath. Turned her head away from Sam with a look of sudden alarm. The blood in Ruth's heart seemingly replaced by a refrigerant, her body became icy cold as Sam's face wavered in and out of focus. Unable to think clearly, her brain frozen, Ruth silently freaked out. *What? How can she know? How can she possibly know?*

Ruth shook her head, crazily at Sam. *Deny, deny, deny!*

'Seriously? Oh come on Ruth, I'm hardly blind.'

Overcome by a foreboding sense of isolation and dread. Painfully aware, Sam was watching her every move, fear twisted and slithered inside of Ruth, like an uncoiling snake. *Sam is not stupid, and she will never give up.*

In the end, answering Sam's question as if she had every right, to cross-examine her, Ruth haltingly said, 'How did you know?'

'It wasn't hard,' Sam scornfully laughed. 'I saw the way he kept looking at you. The way he ogled your every move. Took any opportunity he could, to touch you. He was obsessed with you, wasn't he?'

Ruth shook her head again. She had no idea what Ed thought of her. She just needed to explain, to somehow absolve herself from the sordid truth. 'I don't know how Ed felt about me but you have to know, it wasn't an affair.'

'Enlighten me, then. Just exactly what was your relationship with Ed?' Sam quizzed, sounding eerily calm.

'All we had, was a one-night stand. It was a stupid, drunken mistake.'

'Really? A drunken mistake?'

'Yes.'

Sam's eyes narrowed. 'But Ed was Adam's brother. Why, of all people, would you sleep your husband's brother?'

Ruth cast her mind back, could barely recall any of the details of what had happened that night. Vaguely remembered Ed, on his way back from a short trip to France, calling in by chance. *He* away on business over the weekend, the house empty and she lonely, it had seemed only natural to invite her brother-in-law in, for dinner. A few bottles of wine later though, and they had ended up in bed together.

'Did Adam know?'

Ruth heard her own heartbeat whooshing in her ears. 'No,' she lied, her voice quavery.

Sam's stony gaze fixed on Ruth. 'You're lying again. I know you are.'

Ruth nervously bit down on her bottom lip. Dropped her gaze. The almost untouched drink in front of her was starting to look cold.

'A couple of days before Christmas, we had a massive row.' Ruth stalled. Struggled to think, to recall the detail.

'And?' Sam prompted.

'I lost my temper and in the heat of the moment, things were said.' Need she really say more?

Sam gave Ruth a withering look of disdain. 'So, you did tell him. You told Adam, you had slept with his brother. How could you, Ruth? How could you be so selfish, so cruel?'

'I was hurt and angry. He was going to leave me for another woman.' Ruth stared at Sam intently. Felt Sam was being incredibly unfair on her.

'But there is no other woman, Ruth. You said so yourself. You couldn't find any evidence to prove otherwise.'

'Why is it okay for *him* to screw around, and yet it's not okay for me to make, just one little mistake?' Ruth pleaded in desperation. Hated herself for it.

'*Just one little mistake?*' Sam parroted, giving a sudden, hysteria-tinged laugh. 'Christ Ruth, what sort of twisted logic is that? You steal your sister's boyfriend from her. You lie about being pregnant so you can trick that same boyfriend into marrying you and then, when things get a bit tough in the dream marriage with the perfect husband, you start blaming all *your* issues on a phantom affair and then to boot, you screw your husband's brother. And you call all of that, *just one little mistake?*' Sam shook her head angrily.

Ruth felt her stomach twist and roll. She wanted to crawl onto the floor, curl up into a foetal position and soak into the tiles. Forever disappear.

'Although you seemingly can't remember most of what happened last night,' Sam continued, her eyes flashing dangerously, 'after all these years, you finally admitted it was *you*, who murdered our foster mother and put that *bastard* Burrell in jail. Not that I blame you for any of that as you were a victim, and a monster.'

A monster, she called me a monster!

'Last night, struggling to sleep after everything you'd divulged, I went downstairs to find my book but then,' she hesitated, 'I found Ed, his face battered beyond all recognition and yet still, you expect me to believe you didn't have anything to do with Adam's death? Christ Ruth, it would almost be farcical if it wasn't so unbelievably tragic.'

Neither spoke for some minutes. The only sound was the hum of the dishwasher.

The events of the last twenty-four hours indistinct, and plagued with self-doubt, Ruth felt as though she was sliding into madness.

'Ruth, if you don't tell me the truth about what *really* happened to Adam, I will walk out of this house, right now. Then you can deal with the aftermath of Ed's murder, all on your own.'

'I did not kill *him*,' Ruth said uncertainly, her head pounding. *Did I say that out loud?*

'Yeah, right,' Sam mocked lightly. Looked bitterly disappointed in her. 'You seriously expect me to believe you didn't plan Adam's murder, in exactly the same way as you didn't plan and murder our foster mother… Ed?'

Ruth paled. She could not think of Burrell, or his wife. She could not think of Ed. She could only think of the first time she met Adam. Remembered how the pull was just too strong and how unable to resist him, in one night, she obliterated her sister's life. Experienced a swift pang of guilt for the cold indifference she had shown toward Sam. Told herself it was not surprising Sam was giving her a hard time, after everything she had put her through.

Sam waiting, watching her confusion with an eerie stillness, put Ruth on edge. She stammered out, 'No matter what you think Sam, I d-did not plan for Adam to be murdered. Nor did I kill Ed,' she whispered, uncertainly.

'Ruth, you have to stop lying to yourself. If you don't stop the violence, the dangerous madness, you're going to end up in jail serving a life sentence.'

Sam's words, spoken so calmly, chilled Ruth to the bone. *A murderer, she's calling me, a mad, dangerous murderer!*

Feeling light-headed and weak, Ruth's disoriented and fractured mind was in torment.

Why can't I remember?
This all feels so wrong, so unreal. Off.
Am I in shock?

Has my memory blanked itself out again? Wiped itself clean, like when I fell from the cliff ladder?

Has the horror of what I've so cruelly inflicted on another human being, finally triggered a psychotic break?

Did I really kill Ed… Adam?

Chapter Twenty-Seven

They were no longer talking.

Five nights ago, immediately after their last furious row, Adam had moved most of his personal belongings into the guest bedroom.

Any day now, I will be asked to leave. It was no longer a question of *if*, it was simply a question of *when*.

Through the open doorway of the kitchen, Ruth stealthily studied his face. A handsome face. A face she had stroked and kissed, an immeasurable number of times. *It's a face many people trust, but not me.*

Now strangers, yet they had begun as lovers, who shared every detail of their lives and bodies.

Hah, who are you kidding? A bitter voice silently asked.

When Ruth truly thought about it, when she dissected the time they had been together in detail, they had shared very little. A relationship built on obsession, lies and heartache, from the start, it had been unhealthy, twisted.

'You're wasting your time,' Adam said suddenly. Did not look up from what he was doing. 'I meant what I said the other night. As soon as the Christmas break is over, I will be filing for a divorce.' *And you are moving out,* he did not say, but she thought.

Ruth did not answer. She watched Adam absorb himself in the process of tying the laces of his trainers as if what he had just said, was of no consequence. As if what he had not just ripped out her heart. Bitterly realised that Adam only gave, when he was sure of getting back, twice as much. That he was one of life's takers.

'We can sort out the details of the divorce after the holidays. I'd rather not have to use a solicitor if it can be avoided.'

Yeah, I bet, Ruth thought furiously. Loathed that if she capitulated without a fight, it would be she, not him, who would be forced to leave the marital home. Detested him in that moment. Despised his cold, authoritative manner, his smug certainty in himself, his ruthless egotism.

Struggling not to have to lean against the door frame with the shock of what he had said to her, of what she was being forced to face, Ruth felt light-headed as she realised she could no longer predict with any real certainty, the actions and reactions of her mind and body. Scarily began to realise, just how unprepared she was for the reality, of her immediate future.

Raging inside, Ruth speculated on Adam's real reason for destroying their marriage and again, she wondered who the other woman was? What she looked like? Asked herself whether Adam was screwing someone similar in looks to herself, or whether she was a complete contrast? Was the *other* woman tidy, more organised? Was she taller, curvier, blonde or dark haired, younger or older? Had Adam given her money; treacherously supported the other woman all these weeks and months by taking money from his wife, to give to her?

How, Ruth asked herself, *has he managed it without leaving even a shred, of incriminating evidence?*

Wondering on the intensity of the affair, of a love that had been borne from being underhand, of sharing a dark secret and how heady and exciting it must have felt, Ruth pictured him as a lover. Thought of the intimacies that had been shared between the two of them; she and the *other* woman.

Her thoughts all over the place, the questions bounced liked an Indian rubber ball around Ruth's brain, endlessly repeated themselves. But she needed for them to stop. She needed her hyperactive mind to empty, to leave her in peace.

Adam finished what he had been doing. He looked up, and they stared at each other. For the first time in a long time, Ruth felt Adam really looked at her and she wondered, what he was thinking, what he was feeling?

Anger clenched her up inside.

Then suddenly, Ruth felt the shame and revulsion of knowing she was going to be sick. Her body rebelling at the thought of what lay ahead of her, to her chagrin, she vomited all over the kitchen floor, not far from his feet.

Immediately, Adam got up. Strode toward her and gently squeezed her arm. Led her over to the kitchen sink. Carefully held her hair away from her face as she was violently sick again.

Don't! Ruth silently screamed at Adam. *You can't be this way with me, now. Not after everything that's been said, that's happened between us, that's going to happen. Don't pretend to care about me now, it's too late. Just don't!*

Only bile coming out, Ruth had thrown up everything inside her. She was shedding silent tears.

Adam handed her a clean tea towel. 'Wash your face. I'll take care of the floor,' he said quietly.

Confused, Ruth did not know which was worse, his callous indifference of a few minutes ago, or his unexpected kindness. Told herself not to be a fool. He was a scientist, a clinician. His tender care for her needs was professional, not personal.

Ruth splashed water on her face, then dried it on a musty smelling tea towel. Briefly looked out of the window and saw it was a clear, cold morning. Frost glinting on the lawn in the early morning sunlight, a sparrow forcibly pulled a worm from out of the grass. Swallowed it whole.

Ruth thought of all the effort she had made to please him, of the accommodations she had made. Brought to mind how every time she had sought his reassurance, he had lambasted her as being foolish, over imaginative, *paranoid*. How even with all the issues, she had genuinely thought they had the makings of a good marriage. That their marriage, would be one of the ones that would endure.

But if there was one thing, Ruth could no longer deny, it was that this was happening. Her past and present ruthlessly catching up with each other, they were inexorably colliding as they exacted their revenge on her looming future.

Reaching saturation point, unable to bear the thought of Adam leaving her for another woman, it was then that Ruth told him. Her confession happening almost without her volition, one minute she was standing looking out of the kitchen window and the next, with vomit souring her mouth, she was telling Adam *everything* he needed to hear, but did not want to know.

An hour later, Adam was dead.

Chapter Twenty-Eight

Sam watched Ruth place a hand over her mouth, to smother yet another sob. Her lips bloodless, half moons of mascara beneath her pink rimmed eyes, she wore a ghoulish make-up. Looked confused, and terrified.

No matter how hard she pushed her, Ruth would not admit to being involved in Adam's murder. Whether sober or drunk, Ruth had point blank denied the accusations Sam had levied but now, was not the time to press. Even though she was certain Ruth had somehow been instrumental in Adam's *accident,* time was running out. Down to the last day and the last few hours, she now needed to focus Ruth on the necessary tasks. *Get it over with.*

'What do you want to do, Ruth?' Sam asked, with a heavy sigh. *I am so tired; mentally, physically and emotionally drained.*

Ruth put the heel of her hand to her forehead, briefly massaged it as she nervously chewed on her bottom lip. Looked blankly across the kitchen table at Sam.

'Ruth, you have to concentrate. What do you think we should do?' The state Ruth was in, it felt ridiculous asking her such a question but if suspicion was to be avoided, Sam knew she had no choice, but to go through the motions.

'What do you mean?' Ruth gasped out, her eyes glistening over with fresh tears as she crossed her arms protectively over her chest. Tucked her shaking hands under them. 'Why are you asking me?'

'Well, I take it you don't want me to leave?'

'No,' Ruth gave Sam a weary nod.

'Or call the police?'

Sam heard the breath whoosh out of Ruth's lungs. Almost tasted her terror and for a brief moment, enjoyed a wicked sense of primal pleasure.

'No, no police,' Ruth said, her voice panicked as she violently shook her head.

She's near hysteria, Sam thought.

'Well, we have to do something with the body. We can't just leave it there.'

Ruth stiffened. Her eyes wide and full of fear, she looked on the verge of a near total nervous collapse. She looked furtively away. Said, nothing.

Sam sighed. She needed Ruth's cooperation, her physical strength and her compliance. She tried another tack. 'Look, I know you probably didn't sleep all that well last night and that you're tired and edgy with fear but if I'm to help you, I need you to think. We have to plan.'

Ruth paled. Cleared her throat, but still she said nothing.

'Ruth, would I be right in thinking, there is no significant other in Ed's life? That he's not living with anyone else; a friend, a lodger, a girlfriend? Or someone who would immediately miss him?'

Still, there was a silence.

'Ruth, I can't help you, if you don't help me. Does Ed have anyone living with him?'

'No,' Ruth conceded weakly. 'He was married, but now he's divorced. He lives alone.'

Good, as I thought. Sam nodded to herself. 'Okay, well that works in our favour.' Pausing from what she was saying, Sam glanced down at her wristwatch. 'It's nearly four-thirty already, so if we're going to deal with our little problem, we need to do it soon, before the school misses him and actively starts to chase him down.'

Ruth looked petrified again. Looked down at her tightly laced hands, her white knuckles.

'It's okay, don't panic. I doubt he would have told the school, where he was going. We probably have much more time than we think to come up with a suitable story, but what we do need to do, is get rid of his body before its light. We also need to cover our tracks, just in case…' Sam deliberately left the sentence unfinished. Played on Ruth's angst.

'But what *are* we going to do with him?' Ruth asked apprehensively.

Revisiting what she had already thought through a hundred times over, Sam knew that provided she was careful and kept her wits about her, there was no reason for her idea not to work. Yet studying Ruth's constantly twitching body, the way her right knee jerked ceaselessly up and down, it was obvious she would first need to sort her out first.

Sam got up, walked around the table and placed a steadying hand on her sister's trembling shoulder. 'Look, I know what's happened to Ed is a terrible shock for you, but you'e shaking much more than usual,' she pointed out. 'It's early, have you taken a tranquilliser yet?'

Recoiling in shock, Ruth's cheeks suffused with pink. 'How do you know about my pills?'

'From when I cleaned the house and before you get angry, let me say, after everything you've been through, I don't blame you. If I was in your shoes, I'd take them too.'

Ruth threw Sam an anxious, searching look. One that silently asked, *Can I trust you?*

'What? What is it?' Sam prompted.

'I've decided, I don't need them anymore. So I've stopped taking them.'

Not the answer she had expected or wanted, Sam had to compose herself. 'Oh, since when?' she queried. Strove to keep the building frustration, from out of her voice.

'Since this morning, I think they're messing with my head.'

'But surely that's the whole point of them, isn't it?'

Ruth looked puzzled, momentarily. 'Well, yes. Of course it is but I'm convinced, they're the real reason I keep forgetting things. They make me confused.'

'No,' Sam shook her head impatiently. 'You keep forgetting everything because you have concussion, and a mild amnesia as the result of your fall. I would say that at the moment, regularly taking your pills is probably one of the only things, keeping from totally falling apart.'

'But I don't want to take them anymore,' Ruth said, her voice sounding childish, petulant.

'You do know they're addictive, don't you?'

'Yes, and that's just another reason why I want to stop taking them.'

'Well, you can't,' Sam forcefully pointed out. 'You can't just stop taking those types of pill. You need to be weaned off of them. And that's something you can only do with the help of a professional, a doctor.'

'So what are you saying?' Ruth asked wearily. Her shoulders slumping.

Time to encourage a pragmatic approach. 'I think, today of all days, you *have* to be able to function. You can think about weaning yourself off the tablets, after we've cleared up the mess, talked to the police…'

Wan and sniffling, Ruth's teeth suddenly began to chatter, whilst her knee continued to rapidly jerk up and down.

Ruth's physical symptoms only serving to add weight to her argument, Sam took a breath, then said, 'Look, see what I mean.' She pointed to Ruth's face, her leg. 'Why don't I go and get them for you?'

Ruth hesitated. Looked confused, reluctant.

Time is running out. 'Ruth, seriously? Do you really think you can face what we are about to do, without them?'

'They're in my bedside drawer.'

Sam went to get the pills and whilst she was about it, collected up Ruth's red stained quilt.

A few minutes later, standing in the darkened hallway, it was in hushed tones that Sam said, 'Are you ready, Ruth? If we're going to do this, we have to do it now. We have to go back in there and finish this.'

Ruth stared deeply into Sam's eyes, as though she was trying to figure something out, but then she sighed and nodded.

With Ruth standing directly behind her as she pushed open the living room door, and in spite of herself, Ed's face — or the lack of one — in the harsh overhead light, fully drew Sam's gaze. His face mashed to pulp, cartilage, skin, and bones, had all been pounded down to one horrific mess. His hair matted with blood and brains, his jumper was saturated with a dark red stain. *An attack,* Sam realised, *fuelled by sheer rage.* Felt a funny quiver, low down in the centre of her belly. Then it was gone.

Seeing her turn as pale as sour milk, Sam prayed Ruth would keep down the contents of her stomach. The scene not in quite as much of mess as she had originally thought, as it was, there was already more than enough to clean up.

'I can't even work out how it happened?' Ruth whispered to Sam.

'Looking at his injuries, I think you must have used the base of that empty wine bottle,' Sam replied, pointing to the offensive weapon, innocently lying on the stone hearth.

'But when though? When did I do this?' Ruth challenged back. Looked wary, untrusting.

Sam shrugged. 'How should I know? The odd thing is, you were both fast asleep when I went to bed. I even thought Ed would go home, once he woke up.'

'But you knew he wanted to go home, so why didn't you wake him, before you went to bed?'

'I don't know? I suppose I was tired and not exactly thinking straight. I think, after everything you'd told me about… well you know, I was in shock.'

Jittery and fragile, looking like she was about to disintegrate as she took on board what Sam had said, Ruth started to cry, hard.

Time for some damage limitation, Sam thought.

'Ruth, I know you are upset, but I can't do this alone,' Sam stated. Kept her face seriously resolute, her voice tightly controlled. 'And time's running out…'

Ruth took in a couple of deep breaths. Made a concerted effort to pull herself together. 'But you still haven't explained, *what* we're going to do with him?'

'I thought we'd take him up onto the cliffs. Drop his body over the edge?'

'The cliffs?' Ruth looked nonplussed.

'Yes,' Sam nodded. 'Seems the perfect solution to me. At best his body will get sucked out to sea, and he just disappears. At worst, it will be found in a terrible state on some beach somewhere.'

Ruth looked hopeful, then aghast.

'Don't worry, even if his body is recovered and subsequently identified, his injuries from the fall, and then the sea, should be so severe, they will never know he was murdered,' Sam pointed out.

The two women stared at each other. Each mentally testing the validity of what had been proposed.

Calmer now, and more considered, Ruth banged out her questions with a sudden clarity that was incongruent with the normality of her typically, of late, muddled brain. Quite put Sam on edge, for a minute.

'But after what happened to Adam, what on earth makes you think we will get away with it? And if his body is found, why would Ed, of all people, want to commit suicide? If we don't get this right, the police will be crawling all over me again. And you...' Ruth let drop.

'Who said anything about suicide?'

'What? I don't understand?'

'Look, the police are sure to trace Ed's movements to here, to us. So I think, we need to stick as close to the truth as possible. Don't you agree?'

'Yes.'

'Good, so once the police *do* eventually arrive, I think we should simply say, Ed came down for a visit and that he spent the night so he could have a drink. We can then say, having drunk a few too many the night before, Ed decided he was going to go pull a sickie. That he mentioned, just before he left, he would be going back to London via the cliffs, so he could enjoy the view and clear his head. Lead the police to conclude that because of the terrible weather conditions, Ed must have somehow, slipped; a tragic accident.'

'Seriously, Sam? You think we could get away with a story as crass as that?'

Beyond irritated, Sam gave Ruth a sharp look. 'Look Ruth, I'm sorry if I don't have all the detail worked out just yet but right now, what choice do we have? For now, it sounds plausible enough to me. Believe it or not, murder and dealing with its aftermath does not come as naturally to me, as it obviously does to you.'

Ruth paled. 'What, you, the woman who thinks about everything, and then thinks about it again?' she retaliated rudely.

She's impossible, Sam thought, glowering at Ruth.

'No, but I think you're getting ahead of yourself. We can sit down and think all this through more thoroughly, later. In the meantime, all I do know, is we have a body to get rid of and the cliffs, are right there,' Sam pointed to the curtained windows, 'beckoning.'

For a moment there was a deathly silence. The tension from the last exchange still hanging in the air.

'So you actually think we can get away with it?' Ruth said abrasively.

'I repeat, what choice do we have?' Exasperated, her patience worn thin and about to tear, Sam was struggling to keep hold of her temper. Could quite easily have whacked Ruth one.

'Okay, but how were you planning on getting him up there?'

'Well, it's obvious isn't it? If our story's to stick, we'll have to use his car? Then we'll leave it up there and walk back across the fields.'

'Yes, but I'm telling you, the police won't buy it,' Ruth pointed out maliciously. 'We're bound to leave some evidence, or some DNA behind — in the car, on the cliffs, the fields, this room.'

'You have no way of knowing that,' Sam insisted. 'We'll wear gloves and keep our hoods up. All we can confirm and need to say, is that he came to dinner, left early in the morning and that he was planning to go home, via the cliffs.'

Ruth averted her eyes. Looked pensive for a moment.

But with each passing second, Sam was keen to move the conversation on. 'No one is likely to be up on the cliffs at this time of the day, are they?'

With a timely precision, the panes of glass from the huge living room window, suddenly rattled in the wind. Both of them striding across the room, Ruth was the first one to reach the large bay window; tweaked back the living room curtains an inch or so.

Peeking out of the window, Sam saw it was still pitch-black outside, and that the weather was rapidly declining under a weak moonlight. Invisible hands pushing down the tops of the far trees. Snowflakes, the big clotted kind that melt and disperse as soon as they touch a solid surface, was interspersed with a sleety rain that lashed the garden. The night looking bone-chillingly cold, she shivered.

'In that,' Ruth nodded her head at the terrible conditions outside as she finally answered Sam's question, 'I doubt it.' Firmly snapped closed the curtains, again. 'At least not until it gets lighter.'

'Pardon?'

'As soon as dawn arrives, we'll run the risk of meeting some of the local dog walkers.'

'Even in that awful weather?' Sam asked in surprise as she gestured toward the window.

'Yes.'

'Right, well we'd best get on with it then.'

'They won't buy it,' Ruth muttered under her breath. Shook her head.

Sam bit back her anger, then calmed herself down. Conjuring up what she hoped was a wry and reassuring smile, she shot it in Ruth's direction. 'Yes, they will,' she said firmly. 'Provided we're not seen, and we cover out tracks.'

Tick tock, tick tock. Sam looked at the mantle clock; just after five am. Sunrise just before seven and practically just around the corner, they *had* to get a move on.

Ruth responded with a phlegmatic shrug of her shoulders, followed by a solemn nod of head. Though moving as if in pain and looking exhausted, at least she was now compliant, Sam thought.

Sam pulled a large sheet of plastic she had found earlier, in Adam's garage, out from under her arm and laid it down onto the floor. Then carefully placed Ruth's stained quilt, over the top of it. Together, she and Ruth awkwardly twisted the wing chair round, tipped it forward and with a significant amount of coaxing, eventually managed to eject Ed's body to the floor, on top of the quilt.

Before she could say anything, Ruth bent down to grab the body under its arms but as Sam had already silently predicted, it was too heavy; *an immovable deadweight*.

'Ruth, he needs to stay on the quilt. You go to the head end, grab each corner of the quilt cover and the plastic, and I'll grab the corners at the foot end,' she instructed.

Together, they dragged the body out of the house, and over to Ed's already unlocked car. Ruth unwittingly taking the bulk of the weight, they manhandled it into the boot.

Chapter Twenty-Nine

The car was frigid. Sam impassive and silent in the passenger seat beside her, Ruth felt terribly alone. Barely able to see out of the spattered windscreen, she felt the strain in her shoulders as she hunched forward in her seat. The now heavy rain, sounding like shingle being emptied onto the roof, the wipers thud-thudded as they smeared the cloudburst into a blurred film. The moon hidden, the headlights off, there was only darkness in front and pitch-black behind.

We won't get away with this. How can we?

Though the car was scarcely crawling, Ruth could barely make out the poorly maintained road, or the ploughed fields as they rolled past. Beneath her, the tyres rumbled noisily over the uneven surface as she kept the vehicle tight to the middle of a single-lane farm track that ran parallel with the cliff edge. A five minute drive at most from her house, a couple more, and they would reach their journey's end.

A rabbit shot across the road in front of the car. Ruth braked sharply as the creature darted back and forth across her path again, then wisely disappeared into the blackness of the field. *Shit!* Sam juddered beside her. Said nothing as she manifested one of those solemn disapproving silences which always made Ruth feel so uncomfortable, so miserable.

The rabbit's near miss, propelling Ruth into thinking about what was to come, she shuddered. Dreaded it. Fear clenched her throat like a fist, and she lowered her head for a second. *Breath!*

Sam's hand impatiently tapping the side of her leg, Ruth pulled slowly away again.

How did it get to this? Ruth challenged herself in desperation as she drove. Recalled how she had strained to keep up with Sam's rapid-fire planning, earlier. Felt a chill as she was suddenly consumed by a host of concerns over the actions they were about to take. *But what choice do I have? There is only one road I can go down, now.*

Ruth stared intently at the scarcely visible road ahead. Tried to calm herself down. To think clearly. *To remember.*

Getting the body out of the house had not been quite so easy, as they had hoped. The stiffness of death already set in, it had taken some manoeuvring to release the corpse from the chair. Ruth shook her head in revulsion at the ghastly memory. Flicked it away, and diverted her thoughts.

Bizarrely, nothing about *this* murder, was like the previous one. On that occasion, all she had done, was line up the dominoes and set the first one falling. Yes, it had taken meticulous planning and some timely intervention, but coldly calculated, she had ensured there was no mess to clean up and that there was no need, to touch any dead bodies. She had executed a suitable justice, delivered cleanly and straightforwardly. Which was why this murder, made no sense? Messy, violent, it did not fit.

Yes, Ed disgusted and annoyed me, but he was not a threat. So why would I kill him?

Something had to have acted as a trigger, but Ruth had no recollection to call on. So far, she could think of nothing to explain the atrocity, *she* had supposedly committed.

A headache suddenly claimed her. Briefly interrupted Ruth's thoughts as it pulsated at the back of her neck, her temples. Her jaw felt tight, locked.

Time slipped, looped around itself and then slowly began to unwind. The world around her briefly disappeared as Ruth sharply recalled another time, and another body. Saw Adam's ghost white face as he lay on the mortuary slab. Briefly closed her eyes, and swayed. Hastily opened them again as the car hit a pothole. Held in a sob. Brought her concentration back to the rutted road. *Now is not the time, to have an accident.*

Despite Sam's constant reassurances, still, Ruth could not believe they would ever get away with it. No matter how plausible Sam made it sound, it was madness to think the police would fall for their hastily concocted story.

There will be evidence, DNA, and they will find it.

'Don't worry Ruth, we've got this,' Sam said calmly from beside her as if reading her thoughts.

The knot in the pit of Ruth's stomach hardened.

Why don't I believe her?

Why don't I trust her?

Ruth slowed the vehicle and stopped. Parked on a section of the farm track that ran less than a few metres, from the cliff edge; the nearest point she could get them to, on four wheels. Turned off the ignition.

Her hood up and her face hidden, Sam was instantly out of the car. Immediately, the inky darkness claimed her. Threw Sam's form into nothing more, than a spectral shadow.

Ruth also climbed out of the car. Her hastily snatched lightweight jacket, ill-equipped for the brutal weather coming in off the English Channel, the rain now as sharp as needles, she cringed against its onslaught. Then hearing the death rattle of the wind in the far bushes, feeling its vicious sting across her exposed cheeks, she shrank even further into herself. Realised suddenly, how small, and insignificant she was.

Sam standing near the edge of one of the muddy cliff paths, her diminutive figure pivoting a slow full three-hundred and sixty degrees, Ruth guessed she was looking for dog walkers. In the blackness of what little remained of the night, she doubted Sam could see much. *The cliffs should be clear,* she reasoned, *at least for the moment.*

Lightly stamping her feet as she tried to stay warm, her toes already numb, Ruth felt the chill gnaw deep into her bones as the torrential rain soaked through her hood. Glued her hair to the back of her head.

'I can't see anyone. Let's go.' Sam commanded quietly. 'Don't forget to keep you voice low, we don't want it travelling on the wind. Come on, we *have* to be quick.'

The knot in Ruth's stomach returned, but she gave Sam a grim nod of approval. Helped her to extricate the frozen body in its makeshift swaddling, from the boot of the car.

A black, starless sky, a pale and lustreless moon briefly broke though the clouds. Illuminated the path in front of them as it beckoned like a lighthouse, leading the way.

The track was uneven and several times Ruth slipped as together, they half carried, half dragged the body toward the cliff edge. She at the head end, the heaviest end, her bruised muscles were screaming with the effort of keeping upright, of not dropping him.

A few minutes later, Sam hissed out under her breath, 'We *have* to move faster.'

In spite the injuries sustained from her fall, Ruth was fairly fit. But the rough terrain, the weight of the body, her nerves, the cold air, all combined, they were starting to take their toll. Breathing heavily, perspiring inside her clothes, her coat, Ruth began to silently weep. Her face hurting as the dryness from the salt air ate into her flesh, she was having trouble seeing clearly. Icy rain running down her neck, her back, soaking through her ineffectual jacket, her clothes. Her muscles cramping with fatigues and fear, she was no longer sure, she could make it.

Keep going! Ruth's rational mind pitilessly urged her.

'I can't go any faster,' Ruth gasped to Sam. Heard the tears break through her voice.

'You have no choice,' whispered Sam's ghostly form, the blackness separating them.

Remember, you have to remember, Ruth chastised herself, but that last pill, taken just before they had left the house, had dulled Ruth's brain. Blocked her ability to follow her thoughts through. She could take them so far, but then no further. *This all feels so wrong.*

'We haven't been seen yet but the later it gets, the more likely we will be,' Sam pointed out ruthlessly. 'If we stand any chance of getting away with this, we have to get home and across the fields before its daylight.'

Ruth cast a worried glance toward the left. The dawn beginning to break, she saw the bitumen-black of the night sky was inexorably giving way to a small margin of flamingo pink running along the easterly horizon of an oily sea. Somewhere in the distance, the shrill call of a bird of prey on the hunt, pierced the winter night. Very soon, the sun would fully wake the day and then everything they were doing and were about to do, would become clearly visible.

Forcing her aching legs to move again, Ruth pressed on. Deeply disturbed by the task ahead, she visualised she was safe and sound, back at home. That she was snuggled up in *his* arms. Expunged the last few months as though none of them had happened. But it was magical thinking, nothing more. *He* was dead. His spirit set to haunt her for the remainder of her days. In equal measure, *he* had given her everything and nothing; love, and misery.

Ten arduous, back-breaking minutes later, about a metre from cliff edge, they stopped. In the gloom of a half light, both swept their gazes anxiously up and down the silhouetted footpaths checking for walkers. The cliffs desolate of life, both sighed with a heartfelt relief.

Exhausted, her heart pounding from the effort and the strain, her bruised and battered body screaming in agony, Ruth allowed herself a minute. Dropped to the sodden floor and briefly rested her elbows on her upraised knees. Pulled her hood down and clutched her rain soaked hair into a ponytail. Watched with a nervous apprehension as Sam, now crouching beside her, wasted no time in hastily beginning the task of unwrapping the body.

Her chest tightening, struggling to breath, Ruth experienced a last minute panic attack.

Did I really kill him?

He's not still alive, is he?

Something darted above their heads. Simultaneously, they jumped. A gull screeched down at them. The eerie white form sinisterly shrieking out an unearthly alarm, it circled overhead, then wheeled away.

Her mouth dry with anxiety, her insides jangling with fear, Ruth was hit with a sudden thirst for something strong and calming. *Not now!* Fought with herself, to maintain control.

Gesturing to the mummy in front of her, Sam said, 'I need your help again, Ruth. I can't do this on my own.'

Ruth unfolded herself and slowly rose, joints popping and muscles reluctantly stretching. Bending from the waist, she leant down and grimly helped Sam to roll the body from out of its plastic lined swaddling.

Not wanting to see that obliterated face again, Ruth's stomach revolted, but she withstood her queasiness.

Her pulse thudding at what she would have to do next, Ruth briefly closed her eyes. Tried not to think about it as she studiously watched her sister.

Picking up the wine bottle that had rolled out of the mess of plastic and quilt cover, Sam walked toward the cliff edge and chucked the offensive weapon over with a determined aim. Wiped her blood marred hand on a nearby tussock of wet grass. Then wrenched the whole tuft from out of the earth, by its roots, and lobbed it too, out to sea.

'You ready?' Sam asked.

Sam's gaze too serene, almost amused, Ruth visibly shivered as she contained her silent shrieks.

It was in that awful moment, Ruth had a dreadful clarity of thought. Being up here on the cliffs, with the sound of the sea smashing onto the rocks below, whilst the wind lashed at her body and face, she was suddenly, catapulted into remembering. Unerringly began to recall, in meticulous detail, every key component of her ladder ascent. Remembered the wind whipping around her body as it tried to pluck her from perch; the icy handrail sliding through her chilled palms; her numb fingers as the sea crashed onto the shoreline behind her - Sam snatching away her hand at the exact moment, Ruth had needed it most.

I did not kill him. I know it.

Reeling from an onslaught of memories so lucid she could barely move, Ruth stumbled backward. Then almost fell to her knees at the hideous realisation, on the back of a grim premonition so intense she felt it like a pain in her head, death was only moments away. Every instinct, told her so. *There could be, no witnesses.*

Inching away, her heart pounding, Ruth nervously watched as Sam bent over and began the onerous task of rolling the body lying at her feet, toward the edge of the cliff.

I have to get away from here, from her.

But after only one revolution, unable to finish the job on her own, Sam urgently beckoned for Ruth's assistance.

Petrified, but knowing she could ill afford to put Sam on high alert, and that the body *had* to disappear, Ruth stepped forward. Bent down, to aide and abet.

Ruth's fingers felt hot against his chilled skin.

She locked her teeth and vowed she would not vomit.

Sam now at the foot end, and she at the other, they tumbled the body over once, and then over again. One last, very deliberate push, and it dropped out of sight.

Fighting off a wave of nausea, her eyes wild, her mouth open but no words coming out, for a few seconds, all Ruth could do was stand and hang her head in shame.

She's going to kill me.

Ruth galvanised herself. Suddenly felt more in control of herself than she had been in years.

There could be no witnesses. It was time for Sam to die.

Resolved to finishing this most heinous of crimes, Ruth hastily scoured the landscape for a suitable weapon.

A noise.

Staring up from her search, Ruth suddenly met Sam's gaze.

The look Sam gave Ruth, froze her blood.

So intent, had she been on rolling the body over the side of the cliff, then looking for a missile, Ruth had not noticed Sam picking up the rock that was now swinging toward the back of her head.

The rock slamming into Ruth's skull, she instantly fell to her knees.

Too late, I am too late.

'Always, you've underestimated me, Ruth.' Sam said, her tone calm, cold. 'In your arrogance, your bottomless pit of self-pity, not once did you figure out, *I* was Adam's mistress. But it was *me*, Ruth. I was the *other* woman in Adam's life. For months, he and I were lovers.'

Stunned from the blow, Ruth fell forward from the knees, made a throaty gasp.

In her confusion, her pain, Ruth felt nothing, but utter terror.

'He was going to leave you for me, but then you had him cold-bloodedly murdered and I will *not*,' Sam hissed, 'let his death go unpunished.'

'But I didn't kill him.' Ruth whispered.

'Liar!' Sam yelled.

'But you're my s-sister,' Ruth barely managed to dribble out.

Sam snorted. 'Sister? What sister? You don't know the meaning of the word. For years we lived apart and then, when we were finally together again, instead of welcoming me, you *despised* me. You did everything in your power, to keep us alienated from each other. I tried, Ruth. Really, I tried. Yet always, and after everything we had been through together with losing our parents, with that awful man, still, you would shove me away from you. But then, you did the worst thing possible… you stole and murdered, the only man I have ever been able to love. Who gave you the right, to decide what happens to me, to my life? You're so cruel, so twisted…'

Ruth tried to scream but already, it was too late.

A second, crushing blow from the bloodied rock Sam was holding, and everything went black as the light began to leave Ruth's eyes.

'This time,' Sam said softly, 'it ends.'

Chapter Thirty

Opening the heavy oak door, Sam took a step back in mild surprise. 'Detective Inspector Riley, how are you?' she asked, and although slightly uncomfortable, ensured she bestowed a smile of welcome.

'Hello Ms Smyth, I am sorry for the unexpected call but there is some important information that has come to light,' Riley said, his laser eyes sweeping over her.

Riley, a man of few words, his tone typically soft and slow, with no syllable missed and each carefully weighed, Sam suspected he had the ability to inspire trepidation, in otherwise quite confident people.

'Can I come in?'

Knowing Riley's question was purely rhetorical, Sam automatically moved backwards into the hallway. Allowed him entry.

Riley, in turn, stepped over the doorsill and without instruction, made his own way toward the living room. Left her to follow him.

Sam offered Riley a hot drink, which he politely refused. Observing him settle himself down into a newly purchased armchair, positioned slightly to the right-hand side of the inglenook, Sam inwardly smiled. *If only he knew,* she thought wryly.

Sitting heavily down onto the sofa, Sam folded her hands lightly into her lap. Patiently waited, for Riley to hurry up and convey his *important information.* Silently fussed on why she was getting a personal visit, rather than a polite phone call. Took a deep breath as she fought back her unease.

The sun streaming in through the wide open, living room windows, making it blisteringly bright, Sam could see every line and pore on Riley's permanently sad face. A high forehead, an aquiline nose and a barely noticeable mouth, he had cropped hair, the colour of sand.

Riley's elongated frame dressed in its customary suit of dark grey trousers and matching jacket, a plain white shirt and navy and gold, paisley tie, he exuded an air of unmistakable authority. Flicked his deep set, turquoise blue eyes over the room, then over her as he prepared to speak.

'I am here about Adam Willer, your sister's husband,' Riley stated economically.

The mere mention of Adam's name, even after all this time, had the unfortunate ability to set Sam's insides trembling, her heart pounding. Inwardly concentrating on her composure, whilst outwardly raising an eyebrow, she said, 'Adam? That's a surprise, I had assumed you would be calling about my sister?'

Now, it was Riley's turn to raise a quizzical eyebrow. 'No, Ms…'

'Sam,' she interrupted, hoping to disarm him, if only a little.

'Sam,' Riley corrected himself, without a smile. 'After all this time, I think it highly unlikely Mrs Willer's… your sister's body, will ever be found. And even if it were, well…' Riley left the sentence hanging.

Left slightly unnerved by what Riley had intimated but not said, Sam experienced a swift, sharp shock of memory. Saw in her mind's eye, a graphic image of Ruth in a free fall that seemed to have lasted for hours but had, in reality, taken no more than a few seconds. Remembering how Ruth's body had bounced on, and then off the cliff face, at least once or twice before disappearing into the sea below, she shuddered. Then was doubly discomposed by an equally vivid memory of Ruth's last, almost in-human, scream.

'Are you okay, Sam?'

'Yes, I'm fine.' Sam nodded. Took in a visible, deep breath. 'I just find it so difficult to imagine what must have been going through my poor sister's head, when she…'

For Riley's benefit, Sam allowed her eyes to glisten over.

Riley gave Sam a second. Then quietly stated, 'No, I am not here in relation to the investigation of your sister and her brother-in-law. That investigation, as you already know, was satisfactorily closed a few weeks back.'

Could he be more patronising? Sam shifted on the couch, her eyes never leaving Riley's face. Even after all this time, she still found it hard to believe quite how easily, she had got away with it. Silently congratulated herself, on her brilliance.

Taking time out to plant and erase evidence, Sam had not reported Ruth and Ed's disappearance, until much later that same afternoon. Only to be told, the couple both over eighteen, she would have to wait a full twenty-four hours before her *Missing Persons' Report* would be taken seriously.

It was not until the following morning, the police had finally got to work. Ed's car, subsequently discovered down an isolated side road not far from the South Foreland Lighthouse, the emergency services had combed the surrounding area, the cliffs, the local coastline, towns and villages, the English Channel, and the house.

Over the following weeks, the evidence gathered — the Valium, partially drunk bottles of wine hidden around the house, the journal, a dog-eared photograph of a grinning Ruth found slotted into the glove compartment of Ed's car — had not only shone a bright light on Ruth's declining mental state, but had also strongly implied, she had been having an ongoing affair with her brother-in-law. That, combined with witness statements gathered from Ruth's GP, the A&E Consultant who had treated Ruth following her accident, the National Trust Café, even her gardener — a strong picture of what might have happened to the pair of them, and why, had soon emerged.

Based on the evidence provided, the Coroner's verdict for both parties was ultimately, *Death by Misadventure*. The Coroner explaining, at the inquest, it was still uncertain as to whether the pair had slipped, committed suicide, or whether Ruth being of obvious unsound mind, had taken a deliberate action that had resulted in Ed's death, as well as her own.

'So what was it, you wanted to tell me about Adam?' Sam asked. Sat tense whilst hoping, Riley could not tell.

Riley coughed, cleared his throat. Shifted in his chair as he got more comfortable. Watched her keenly. Took his time. Finally said, 'A witness has come forward.'

'*A witness?*' Sam parroted, her voice slightly rising with her nerves. Riley's news was startling. Left Sam with a vague, unsettled feeling as she tried to imagine, what he meant.

No, not after all this time, surely?

I can't believe…

We were so careful.

Sam's agitated brain skittered onto the arrangement they had both, so carefully settled on. Thought on how, from that very first encounter, they had been so very cautious. How they had left *nothing,* to chance.

'Yes,' Riley nodded. Swept his eyes over Sam's burgeoning stomach as she sat up a bit straighter.

Adam, concerned for Ruth's rapidly declining mental health and what she might do to him and his finances should she ever find out the truth, had been so determined to hide their affair, to make it untraceable. Deliberately avoiding all forms of technology, he had insisted they not use a single mobile, phone, or computer. Every single one of their liaisons was carefully prearranged, at the end of the last one. Discreetly meeting in the studio flat Sam had found, and that Adam had paid for — always in cash — they had secreted themselves and their love, away from prying eyes. Kept it hidden from Ruth, and the rest of the world. Then sought to slowly destabilise Ruth, enough that she would eventually leave Adam or preferably, take her own life.

I have to play it cool, Sam thought. *Riley can't know anything, we were too careful.*

'With all the press coverage on the disappearance of your sister, her brother-in-law, and the manner of their deaths, an inmate of Belmarsh Prison has come forward with information on Adam's death,' Riley continued on, in the same low, slow tone that betrayed nothing.

In the silence that ensued, the floor seemed to dip and wave like a roller coaster as in spite of herself, Adam was instantly and painfully, brought into sharp focus.

Harrowingly recalling the broadness of Adam's smile, the length of his stride, of lying in the crook of his arm whilst he slept, the delicious touch of his fingers as they ran up and down her naked back. How he did not like foggy days, London traffic, clutter or mess, Sam fought to hold in the tears. She would not acknowledge the dreadful pain; a pain as deep and as agonised as an amputation. She had to concentrate. *I can cry later.*

'Belmarsh prison?'

'Yes,' Riley answered.

'But isn't that…'

Riley's mouth was set in a hard line. 'Reinvestigating Adam's death in line with what we now know to be true, we can confirm we have identified a credible witness who has stated that Karl Burrell, hired a professional hitman to murder Adam.'

The ride picked up speed and dropped a few tens of feet. Sam felt light-headed, dizzy. *But that can't be right?*

The child within Sam's swollen belly cramped for space, head down low in her pelvis and soon to be born, twisted like a corkscrew. Shot a bullet of sheer torture through her lower pelvis.

Wincing in pain, Sam cleared her throat and in spite of her bulk, sat up straighter. Rubbed a hand protectively over her protruding stomach.

'I'm sorry, are you saying Adam was murdered by Karl Burrell?' she asked carefully.

'I am saying, Adam was taken out... killed by a hitman who was hired by Burrell.'

There was another long pause. Silence did not bother Riley.

Sam's mouth went dry, and she licked her top lip. She paled.

Always observant, Riley was watching. He got up out of his chair, and looked around him. Gesticulated to the brandy and whisky decanters sat on top of the coffee table. 'Where do you keep the glasses?'

Sam pointed to the sideboard. Riley strode purposefully toward it, found a glass, poured out the smallest shot of brandy and handed it to her, but she could not hold the glass steady. Riley braced her fingers, whilst she took a tiny sip. Withdrew the glass again, placed it on the coffee table in front of her. Retook his seat.

Having to acknowledge Adam's death was not down to Ruth, Sam vacillated between shocked surprise and a guilty horror. *All this time, all these weeks and months, and I never knew.* Karl Burrell culpable for Adam's death, all of them - Adam, Ruth and herself — had been played like pawns, in someone else's sick game. Even Ed — spat out by the sea onto the strip of shoreline that ran between Deal and Kingsdown, his mutilated body physically unrecognisable and left to the Coroner to determine a formal identity — was just another, of Burrell's unwitting victims.

But do I have any regrets? Sam asked herself. *No, I don't think so. I may not have Adam, and my baby may not have its father, but I do have everything else that was always destined, to have been mine.*

Her hands steadier than they had been, Sam took another tiny sip of brandy. Coughed. Settled the glass back onto the coffee table. 'But why?' she asked Riley. 'Why would Karl Burrell want Adam, of all people, killed?' A silly question as Sam already knew the answer, but it would look odd, if she did not ask.

'It seems Burrell wanted his revenge on your sister.'

Riley paused for several seconds.

Sam held her silence.

'He told our informant he wanted Ruth to suffer in the exact same way he had done, when she murdered his wife.'

'What? But that's preposterous,' Sam ejected.

'They are Burrell's words, not mine,' Riley clarified.

Sam tried to read Riley's inscrutable eyes. 'You do know that Ruth was only child when our foster mother was murdered?'

Riley gave her a considered look. 'Tell me Sam, what do you remember of the events that took place that day?'

Well, I walked into that one, Sam thought.

Now it was coming, Sam was not afraid exactly but she was nervous. Her life finally on track again, the last thing she now needed, was for Riley to open up their old case. Innocently shook her head at him. 'I'm sorry, what day?'

'The day Burrell's wife died? I believe you and your sister were in the house at the time.'

The police cannot act unless there is evidence a crime has been committed, Sam reminded herself.

'I'm sorry DI Riley but you have to remember, I too was just a child and at the time, even younger than Ruth,' Sam pointed out politely. Guarded, she then sat silent for a moment or two. Waited for Riley to continue his interrogation.

'But you would have to admit, it does seems rather strange that Burrell would go to all the trouble of killing Adam, unless of course, there was something in his story.'

Sam felt herself redden. If Riley thought she was about to help him in anyway, he was sorely mistaken. Felt a sudden and almost fierce dislike, for him. Wanted him gone from her home.

'I'm afraid I can't help you with any of that. As far as I'm concerned, Burrell had to have been extremely disturbed at the time of his wife's death.'

'Okay, well tell me then, what do you remember of Burrell?'

'How do you mean? I thought I'd just answered that question.'

'Sam, all I am trying to do, is get a sense of the man, from your perspective. Was he a good foster father?'

'Why are you asking me all these questions, now?'

'I should have thought that would be obvious?'

'Not really Inspector, as I've already tried to explain, I was a young child at the time. Plus, I had only been living in the house for a few weeks, when my foster mother was murdered. As a consequence, my memories of Burrell are pretty sketchy. Ruth would have been the better one to ask. She was living there a good couple of years, before me.'

Riley gave Sam a good hard look. 'Even after only a short amount of time, you must surely have formed some sort of an impression of Burrell?'

He is obviously not going to let it go. 'No, not really, his job took him out of the house for most of the day.'

'And Mrs Burrell?'

'She didn't work, but Ruth and I were obviously in school during the week, so we didn't see that much of either of them.'

'And in the evenings? On the weekends?' Riley asked, staring intently at Sam.

The hairs on the back of Sam's neck prickled. It wasn't what Riley knew that bothered her, it was more what he suspected… Realised, if she was to get him off her back, she would have to get into the spirit of whatever this was; *throw him a bone.*

'It was rules… and fear,' said Sam, hesitantly. Gave a disheartened sigh. 'That's my abiding memory of Karl Burrell, the man who was entrusted to be my foster father, the carer of my physical and emotional needs. The same goes for his wife, but she's now dead and he's in prison. But in my present condition,' Sam pointedly dropped her eyes to her bulging belly, 'I really don't see the point of putting myself through the pain of having to remember what was a difficult, and uncomfortable time.' Rubbing a hand across her stomach, Sam faked a grimace as she moved to get more comfortable. Threw Riley's cold and suspicious eyes, a weak, *do we really have to do this now*, smile.

Riley finally gone, Sam felt a lightness of relief. That Detective Inspector Riley did not like her, was obvious. *No, it's more than that, he distrusts me,* Sam sensed. Briefly wondered if Riley disliked and distrusted all the victims of the crimes he investigated, or whether his attitude toward her, was more personal?

Not that it matters, Sam thought. *Riley might have his suspicions about Ruth, but he has nothing on me. There is nothing to connect me to the unlawful killing of Burrell's wife, and there is certainly nothing to tie me into the disappearance of Ruth and Ed.*

Murder doesn't have to be hard, it can be easy, and I have Ruth to thank for showing me that, Sam thought, a broad self-satisfied smile playing at the edges her mouth as the baby turned and twisted.

ABOUT THE AUTHOR

Kim used to work in internal business until she retired. She currently lives with her husband, in a small village just outside of Dover, England. *Twisted* is her debut book and hopefully, the first of many.

Printed in Poland
by Amazon Fulfillment
Poland Sp. z o.o., Wrocław